I0719904

Dragon Thunder
Coddiwomple: Book 3

By Lea Carter

ISBN 978-1-951248-05-5

Learn more about the author at
leacarterwrites.wixsite.com/flinch-free-fiction

Chapter 1

Leuna and Sati burst out of their rooms at almost the same moment and stood, staring at each other in the hallway. Sati's gleeful adaption to some parts of city life was abundantly evident in the frilly, lacey nightgown she wore, while Leuna's no-nonsense soft britches and shirt marked her as the country doctor she was. And had been, for the past ten years.

"Is the house afire?" Sati asked, still rubbing the sleep from her eyes.

"I don't smell any smoke." Leuna shook her head and looked downstairs to the front door, which rattled under a fresh barrage of knocking. Spotting herself in the hallway mirror, she grimaced. She was modestly dressed, but she'd foregone her nightly braid and her brown hair stuck out every which way.

"Should we answer it?" Sati eyed the door with trepidation.

"At this time of night?" Xelebre, Leuna's grandfather, stood in the doorway to the master bedroom, pulling the sash tight around his dressing robe. "Never. Let the servants get it."

Gently, he took the young women by the shoulders and pulled them back to where they couldn't be immediately seen from downstairs. Merezi, his wife, was just joining them when whomever was pounding on the door began shouting as well.

"Jaurle Izan! Open in the name of King Txoko!"

Leuna's chest constricted painfully and her hands dropped to her sides from where they'd been smoothing her hair. Up until five days ago, she'd known the Marroi 'King Txoko' as Neba, her amnesic patient with intense golden eyes. His dark skin had been their only clue as to his identity when he turned up on the outskirts of Herrixka, her town and arguably the middle of nowhere.

"Open in the name of King Txoko!"

"He'll rouse the entire quarter," muttered Xelebre, formally known as Jaurle Izan. He didn't have to look at a clock to know it was dark outside and that all sensible people were fast asleep.

"Darling." Merezi caught his hand, stopping him from going down. "What if it's a ruse?" As one of the more practical jaurles in Ibilia, he drew both admiration and ire from those who worked with him.

"To what end?" Xelebre squeezed her hand gently. "The few enemies that I have are all too smart to call this much attention to themselves."

Leuna winced as the door shook again, almost coming loose from its hinges. Stepping forward, she swung onto the stairway banister and slid down to the house's first level. Some of the tension left her as she saw a bleary-eyed footman approaching from the servants' quarters.

"Open it," she instructed, pointing at the door when he hesitated. Moving back into the plentiful shadows of the house's sitting room, she waited to learn what was going on.

"Enough of that racket!" barked the footman as he swung open the door.

Ignoring the footman, the knocker shouldered his way inside. "Jaurle Izan! Show yourself!"

Leuna allowed herself a moment to assess the messenger. Dark-skinned and on the burly side, he nevertheless carried only a short dagger at his belt. No other weapons were in evidence and he was breathing heavily, as if he'd run all the way from the Marroi embassy.

"How dare you come here in the middle of the night and demand audience with the jaurle?" She stepped out of the shadows, letting him get a good look at her. Not that there was much to see. To her extreme surprise, the man had barely gotten a glimpse before he dropped to one knee.

"Doctor Oneko." His right arm across his chest, he lowered his eyes. "Prince Zain begs you to come at once."

Leuna's eyebrows raised so far so fast that she almost didn't have to look up the stairs to see her grandfather and the others descending. She flung up a hand to stop them.

"Why?" The one-word question brought his eyes to her face.

"The king is not well."

"Has the embassy no physician?" His lips tightened and Leuna got the distinct impression that she was dangerously close to being tossed over his shoulder and taken to the embassy whether she liked it or not.

"You have been called for."

She sucked in a breath, easily reading between his words. As Neba, King Txoko suffered from incapacitating mind fevers. That was part of how she'd come to diagnose his condition, to realize his mind had been intentionally manipulated. His old memories had recently been restored by the logura, or doctor of mental health. In the process, he'd lost all of his new memories. So unless King Txoko was up in the middle of the night calling for a woman he'd barely met, some small part of Neba's memories must've surfaced.

"Sati." She looked up at her former apprentice. "Please bring me my medical case."

"Are you sure that's wise?" Xelebre asked Leuna. He frowned and came down the stairs, ignoring the glare of the massive messenger. Xelebre had never met the Marroi king, but he'd liked Neba—for the two or three days that he'd known him.

"At the moment, I probably have a better understanding of the king's situation than any doctor in Ibilia," Leuna reminded him gently.

"More than a logura?" Xelebre countered quickly.

"Perhaps not," Leuna amended, smiling at Sati as she accepted her medical case. "But under the circumstances," they'd all promised the prince that they'd keep the bizarre events of the last lunar quiet, "I'd like to examine him myself before I recommend bringing in another doctor."

"If you are ready?" The messenger's words were half-question, half-command.

Leuna saw her grandfather's face begin to settle into a familiar, stubborn expression, and hurried to wrap him in a hug. "I'll be back as soon as I can," she promised.

"Wear this." Merezi caught up her cape from where she'd left it for cleaning after the concert they'd gone to. The tiny smudge of dirt on the hem didn't seem important as she slipped the cape around her granddaughter's shoulders.

"Thank you." Leuna hugged her as well, then followed the messenger out the door, where, much to her surprise, a dragon waited.

"I'm told you've flown before?" The messenger tossed the words over his shoulder as he stepped aboard.

"A little." Leuna hated how timid she sounded, but this wasn't Sparks or Presa, the dragons she was used to and had even—sort of—helped to train.

"Nothing to it." Anxious to be away, he offered her his hand. "Just hold on and we'll be at the embassy before you can blink."

She tried to smile bravely as she clambered onto the back of the black and gold striped dragon. Its spiked tail rattled against the stones of the street for an instant; then, as soon as she had her arms wrapped securely about the messenger, they were off!

The creature's massive wings beat so furiously that they raised columns of air about its sides, buffeting her until she hid from them against the unperturbed man's back. She seemed barely to have gotten her breathing under control before the muscles and scales underneath her stopped moving. Her arms tightened spasmodically around the man, though not yet enough that her hands could touch. Were they going to fall out of the sky? How many of Ibilia's fine buildings would be crushed under the weight of the dragon? Would the dragon be alright or was there some small chance it would be injured in the crash?

"We've arrived."

Leuna jerked upright and looked around, blinking. Her cheeks burned as she realized that they hadn't just arrived, there was a small audience in attendance. Most of them wore knee-length batas with the royal crest on each sleeve, indicating their role as house servants, but that didn't make it any less embarrassing.

"Thank you." Forcing herself to let go of him, she decided to slide off the dragon's back as she would have either Spark's or Presa's. Only this was a much longer, *much* bumpier ride. This dragon must've been kneeling or lying down at her grandfather's, because it hadn't seemed nearly so far up as it now was down.

"Are you alright?" asked a woman, separating herself from the others and coming closer.

"Close enough." Leuna winced, then sighed, her legs and back thoroughly bruised from her experiment. She didn't miss that the woman spoke in slightly stilted Lurrakian instead of Marroi. "Can you take me to my patient?" A tall, thin man with a long, thin nose, stepped forward.

When he spoke, his words were deliberate and heavily accented, as if he spoke Lurrakian only grudgingly. "I will take you to the king." The short Lurrakian woman's messy hair and the battered medical case on her hip did nothing to reassure him about the prince's decision to send for her. A sleeping tonic would have soothed the king's frenzied mind just fine. He bowed stiffly. "Follow me."

She did her best, though he made no effort to adjust his stride to hers. The marble rooftop where she'd landed gave way to a marble staircase—no banister. Gritting her teeth, she placed one hand on the wall and tried to ignore the way the man's embroidered, silk bata swirled around his knees as he rapidly descended, making it seem almost as if the steps were in motion. Finally, on the third level down, the man turned to walk down a hallway where every window that would've let in fresh air and sunshine during the day was shuttered, the only light coming from the firestones embedded at intervals in the walls. That seemed odd given that the first of Jatorri's three moons was entering its full stage and its soft, orange light would've lent the dim hallway a cheerful air.

Her step faltered at the first sound of shouting. A glance at her guide showed that his face had gone even blanker and stiffer than before. The voices continued to rise and she recognized one of them. It was coming from behind a heavy door, which a muscular guard opened at a signal from the man beside her. She started to rush in, but the man spoke.

"Wait here." The man was resigned to announcing her, but he hoped to make one more argument against her interference.

Hearing the almost-sneer in his tone, her lips tightened. Brushing past him, she dodged the startled guard's grasp, and plunged into the room. She stopped abruptly, taking in the scene before her. There was a fire burning in the large fireplace on the far side of the room. Luxurious chairs were strategically scattered throughout, their elegant brocade and stiff backs clearly of Lurrakian design. Perhaps that was why the room's only two occupants, remained standing.

"I told you!" Fully clothed, Txoko half-stood, half-leaned against a wall to her right. "I want nothing to do with that cursed stone!"

"Your Majesty." Prince Zain ran his fingers through his hair, the action causing the muscles in his bare back and side to visibly ripple. "You're right. That stone is worthless. *Less* than that. It should be destroyed."

Leuna's eyes followed Zain's gesture to where a small, gray ash stone sat in state on a marble table. A brick sat beside it, ready and waiting to smash the stone, releasing the secrets stored there by Jabea Burua. It was an old trick of logura, or mind manipulation.

"He's right." They both swung around to look at her as she came further into the room. Something medically unnamed flared in Txoko's eyes, almost knocking her back a step.

"Ah, Doctor." Zain smiled tightly, unhappy at having to involve a stranger. "Kolo found you."

"Leuna." It was more sigh than word, and Txoko was suddenly in motion. Vaulting over a table that stood between them, he crossed to her in an instant. She barely had time to raise her hands to the height of his chest before he'd taken her in his arms. Without waiting for permission, he kissed her. Tenderly. Possessively.

Leuna forgot about the others in the room as she curled her fists in the soft, silky material of Neba...*Txoko*'s shirt to keep from wrapping her arms around his neck. The same arms, the same lips. She'd only had the pleasure once before, but her senses screamed that it was Neba, though she knew it wasn't. Her heart, still grieving her loss of Neba, threatened to explode in rebellion as she struggled not to kiss him back.

The pain that pulsed through her with every erratic heartbeat was reflected in his golden eyes as he slowly released her.

"Don't you love me anymore?" He didn't understand. Not her, not himself. Kissing her had seemed as natural as sunlight. He'd expected more of a response, though. Had he misunderstood his memories of their trip together from Herrixka? Why was she staring at him like he was a stranger?

Confused and disoriented, Leuna willed her hands to unwind from his shirt so she could step back, breathe a little Txoko-free air. *I have to remember he's Txoko, even if he doesn't!* She had to clamp her lips shut to keep from saying, *I loved Neba. And he wasn't real.*

"Thank you for coming so quickly."

She swung around to find Prince Zain staring at her, his thick, dark eyebrows drawn in so far that they looked like a single, fuzzy caterpillar. Licking her traitorous lips—for she had kissed Txoko back, at least a little—she nodded.

"Of course." Maybe she was still reeling from the effects of Ne…Txoko's kiss, but she had to remind herself that Prince Zain was Txoko's cousin. They were so similar! Zain's piercing amber eyes were only a shade more orange than Txoko's. He had the same firm jaw and straight nose. Even the way that he stood, shoulders back and hands quiet at his sides reminded her of Txoko.

Txoko stared back and forth between them for an instant before he strode to the marble table, his handsome features twisting in anger. Snatching up the brick, he brought it down hard on the ash stone. Abruptly, he was wholly absorbed in what he'd just done. Lifting the near edge of the brick, he peeked at the dust underneath it. Slowly, he straightened, his free hand rising to cover his eyes as he swayed. The brick slipped from his fingers and bounced twice before coming to rest on the plush carpet.

"No, no, no!" Leuna rushed forward, catching him about the waist and easing him onto the couch behind him. "Get his feet," she ordered.

To his credit, Zain leapt to obey, lifting Txoko's sandaled feet onto the expensive brocade without hesitation.

"What is wrong?" he asked in flawless Lurrakian.

"So many things," she muttered under her breath. She reached for her medical case, but it wasn't there. Zain must've followed her bewildered gaze to where she'd dropped it in the middle of the floor, because he retrieved it before she could ask.

"Stand aside," ordered the tall, thin man, appearing at her elbow.

Leuna didn't even look up from what she was doing. She'd completely forgotten the man existed and wasn't about to give place to him now.

"Hold these." She handed him three glass bottles from her case. The next time he spoke it was in rapid-fire Marroi and she only caught the gist of it. Something about how he was the royal physician and how dare she—she missed a few of the adjectives he used to describe her—presume to do what she was doing?

"He called for her. Not you." Prince Zain's response was delivered in a perfectly calm tone, but still in Marroi.

Leuna surreptitiously wiped a tear from her cheek

and bit her lower lip to keep it from trembling. Neba's transition to Txoko had happened so quickly and so completely once he began regaining his memories in Ilun that she'd never expected to see him again. His face would taunt her from every Marroi coin that passed through her hands, but the man she'd come to know and love? Replaced by a stiff, formal stranger. So what could possibly have happened to make a few weeks of memories take precedent over a lifetime of identity?

"Mind fevers are dangerous," she said aloud. "If you know more about them than I do," she lay a square of gauze flat on Txoko's chest, "then stop stalling and get to work." She took the bottles back from the physician and shoved her chin in the direction of the door. "If not, we need water. Quickly."

Deftly she poured a drop each from two of the bottles onto the gauze. Much to her relief, Prince Zain remained while the physician stomped off to get water. Deliberately, she worked the oils together until they had soaked through the gauze. It had all taken less than a minute, yet she was worried as she held the gauze to Txoko's nose. Patting his open-front bata until she found a handkerchief tucked into the wide gerri he wore wrapped around his waist, she began gently dabbing at the sweat that had broken out on his face.

"How can I help?" Zain dropped to one knee beside his king's head and looked up at her.

She almost dropped the bottles she was corking. The resemblance between the two men was absolutely uncanny.

"Hold these?" she suggested timidly. He smiled as he took them and she tried to focus on the gauze. "If we're lucky, this," she nodded at the gauze, "will force a redirection of his thoughts and King Txoko will resurface."

Zain frowned. "I had no idea that smashing the stone might harm him."

"I don't think it did. He was already behaving strangely, remember?" Then, answering the genuine regret she'd heard in Zain's voice, she tried to smile. "Logura is as much an art as a science. Perhaps if he hadn't been so upset," she felt a slow heat rising from beneath her shirt collar and did her best to ignore it, "it would've gone much more smoothly."

Zain's eyes dropped to her neck, widened almost imperceptibly, then rose to meet hers again. He knew so little about her. Much more now that he'd witnessed the passionate exchange of a few minutes before. He admired her efforts not to participate, sensing strength if not fully understanding it. All he was sure of at the moment was that this Lurrakian doctor was very different from King Txoko's first wife, Nire.

"You know the logura who did this to him."

Leuna closed tired eyes. Now that she was semi-comfortably perched on a non-flying seat, it was all starting to catch up with her: the shock of being woken in the middle of the night; the unadulterated fear of riding a strange dragon; Txoko's devastating kiss.

"I know her name, yes." She opened her eyes and looked directly at the prince. It might've been too bold; she had next to no idea how the Marroi culture worked, but she needed to know he believed her. "As I told you before, I gave Jabea Burua some money and suggested she go to Herrixka, the town where I serve as doctor. We were under attack from the poachers and she was afraid to return to Ibilia."

"Because of her prior offenses."

"While a student at the university, yes. Her offenses, her logura experiments, were what drew my attention when I was trying to help him regain his memories." Absent-mindedly, Leuna put two fingers on N…*Txoko*'s neck to check his pulse. It was still racing.

"Yet you believed her when she said she only took his memories to protect him." Zain's carefully modulated tone was the only thing that kept the sentence from being an accusation. "Do you still believe her?" He gestured at the king, then laced his fingers together and leaned forward slightly, one elbow propped on his elevated knee. "Could this not be the work of an enemy?"

Txoko groaned and stirred. "Enemy?" he rasped. "Where?"

"Not here," Leuna soothed, patting his chest. Prince Zain watched her closely as she lifted the gauze from Txoko's nose. "Take a deep breath, please." The acrid scent of the mixed oils had roused him before he could slip fully into the mind fever and now he needed to clear it from his lungs. "Good. Another." Her hand, still on his chest, rose and fell with his breaths. "How do you feel, Your Majesty?"

"Like I've been hit with the clubbed tail of a kisket dragon." Lifting his hands to his head, he blinked up at her. "I…know you."

"Not really." Leuna busied herself with returning the two bottles to her case. Where was the physician with the water??

Zain's head tilted to the side as he watched her reaction when the king sat up. Txoko didn't actually touch her, but that was largely because she leaned clear of him while he moved. Having seen the way she responded to the king's kiss, Zain found that very interesting.

Chapter 2

Txoko ran his fingers through his hair and tugged on his collar. Why was he soaked with sweat? What was he doing in the second floor reception hall? Who was this woman? Pinching the bridge of his nose between his finger and his thumb, Txoko tried to force his headache to ease.

"The last thing I remember is sitting down to watch the sunset."

"Two servants found you on the roof." Zain paused, choosing his words carefully and not just because of the pretty doctor. He had no desire to trigger another 'mind fever,' as she called them. "You were holding the last ash stone and mumbling to yourself about hunting schelch."

"Will this nightmare never end?" Txoko came abruptly to his feet, then just as quickly sat back down, the room swimming before his eyes.

The door opened and the physician sauntered in, a servant at his heels.

"And where have you been?" Txoko asked the physician sharply, reverting to Marroi out of habit.

"I sent him for water," Zain hastily explained.

"Here." Leuna pointed at the table and the servant obediently set the silver tray they were carrying down.

"Will that be enough water?" Zain asked doubtfully, eyeing the tiny pitcher. He lived in an arid section of Marroi and routinely drank three times that amount in a single gulp.

Leuna decided then that she would keep her understanding of their conversation to herself. There hadn't been an overlap as yet, and she was a little miffed that they were excluding her so casually.

"I trust the doll you took this from didn't put up too big of a fight," she told the physician, pointing at the water pitcher. Opening the final bottle, she shook a little powder into the pitcher. There was no spoon, so she poured the water into the waiting goblet, then back into the pitcher while the physician ranted in Marroi.

"This will help with your headache," she told Txoko, offering him the pitcher.

His eyes narrowed as he reached out to take it from her. It felt so familiar, as if he'd done this—or something like it—many times before. He trapped her fingers beneath his own and stared into her eyes. Her wide, hazel-green eyes.

"Who *are* you?" he breathed. Her name seemed on the tip of his tongue, yet obstinately it refused to reveal itself.

"She is a local physician," Zain interrupted smoothly, grateful when the physician decided at last to be quiet. "Highly recommended." He omitted the fact that it was Txoko who had 'recommended' her.

"Yes." Leuna cleared her throat, leaned back, and nodded. "Leuna Oneko, at your service, Your Majesty."

He transferred the pitcher to his free hand and continued holding the hand he'd captured. Her white palm and fingers were rough with callouses, like his own.

"I'll escort you out," offered Zain.

Leuna tried to control her enthusiasm as she tugged her hand free and got to her feet. The medical case settled into its place at her side almost on its own.

"Please." She grinned to cover how unsettled she was. "No dragons."

Zain smiled back and offered her his arm in Lurrakian fashion. A slight nod to the king and he quickly led her from the room. Once the door had closed behind them, his walk slowed perceptibly.

"I cannot thank you enough for your assistance," he said quietly. "Marroi owes you a great debt."

"No, not at all," she disagreed hastily. "I'm a doctor. Ne…um, he was my patient."

"I see." He slowed his pace even more. "I do not ask to pry, Doctor, but why didn't you tell me your relationship was also romantic?" It hadn't occurred to him to ask such a question during their interview of a few days ago.

She was blushing. She could feel it. How she envied Marroi women in that moment, with their darker skin color that hid their blushes.

"I…we weren't…" She shook her head, trying to gather her thoughts, and realized they'd stopped near the door to Zain's office. She recognized it from her first—and she'd assumed, last—visit to the embassy. Of course, he'd been wearing a shirt that time. She'd been in such a hurry to leave the reception hall that she'd willingly overlooked Zain's bare, broad chest. Now she winced and averted her eyes. She resisted the urge to rub her face in frustration and inadvertently squeezed his arm instead. Embarrassed, she snatched her hand back.

"Perhaps we could discuss it over a plate of fried bread and honey?" he offered. That would also give him the chance to don a shirt and open bata, neither of which had seemed terribly important before. He waited and, when she didn't respond, observed gently, "You do not deny there is something to discuss."

She sighed. She wished she could, but a half-nod later, she found herself inside the office. Unlike the opulence of the Lurrakian furnishings she'd seen elsewhere, this room was quiet. Restful, even. A few simple reclining lounges were spread in a semi-circle before Zain's desk, where they could be easily rearranged for formal or friendly visits. Slightly faded shapes on the walls marked the places where pictures had been removed and replaced with Marroi tapestries and, in one case, a pair of curved, crossed swords.

"Make yourself comfortable," Zain invited. "I will be only a moment in summoning the refreshments."

Leuna almost took him at his word. The lounge she longed to collapse into was a lot like the chair in her garden back in Herrixka, where she'd fallen asleep many times. Instead, she rubbed the sleep from her eyes and pushed back one of the curtains. The window where she stood had a commanding view of the public courtyard, where the only light still came from the moons and firestone poles. Outside of the Marroi embassy, the rest of Jatorri slept on.

Sinking down onto the lounge, she inhaled and exhaled slowly. The strap on her case slid down to her elbow when she put her head in her hands. She'd never experienced such exquisite agony as being in the same room with Txoko just now. *That kiss.* Her pulse raced just thinking about it. Actually, the kiss had been all Neba. Txoko hadn't even recognized her. Wearily, she wrapped her grandmother's cape more tightly around her shoulders.

She'd known there was a chance that his memories from their time in Herrixka might merge with his memories from before. *Might.* Jabea had mentioned it. And that would've been fine with Leuna. But instead, the two sets of memories seemed to be fighting for dominance. A doctor of logura would probably know what to do. She certainly hoped so, because her old professor had recommended one and she was finally desperate enough to seek their advice.

"My apologies." Zain smiled as he re-entered the room, a tray in his hands and a long-sleeved wintergreen bata over his plain white shirt. "The cook was asleep, so I'm afraid I just stole some of the breakfast bread dough and made these myself."

Leuna couldn't help laughing despite the ache in her chest. "Cooking must run in your family."

"Did he cook for you?" Zain asked conversationally, setting the tray on his desk.

She watched for a moment as he drizzled generous spoonsful of honey over the lumpy, delicious-smelling bread.

"Yes." She accepted the plate he handed her and spread a cloth napkin on her knee. Leaning over the plate, she inhaled wisps of steam as they curled off the bread. "He cooked for all of us on the trail between Herrixka and Gertuk." It had taken them days to reach Ibilia, more than two weeks. "He's especially adept at cooking with dragonfire."

"Yes." Zain nodded and took the lounge opposite her. Leaning one elbow on the back of the lounge, he propped his feet on the lounge for balance and set his plate on the seat in front of his hips. He looked so comfortable that Leuna decided to try it, too. "We began learning to cook over dragonfire at a very young age."

Leuna's desire to hear stories about Txoko's youth were preempted by Zain's sudden shift of topics.

"Tell me, Doctor. How long do you think this will go on, his switching from my king to your…friend?"

Leuna grimaced at the thinly veiled question about their relationship.

"A logura would know more about that than I do," she answered honestly. "And yes. We were more than friends."

Zain lifted a bit of bread from where it sat in a pool of honey and watched the honey drip back onto the plate. He knew what he wanted to accomplish with this conversation, but had a hunch she would reject it if he proposed it directly. He decided to try an ambush instead.

"What do you know of his wife, Nire?"

Surprised, Leuna sucked in a breath. "I heard him mention her once during a mind fever. Though I had no idea who she was, I can assure you that our *relationship* was honorable by the traditions of both our cultures."

Zain abruptly stuffed some bread in his mouth to hide a smile. In the process, he got honey on his mustache, which he hastily tried to remove with his napkin.

"Why am I here, exactly?" She took advantage of

his not being able to politely respond while chewing to continue. "I've done what I can for him as a doctor, and frankly, I'm surprised that seeing me just now didn't make the situation worse. He's smashed the last ash stone, which means his memories are completely restored." She noticed a slight twitch of Zain's eyebrow at her mention of the ash stone. "I'm returning to Herrixka in a few days, he's going back to Marroi for the dragon festival soon, and we'll never see each other again. End of story. End of romance." She sank back, feeling deflated.

"A thousand pardons. If I may be permitted to explain," Zain somehow managed to bow while reclining on one side. "I wished only to ascertain what you knew of the...politics of his first marriage."

Well, that knocked her back even further. Politics? *First* marriage? Speechless, she shook her head.

"Nire Baden was a beautiful woman. Highly intelligent, strong and possessed of a wide array of skills." Zain shrugged. "She was also the youngest daughter of a wealthy, powerful buru."

Leuna saw his eyes flick up to her face, but was too busy trying to unravel what he'd just said to worry about her expression.

"A buru," she repeated. "That's a...military position?" She wasn't sure. While her education hadn't spent much time on the finer points of Marroi politics, she thought she remembered that the Marroi culture had one king, and many 'burus.'

"Not quite." Zain smiled. "They serve the king and yes, that includes providing military support in times of war. However, a buru also acts as the king's representative for their locale, maintaining order and seeing to the king's justice. Something like your magistrates."

"Oh." While Lurrakian magistrates had nothing to do with the military, she thought she saw what he was driving at. And though she didn't understand how the buru of one city could pose a credible threat to the Marroi crown, she was no political expert. Now, marriage versus unrest and possibly armed conflict? That she could figure out easily. So…what? "Why are you telling me this?"

"To be blunt," Zain laced his fingers together and looked at her steadily, "while Txoko may not remember your name, his heart cries for you." He watched her blink. He didn't know her well, so he could only hope he'd laid the right foundation. "I fear for him, should we return to Marroi without you."

Leuna couldn't swallow around the painful, egg-sized lump in her throat. Rising, she turned toward the door, her case banging painfully against her legs.

"Wait!" Zain leapt to his feet and touched her arm. "You must listen to me."

"Listen to what?" She rounded on him, suddenly angry. Too tired to care, she told him exactly what she was thinking. "I loved Neba. I would've married him," her voice broke, "if…if he'd asked. Except he never really existed, so I'm twice heartbroken. And you have the unmitigated gall to suggest that…"

"That you stay at the embassy until we leave for the upcoming festival." Zain would have offered her his handkerchief if her damp, hazel-green eyes weren't still spitting fire at him. "Let him see you. Be with you. His memories must have the chance to knit together if he is to remain king." He finished in as grave a tone as he could muster.

"Remain king?" Confused, she shook her head. "What are you talking about?"

"What happened tonight?" Zain pointing toward the room where he'd hurriedly sequestered his cousin after realizing something odd was going on. "A relapse like the one tonight would throw the court into an uproar. Two such episodes and he could be judged unfit to rule."

"What…" she spluttered. "But it's not his fault. Jabea *had* to hide his memories from him so the poachers wouldn't kill him. And neither of them could have guessed they would be separated for so long."

Zain cut her off with a slashing motion of his hand. "Irrelevant. Worse," he threw up both hands, "he was supposed to be in mourning. Instead, he comes to Ibilia and tries to uncover the poachers himself? The Baden family will be offended if they learn of this."

"What happened to Nire?" Leuna couldn't help the question. Couldn't help wondering why she hadn't asked it before. "How did she die?"

Zain's arms dropped to his sides. His chin lowered toward his chest.

"I should not speak of it." He gestured for her to take her seat again. "However, I can see that you need to know." He carefully smoothed the front of his knee-length bata as he took the seat opposite her once more. "Nire was bored at court. Her childhood was spent in one of the wildest areas of Marroi, her days full of flying and hunting and outdoor pursuits." He spread his fingers. "When it was discovered that she was with child, she tried to convince Txoko to allow her to raise the child there, in the region of Gordinak."

Leuna barely restrained an exclamation of horror. Admittedly, she'd never been in a loveless marriage, but what would a suggestion like that have done to Txoko's pride? As a man, let alone as a king?! Her arms found their way around her stomach as she tried to ward off empathetic devastation.

"The entire royal family, myself included, tried to dissuade her. Txoko's mother went so far as to forbid it." He sighed heavily. "Then one morning, Txoko awoke to an empty bed. Uneasy, he sent for me and we discovered together that she had taken a dragon from the stables hours before dawn."

"So you went after her." Leuna gently filled in the story when he seemed unable to continue.

"She made no attempt to hide. Rather, she set out on the most direct route, and refused to respond to our hails."

"Until we caught up with her." Txoko felt no satisfaction at their startled expressions as he looked back and forth between Zain and the physician. He'd come to discuss the ash stone's secret with Zain, to plot how to catch the poacher's leader. Never in his nightmares would he have expected this. "I trust you with my life," he addressed Zain in Marroi, stepping out from the secret passageway where he'd been listening. "But this I will need you to explain."

"Your pardon." Zain rose and bowed. How much had Txoko overheard? "The physician and I are concerned that you will continue to suffer from these mind fevers."

"How will her knowing of my shame help with that?" Txoko demanded coldly.

Leuna sat, frozen in place, on the lounge. Before she could rally herself to answer him, Zain stepped closer and whispered something she couldn't quite catch. Whatever it was, it made Txoko catch his breath and ball his hands into fists.

"You presume too much, Brother."

Leuna closed her eyes as yet another wave of shock rolled over her. *Brother?* She hadn't misheard. The Marroi words for 'cousin' and 'brother' were nothing alike. An endearment, perhaps? Mixed with a rebuke to take some of the sting from it, like when she added a pinch of sweetener to her potions for the children she treated?

"Are you alright?" Txoko's tone was gentle, the words in flawless Lurrakian.

She opened her eyes and looked up at them. *Brothers?* It would explain so much.

"I'm not sure," she answered at last. "Your…" She stopped herself in time to keep from blurting the secret she'd inadvertently overheard. Likewise, the subject of her heart was off the table. Safer by far to deal with the medical aspect of the situation. "Since regaining your memories, you have been unable to recall where you were and what you were doing between meeting Jabea and returning to Ilun, correct?"

"Yes." Txoko frowned fiercely, but she didn't even blink. Was he losing his touch?

"You spent some of that time with me. It is possible that," she swallowed, her throat constricting painfully, "I could help you regain those memories."

Curious, Txoko had to remind himself to continue frowning. "How?"

"By recreating, at least partially, some of the events. Working with Sparks, for example. Fishing." She almost suggested chopping wood, too, but decided to hold that back as a last resort. Come to think of it, where had a king learned to wield a woodcutting ax? He'd done a marvelous job of splitting her woodpile before they left Herrixka, turning dozens of fireplace-length logs into neat wedges of firewood. She closed her eyes and took a deep breath. It was only reasonable that she should be feeling a little overwhelmed by now.

"Fishing." Txoko fought to maintain his frown. He loved fishing. "You truly believe I have time to go fishing. The dragon festival is less than…"

"I can oversee the embassy's preparations for the dragon festival," Zain volunteered, smiling broadly.

Chapter 3

"Are you sure this is a good idea?" Merezi asked as she brushed Leuna's hair later that day.

"No." Leuna kept her eyes closed instead of looking her grandmother's reflection in the eyes. Nothing soothed her headaches like having someone else brush her hair while she focused on relaxing her tense shoulder and neck muscles. Usually.

"Well, I don't want to meddle." Merezi set the brush aside and swept her granddaughter's soft, brown hair into three separate sections. "Your hair is so thick!" she laughed, momentarily distracted. "You must get that from your father."

"Yes." Leuna smiled. "Mother used to say the same thing." It was one of the few things she still remembered clearly about her mother, who had died when Leuna was very young.

"Mmm." Like Leuna, Merezi allowed her mind to drift to thoughts of her daughter, Desa. What would Desa have said to Leuna? She sighed and deftly wove Leuna's hair into a braid.

"Grandma?" Leuna's eyes were open now. "What's wrong?"

"Oh…" Merezi selected a sturdy hair tie and slipped it around the end of Leuna's braid. "The usual, I suppose." Resting her hands on Leuna's shoulders, she smiled at her granddaughter's reflection. "I don't want you hurt."

Leuna rose and hugged her grandmother. Hard. She was tempted to remain there. To hide there from the difficult decision she'd made.

"Thank you." Reluctantly she straightened away from her grandmother's arms. "I have to help him. If his memories don't merge before he returns to Marroi, there could be very serious consequences."

"Yes." Merezi clasped her hands together and watched as Leuna sat on the freshly made bed. At least there'd been time for a short nap before Txoko's first appointment. "Have you given thought to the possibility that the man you came to love is still there, buried inside Txoko?" She walked over to sit beside Leuna, who'd paused in the middle of putting on her slippers. "Although, what worries me most, I think, is that you might fall in love with King Txoko."

Leuna pretended to be engrossed in sliding her right foot into its leather slipper. She had fancier slippers and clothes, items she'd left behind as impractical after accepting the invitation to serve at Herrixka. Rising, she wriggled her toes and tried to smile. These were perfect for spending an afternoon at the dragon stables with Txoko.

"I can't say that I won't fall for him," she admitted, turning to her grandmother at last. "My impression of him so far is that he's overbearing and a little pompous." *And in terrible pain.* She'd never forget the look in his eyes at the mention of Nire's name. "You may recall that he tried to take one of the dragons and leave me on the *Skimmer.*"

Merezi waved that aside. "His memories were just restored and he'd forgotten you completely at that point. I suppose as king, he might easily have assumed the dragons were his, you know."

Leuna wrinkled her nose at her grandmother. Confound her for being right. "I hadn't thought of that," she admitted unhappily.

"You see?" Merezi rose and slipped her arm about Leuna's shoulders. "You are in more danger than you realize."

"Be that as it may." Leuna picked up her medical case and slung the strap over her shoulder. "The logura I spoke to earlier agrees with Prince Zain. With me as a catalyst for his memories, King Txoko's mind should heal much more rapidly." A knock sounded from downstairs and Leuna smiled brightly. "He's early."

Merezi caught her hand as she turned to go. "I know that knock." Her eyes narrowed as she tried to recall to whom it belonged—and why it mattered.

A male voice floated up the stairs to them.

"Is Doctor Oneko in?"

Leuna grimaced. "And I know that voice. What is Mardul doing here?" She hadn't seen him for over ten years, but she had no difficulty picturing as she'd last seen him, down on one knee at the railway station. She'd never figured out why he'd waited until the last second to ask for her hand—well, actually, why he'd done it at all was a complete mystery to her.

"I have no idea." Merezi paused. "Unless… He may have seen you at the concert last night."

"At the *concert*?" Leuna strangled a laugh. The Mardul Ospe she'd known had been more interested in his own biceps than music.

"Now that's enough," Merezi scolded. "He's not the immature boy you knew. Since you left, he's gone into business and is doing quite well for himself."

"That's wonderful." She meant it, too. "But what's he doing here? Asking for me?"

"He's, um," Merezi took a deep breath, "single."

Leuna did laugh at that and clapped both hands over her mouth to smother the sound.

"Miss Leuna?" A footman appeared in the open door to her bedroom. "You have a guest."

"Yes, thank you." Merezi stepped between Leuna and the footman. "Ask him to wait in the sitting room."

"Very good." The footman's lips twitched as he headed back down the stairs, for he, too, recalled Mardul's attempts at courting Miss Leuna while they were attending university. And Miss Leuna's barely stifled laughter didn't bode well for the amorous young man already waiting in the sitting room.

"Now you get control of yourself, young lady," Merezi hissed, not wanting the footman to overhear. "I know Mardul was an inept suitor in the past."

Also known as self-absorbed, conceited, arrogant... The list of synonyms faded from Leuna's mind as she considered her grandmother's next words.

"But if he's willing to take the time to visit you, you can at least be gracious."

Leuna inhaled deeply and lowered her hands from her mouth. A giggle or two tried vainly to escape, then dissipated as she called on her early training to get control of herself.

"Of course." She nodded. "I'm sorry, Grandma. I'll behave, I promise."

"That's better." Merezi relaxed and kissed

Leuna's cheek. "Now, hurry along."

Leuna reached the bottom of the stairs before she'd quite decided between shooing Ospe off or chatting politely with him until Txoko arrived. Txoko was technically her patient still, which made him a priority.

"Leuna." Mardul came to his feet as she entered the sitting room. He flexed slightly, knowing that would make his tailored suit coat bulge. Unlike many 'former' athletes, he worked hard to stay slim and muscular and paid good money—too much, some said—for clothes that accented his physical attributes. He'd chosen this suit because it was made of the finest cloth money could buy and died a rich, tyrian purple. The color of royalty.

While her casual dress would've irked him under other circumstances, right now he was too busy appraising the rest of her. His glimpse of her last night hadn't done her justice. She might weigh a little less than she had during their time at university, but that was easily fixed. He'd never been the type to enjoy a skinny companion—might as well try to date a stick as a woman with no flesh on her bones. And he thought her tan was a huge improvement over the pasty-white complexion he remembered.

"How are you?" Crossing the room in a few strides, he swept her into a possessive hug. Something hard rammed him in the ribs. "Ow!" Jerking back, he glared at her.

Leuna retreated to a safe distance the instant his hold loosened.

"What is that thing?" he frowned, rubbing the sore spot on his side.

"This?" She patted her case fondly. "It's my medical case. I carry it everywhere."

"Even in your house?" he parried, eyeing it with some malice.

She chuckled. "I'm on my way out, actually. My patient will be here in just a few minutes."

He frowned. "Have you moved back to Ibilia?" he asked, cautiously hopeful. He'd offered her a comfortable city life all those years ago and she'd turned him down flat.

"No, nothing like that." Still smiling, she retreated to a chair and seated herself, thinking quickly. She could hardly tell him how she'd brought Neba-Txoko from Herrixka, so what should she say? "I escorted my apprentice to town for the entrance examinations and decided to stay on a few days to help a friend." That was technically true, but by now she was rather wishing she'd followed Jartz' lead and left for Herrixka immediately after returning from Ilun.

"Oh." Mardul sat back down on the couch, which he'd selected in the hopes that she'd join him. "Well, that's awkward."

Surprised, Leuna tilted her head to one side. "How so?"

"It's…nothing, really." He resisted the urge to run a finger under his fashionably-tight collar to loosen it. "After I saw you last night, I arranged a few days absence from work. Thought we could spend some time together." He added that last in a poor-little-boy tone that he'd learned worked well on women, providing it wasn't used often.

Leuna leaned against the back of her chair and

studied him. His rash decision was not her fault. Why then had he brought it up?

"I suppose we'll be able to go to a few concerts, at least." He hoped so. At least one of his major business deals was stalling because the head of the other company preferred to work with married men, claimed they were more stable or something. If he couldn't get her to agree to date him outright, he could at least introduce his dear old friend, who just happened to be a doctor and everyone knew how sensible they were.

Leuna shook her head. "I can't commit to that, I'm afraid." The corners of his mouth turned down and she continued hastily, "Between plans with my grandparents and my patient, I have very little free time." *That was close.* Among her reasons for declining his offer of marriage so many years ago had been his tendency toward making decisions for her. What was even worse, however, was the way he pouted when she refused to go along. He didn't seem to have grown out of that, either, judging by his reaction a few moments ago.

A knock on the door brought both their heads around. Leuna silently exhaled in relief.

"Another visitor for you, Miss Leuna," the footman announced, omitting the name he'd been given. Years of service in a jaurle's house had taught him discretion, to be sure.

"I'll be right there." Leuna was on her feet in an instant, but Mardul was just as fast.

"This isn't fair. You can't let your patients rule your life." Desperate and unwilling to admit the real reason why, even to himself, he rashly caught her by the shoulders and stepped close. "You deserve to have a little fun, don't you?" Eagerly, he waited for her to agree. Women always agreed with him. Always.

Stunned, she just blinked up at him. This was completely out of character for him to put her over his own concerns. Except… Her eyes narrowed.

"I suppose you're right." As expected, his eyes brightened at her concession. "I'll ask my patient if he can join my grandparents and me for dinner this evening."

"What?" His handsome face had gone blank.

Extricating herself with a slight twist of her shoulders, Leuna backed away from him toward the door.

"Sorry I can't stay," she offered insincerely. "So nice of you to stop by." She backed into something solid and stopped, stiffening. Using her peripheral vision, she double-checked that the walls were still on either side of her. They were. Then what… She gasped as hands settled on her waist and a baritone voice spoke.

"Forgive me for intruding." She tried to look back at him, but Txoko's hands were still on her waist, leaving only her shoulders free to turn. She found herself staring up at him, her shoulder braced against his chest as if they had frozen in place mid-dance move.

Mardul bristled. "You." He addressed the interloper imperiously. "Release her at once. Then take yourself back to your master and tell her the doctor will be out when we are done talking."

"Mardul!" Leuna snapped out of her trance to gape at him. Txoko's hands tightened on her waist in the briefest of squeezes before he took a half step back.

"I did apologize," Txoko observed mildly. "And if you wish me to wait outside," he looked directly at Leuna, "I shall."

Leuna managed to shake her head *no*. The only thing she dared want right at that moment was to get away from Mardul without disclosing the identity of her patient.

"I—I guess we're done talking." She smiled at Mardul. "Enjoy your vacation?" Txoko's hands nudged her to his left and she followed his cues as easily as if they *had* been dancing. In an instant, they had exited the sitting room and were out the front door, the footman closing it firmly behind them.

"Well." For propriety's sake, Txoko lowered both of his hands to his sides. "That was different."

She burst out laughing and linked her arm through his. "Come on. Let's go see Sparks."

"You're sure?" he hesitated. He hated to do it, but… "Perhaps your friend would like to come with us?"

Leuna tugged on his arm, literally pulling him away from the house. "Not so loud." She looked over her shoulder to confirm that Mardul wasn't out of the house yet. "He's not my friend. Or at least, he's not that kind of friend."

"I beg your pardon?" Txoko shook his head to clear it.

"I mean," she clarified, "he's someone I knew from university, but we were never close. Definitely not in the way he seems to think."

Though she muttered that last under her breath,

Txoko heard it quite clearly. For some reason, it made him feel better. "I hope you don't mind walking." He smiled down at her, nearly walking into a street sign in his distraction. "I can call a cycle carriage, if you'd rather."

"No, this is fine." She tightened her grip on his arm just in case. Now that she could see him better, she had to admit that he wasn't dressed like royalty. His tan, thigh-length jacket was unbuttoned in front and flowed down in straight lines around his berry blue shirt. Nondescript tan pants were pulled over the top of Marroi riding boots that sported worn spots. In short, she could see how he might be mistaken for a servant. It was Mardul's tone that she would struggle to forgive.

"Tell me about this dragon," Txoko invited.

"Sparks?" She smiled a little sadly, thinking back on how Neba had come to call him that. "He's a gailen dragon." She paused, shook her head. He'd tried to 'borrow' Sparks after their adventure at Ilun, so he already knew that. "I mean…um…what did you want to know?" she asked lamely. Talking had *never* been this difficult with Neba.

"How old is he?" Txoko responded helpfully. "Has he had any training?"

"Oh." *The dull stuff.* "He's about ten months old. I'm not sure what sort of training you mean, though."

"You're not sure of his age?" Txoko didn't bother to try hiding his surprise. "He's truly wild, then."

"Yes," she nodded. "We only became aware of him after he'd been raiding Jartz'—that's a friend of mine in Herrixka," it felt so weird to have to explain who Jartz was that she had to pause to swallow a lump. "After he'd been raiding a trapline for a while."

"An orphan." Txoko couldn't help wondering if Sparks' parents had fallen prey to poachers. Admittedly, it was unlikely given the location of Herrixka. His mind, once on the subject of poachers, returned to the most recent developments. He'd finally gotten Zain alone and revealed who the head of the poaching ring was. Sad to say, if not for the irrefutable evidence he'd personally uncovered, Txoko would've never accepted the truth of it. Now here he was, going to play with an orphan dragon—and an admittedly attractive doctor—instead of making plans to capture the villain.

"That's right." Something else was on his mind; she could tell. It made sense…he *was* a king. Leuna bit her lip, then hurried on. "I know you rode him once before Ilun, to take him up to the top of Firedrake Crags. We were all hoping he'd find a home there."

"A sound idea." Txoko quirked an eyebrow at her. "What went wrong?"

She laughed and shrugged. "I have no idea. I'm sure you wouldn't have left him if you weren't satisfied that he'd be safe, but I really don't know much more than that."

"I…see." Txoko repressed a groan. He did see. And he didn't. Naturally he liked the idea that, even without the faintest notion of his own identity, he'd behave so honorably. If only *he* could remember it, too. Would his memory ever be whole again? This business of playing with a dragon and going fishing…it was all too ridiculous.

"He showed up on the trail when we were leaving Herrixka. With a friend." Leuna had a terrible feeling that Txoko's too-calm expression was hiding nervous frustration. That wouldn't help his situation at all. Actually, according to the logura she'd consulted earlier that morning, trying to force things could make his condition worse, potentially fracturing his memories forever. "She was a lovely yellow dragon that I named Presa."

"Yes. Yes, of course." He nodded. "Excellent conformation."

"A bit skittish still." She was disappointed to hear him refer to Presa as though she was devoid of personality. It gave her an idea, though. Perhaps she could use the dragons as a distraction. Get him thinking about something other than how much he was missing. "I really don't know what I'm going to do with them when we get back to Herrixka." For the first time in several minutes, he looked directly at her.

"Oh?" Txoko couldn't imagine. Especially since he didn't recollect anything about Herrixka. "I suppose you could sell them." He held up both hands to ward off the hurt surprise on her face. "There is always a market for young, healthy dragons in Marroi." She said nothing, so he rushed on. "There are so many domesticated dragons that it's generally unnecessary to raid the wild kabis—nevertheless, there is always the danger of letting a bloodline grow stagnant. And under ordinary circumstances, any breeder applying to the Marroi crown for permission to claim a wild dragon in the five year lustrum must be willing to release two healthy young dragons—one male, one female—in exchange. These two," he gestured toward Sparks and Presa, "would seem a bargain to them at nearly any price."

Indignant, Leuna spun on her heel and walked away. It was better than making a fool of herself in giving him a lecture she'd only regret later. But sell Sparks and Presa? How could she? They were almost all she had left of Neba.

Txoko followed silently. He saw her wipe away a tear and berated himself for making her cry. He had a grandmother, a mother, three sisters, one sister-by-law, and spent nearly three years as a husband. Yet he still had no idea how to talk to a woman.

"Gailens, in particular, are such favored mounts that some Marroi keep their names perpetually on the lists with the breeding houses," he said, still trying to explain.

"Yes, I know. You told me."

He stopped, surprised, then hurried to catch back up. "Wait." He took her arm, drew her to a stop at the door to the dragon stables. "Please forgive me. I only meant to offer a solution."

Leuna blinked a few times and took a deep breath. "I know." Suddenly she was smiling. "And please don't apologize. You did nothing wrong."

"I made you cry," he pointed out, even more confused by the appearance of her sunny smile.

"You also made me smile." She stepped closer, looking into his deep golden eyes and trying not to fall into them. "I just hadn't even considered selling them because, well, because I never felt that I owned them.

I'm still not convinced that I do."

"And that lovely smile?" Txoko ordered his hands to remain at his sides, which wasn't easy. At this distance, he could smell the soft scent of her perfumed soap and see loose strands of hair that were practically begging for him to smooth them.

"You made me think of my father." She leaned lightly against the door. "My mother died when I was quite young, so it was just the two of us. And the entire village," she amended fondly. "Anyway, my father and I would sit up late on winter nights, solving Jatorri's problems."

"Did he make you cry?" Txoko rested one hand against the door.

She looked away from her memories and up at him. Her throat tightened like wet buckskin under a hot sun at his nearness. "Sometimes."

"Didn't you mind?" Txoko allowed his eyes to roam her face, taking in the tiny dots of darker skin that were sprinkled across her fair nose and cheeks. Freckles? He thought that was the Lurrakian word for them. The crazy thing was, he would've been perfectly happy to stand there and count those adorable dots until the sun set.

"I… Well, we…" Leuna cleared her throat and straightened away from the door. Some doctor she was. Why, during her time at university, she'd been face to face with dozens of handsome athletes while she treated them and never had any trouble stringing words together to make a coherent sentence! "We understood each other. I knew so little about the world beyond Herrixka and he was trying to teach me."

Txoko hesitated, then reached for the door knob. "Come on. Let's go inside and meet these dragons." He might not know what women were thinking, but dragons were easy. Simple. Straightforward. He could use a little of both.

Leuna entered through the door he'd opened for her and immediately spotted Ordez, the groom who'd helped out when they first brought Sparks and Presa to the stables.

"Morning!" Ordez grinned at them as they walked over to where he was scrubbing out buckets. While dragons adored the pressed cakes of mixed animal meat and fat, the buckets quickly came to smell rancid unless they were kept meticulously clean. "Come to see them, have you?" He pointed with his elbow toward the indoor-meadow. "Gang's got a game of keep on," he laughed. "Might be a bit before they settle enough to notice you."

"That's alright, Ordez." Leuna smiled and took Txoko's hand. "We can watch for a while."

The indoor meadow before them was large enough to have harbored a small village, but Txoko thought he rather liked the rolling green meadow just as it was—covered with frolicking dragons.

"It must cost a fortune to keep this meadow looking so pristine," Leuna observed, wincing slightly as one of the dragons began digging a hole, apparently because they could.

Txoko chuckled. "Yes, I think you're right." The movement above them caught his attention and he observed the game of keep until he was dizzy from tracking their darting and dodging, all while passing what looked like a large chunk of wood about. He could guess which dragons were on which 'team,' as the stick was only shared willing between some of them, leaving the others to try to snatch it away.

His lips twisted wryly. It rather reminded him of some of the trade negotiations he'd attended in the past.

Chapter 4

His eyes dancing with humor, Zain waited while Txoko gingerly lowered himself onto his favorite lounge. "Getting stiff in your old age, I see," Zain teased as he seated himself on the balcony's only other lounge.

"Laugh if you will," Txoko grunted as he shoved another pillow behind his back, "but I'd like to see you take two falls off a wild gailen and walk away from it." Bruised, battered, and sporting several brand new grass stains on his clothes, he'd been lucky to endure escorting Leuna home. Even with all of that, though, he was more interested in the startling discovery that she spoke Marroi fluently. How much had she heard that she wasn't supposed to during her visits to the embassy?

At that, Zain did laugh. "To think we used to spend our summers doing that sort of thing for fun!"

Txoko shook his head ruefully. It was true. Every summer for five years they'd claimed at least one ride on a freshly-caught dragon. There were enough domesticated dragons to make it generally unnecessary to raid the wild kabi's. On the other hand lay the danger of letting a bloodline grow stagnant.

"I suppose I am getting old." Txoko sighed as he settled a cold pouch on his bruised shoulder. "Was the ground always so hard?" Rotten luck, really. He hadn't expected her to invite him to supper at her grandparents' and wished he could've accepted. What had possessed him to counteroffer with an invitation to the concert tomorrow? He'd been far too happy when she accepted, he knew that much.

Zain chuckled again, then arranged a second cold pouch on Txoko's knee. His king had tried to conceal his limp when he arrived back at the embassy for the evening meal, but Zain knew him too well to be fooled.

Txoko waved away the servant that waited on them and instructed Zain, "Tell me what you've learned."

Zain spread his hands before him. "Nothing. We have almost no records here at the embassy that would contain anything useful in this matter."

Txoko growled angrily. "I cannot publicly accuse them based solely on the testimony of a dead smuggler."

Zain's eyes narrowed. "Dead?" He waited, but Txoko just stared at him. "You didn't tell me the smuggler was dead."

"Didn't I?" Txoko frowned, then shrugged. "What difference does it make?"

"As you say," Zain neatly parried the question, ignoring the aggressive tone, "a dead witness is no witness at all." His eyes on his king's face, he nevertheless noticed that Txoko's hand had moved to cover his abdomen, almost protectively.

"That isn't exactly what I said." Txoko's lips twisted in wry amusement at the clever rewording. "However, you are correct. We require proof and we have none." He didn't regret killing the smuggler, since the alternative was his own death, but he did wish there had been another, more cooperative smuggler on hand who could've corroborated his story.

"Some council members would not require proof beyond the king's word," Zain pointed out.

"Yes, and they're the same ones that nearly got us in a war with Bizil three years ago over the new nesting grounds." Txoko gave his cousin a long-suffering look. "Spare me from a return to the days of war and blood."

Zain smiled back, relieved. "Agreed."

"Well, out with it," Txoko ordered when Zain went on grinning at him. "What clever solution have you found to our problem?"

"The dragon festival." Zain routinely assisted Txoko in selecting those to be members of the royal Marroi party for the festival. "I've invited their entire family."

The air left Txoko with as much force at this announcement as it had earlier that day, the first time he'd unexpectedly come off of Presa.

"You invited Lady Adeita?" He couldn't believe it. The last time he'd encountered their old teacher of cultures, white hair had been creeping in around her temples. "I cannot spring a trap on her child while she watches!"

Zain glared reprovingly at him and motioned for him to speak more softly. "Of course not," he agreed. "Do you think you're the only one who remembers her fondly?" Zain had struggled to learn Lurrakian until she'd introduced some of their mouth-watering dishes in their classes. She'd also invited them to practice Lurrakian with her freely and allowed them to discuss topics that actually interested them, something that their much stricter teacher of languages apparently never considered.

"No." Txoko rested his head against the pillow. "No, of course not. Forgive me." He rubbed one hand over his face. "So. Continue. Tell me the rest of your scheme."

In low tones, and accompanied by a glass of hot chocolate, Zain did just that. The sun was setting by the time he'd finished laying out his plan and Txoko had given up trying to hide his yawns.

"I can't think of anything you've missed," Txoko congratulated him. "Still, let's sleep on it and go over it again in the morning."

"You've got a head start on sleeping on it," Zain needled him good-naturedly. He caught the pillow that Txoko lazily tossed at him and set it aside. Collecting the dishes, he set them back on the tray they'd come from. "Need any help?"

"No." Txoko stood and stretched. "I'm not that sore."

They grinned at each other, thinking back on the times when they *had* been that sore. Dragons hadn't been their only endeavor, after all. Wrestling. Swimming. Rock climbing…and occasionally falling.

"Go on." Txoko waved him away. "I know a courier arrived from Koroa just ahead of supper. Go read your letters." Zain had left his wife, Min, and three children at their estate when news reached him of Txoko's disappearance, and now letters seemed to arrive for him with each diplomatic pouch.

As the door shut behind an exuberant Zain, Txoko stubbornly shoved away the self-pity that threatened to swallow him whole—the way the shadows were engulfing entire buildings now that the sun had settled in for the night.

Stripping off his shirt, he threw it aside and stepped into the rain booth. With soap and hot water, he washed away the day's dirt and sweat. Eventually, the water ran cold and he knew he couldn't postpone going to bed any longer.

Soft, lightly-scented sheets stretched smoothly over the length and breadth of the empty bed. Empty…as his every bed had been each night since Nire abandoned him. Tonight the memories stormed in, filling the emptiness and tearing at his heart.

He could hear her querulous voice starting or restarting an argument. The derisive way she spoke of the various ambassadors' wives: their clothes; their food; their entertainments. Nothing was good enough for her. Not her life at the palace. Not her life here at the embassy. Not…her life with him.

Breathing hard, he abruptly turned his back on the bed. He couldn't sleep there. He might lie there, staring up at the canopy until the memories drove him mad. But he couldn't sleep there.

Making his way out to the balcony again, he shoved two lounges together and piled the pillows at the slanted end. As a small concession to the lowering temperature, he grabbed a blanket from the locker at the food of his bed.

Nire would've scoffed at him, called him soft for not sleeping on the balcony floor. He shifted to ease the pressure on his sore shoulder and sighed. She'd seemed like the best option when it came time for him to marry. Young, healthy, easy to look at. Strategically, the marriage offered renewed loyalty from her prosperous city. If he could change one decision—just one—from his entire ten years as king, it would be to have selected a different wife.

An image of Leuna sprang unbidden into his mind…not one he could remember seeing. She was standing over a cook fire, her face flushed with the heat, a smile curving her tempting lips. He blinked, and the image was gone, replaced by images from that day, complete with sounds and smells from their time at the stables.

Smiling, he began to relax. It was impossible to be upset with the pleasant sound of Leuna's laughter ringing in his ears. He was still thinking of her when he drifted off to sleep, where more forgotten memories surfaced. He dreamt of their time together throughout the night, then lay, half-asleep, for several minutes the next morning, afraid that waking completely would banish his memories to their hiding spots again.

Rising at last, he seated himself at his desk and began to draw. Working quickly, he filled several pages of his sketch pad with images from his dreams. *His memories.* He could taste the bean and tomato soup Leuna had prepared over his campfire. Hear the birds near the stream where he worked with Sparks. Smell the smoke from the fire where he dried the schelch meat. Feel the steel of his enemy's blade cutting into his side as he dueled feverishly—for their orders were to dump him where no one would ever find him.

He added a final detail to the image of the clearing where he'd woken up after that fight, wounded and thoroughly confused, before setting the sketch pad aside with a sigh. Light was beginning to creep in through his window, telling him it was time to get on with the work of his day.

Dressing in the traditional Marroi style of comfortable pants and a thigh-length bata, he began mentally preparing himself for the day's activities. He had two appointments with foreign dignitaries after lunch, but would spend the morning with his own advisors, discussing the weekly updates that had also arrived in the diplomatic pouch last night. Opting for formal yet comfortable, he chose a slate gray sleeveless jacket. He buttoned each of its dozen iridescent-yellow dragon scale buttons carefully, for each of them represented a memory with his first dragon. When the jacket was eventually discarded, the buttons would first be carefully removed so that they could be used in another item for his wardrobe.

Assessing himself in the mirror, Txoko straightened the jacket so that the embroidered royal Marroi crest rested over his heart where it belonged. The crest was simple: a powerful gailen dragon perched atop a pile of precious stones, looking out over a small oasis. Marroi was an arid, mountainous land, but her few habitable areas were small paradises of water and lush vegetation. A plentiful supply of gemstones and legal dragon goods allowed the people to live comfortably.

He went directly to breakfast, where he listened carefully as his advisors took turns reading from their official mail and discussing it. It was a little tedious, mixing business with roast fruit, soft cheese, fresh bread, and spiced milk.

"Your Majesty." Txoko's eyes narrowed at the security advisor's grim tone. "There has been a raid on a suspected poacher refuge."

Txoko waited as long as he could before prompting, "I assume it was a failure?" He hated to use that word, but how else to describe carefully planned movements that culminated in empty rooms, the occupants long gone and no eye witnesses? He frowned. On a few rare occasions, it had been necessary to punish 'ignorant' and 'innocent' neighbors, whose connection to the poachers or smugglers had already been proven by spies. All of which told him much of how his officers were viewed outside the central cities.

"One could term it such, yes." The advisor tapped the report he was holding on the smooth wood of the tabletop, then handed it to one of the young pages who carried it to the king. "We took no prisoners, yet undoubtedly their organization is…disrupted."

"No prisoners?" Txoko took the report, smiled at the page, and began to scan the document. *Thirty dead.* The words leapt off the page at him, leaving him feeling as though he'd just been unceremoniously dunked in the Izotz River, where ice floated until the mid-summer months. "Thirty dead," he read aloud.

"Poisoned," announced the advisor helpfully. "The officer in charge indicates that they were all gathered around a table still laden with stale food, indicating that they'd been there for a day or two at least." The following silence was only broken by clinks and thuds as utensils and glasses were abruptly lowered to the table.

"Keep your seats," Txoko instructed absent-mindedly. He'd resumed reading, more slowly this time. "The report notes that every purse was turned out, every pocket emptied." Shaking his head, he handed the report to another page, who returned it to the advisor. "We are not in danger as yet."

"How can you be sure?" asked a portly advisor, eyeing his second helpings warily.

"Because." The security advisor leaned heavily back in his chair. "We don't know nearly enough about this," he waved vaguely, "this maniac for him to want to kill us."

"Yet we are getting close." Txoko clasped his hands together and leaned forward. This was hardly the time to tell them that he knew exactly who the 'maniac' was. He didn't have enough proof—and none at all so far as the murders were concerned. "In the past, the organization has simply packed up and moved, perhaps targeting another breed of dragon in the process, but never really suffering a loss. This time, though. This time, thirty well-dressed poachers were murdered in cold blood, then stripped of every item of value."

"The maniac," the security advisor smiled darkly, "is running scared. Getting out while they still can."

"Not without first robbing the victims," Txoko pointed out severely. "Proving that they're still a black-hearted, greedy piece of scum." Silence followed his declaration and he let it stand. Bits and pieces of what was said in these confidential meetings always filtered out through the gossip chain, so for once he was going to use it to his advantage. Now that he knew—not postulated, not deduced, not believed, but *knew*—who was running things, he also knew how to get under their skin.

"He must be stopped," announced the portly advisor who'd spoken earlier.

"He?" The security advisor repeated the specific pronoun curiously. Most of the poachers were male, it was true. The reports as to the identity of their main target, however, were mixed, even as to their gender. Undoubtedly at least one lieutenant of the highly successful organization was a woman. The portly man stared at him, mouth slightly open so that he looked something like a fish, so he spelled it out for him. "You said *he* must be stopped."

"Slip of the tongue, I'm sure." Txoko gestured dismissively. "As a boy I called my teacher, Lady Adeita, by the male pronoun several times while learning Lurrakian."

Several of the advisors laughed, glad for the distraction. Discussing poisoning while eating, well, it was bad for the digestion!

Txoko laughed with them. "If that's all for security?"

The meeting continued, though thankfully it was nearly done. With an effort, Txoko forced himself to let the rest of the meeting proceed at its usual, sedate pace despite his impatience to be away. Anywhere but here. The dragon festival was still three weeks away. What might happen during those three weeks? How many more lives might be lost, human and dragon? Should he act now? These and other concerns made it difficult for him to focus, until at last he was able to dismiss them.

Zain touched his arm lightly. "You look like you need time to think. Would you like me to meet with the ambassadors today?"

Txoko cocked an amused eyebrow. "I thought they insisted on seeing me?"

"They did," Zain agreed. After a moment, they grinned at each other, knowing well enough that ambassadors tended to ask for the highest ranking official they thought they could get, regardless of what needed to be discussed.

"Thank you." Txoko walked casually down one long hallway, turned a corner, then swiftly crossed to a door that led to the garden. His hand on the knob, he eased the door open…

"No, no, no." The strident voice of the embassy tutor invaded the hallway. "Observe. The tantaka tree does not slouch. It bends, gracefully, as though weight down by the sun's rays on its slender petals."

Wincing, Txoko closed the door on the art lesson. "Blast," he muttered under his breath. The library and his own suites were the first place they would look for him. Where could he go to think? Clasping his hands behind his back, he strode unhappily down the hall…and stopped at the sound of street noises.

His mind made up in an instant, Txoko removed his jacket and tucked it behind a fancy chair that stood almost flush with the wall. Now suitably nondescript, he slipped out the servants' entrance to merge with the foot traffic. Surrounded by dozens of strangers, he walked and walked, trying to sort through the latest developments.

The dead poachers. Was it as simple as it appeared? Wiping a slate clear of any who knew the identity of the poaching-smuggling ring's leader? He frowned. Or was it a subtle warning to stay away? As evil as the victims were, they were still victims. Possibly leaving behind widows and children. One could argue that the poisoning had saved a great deal of time and expense for the courts, yet it would be stupid to believe that was the end of the matter.

Txoko was so engrossed in his thoughts that he failed to notice when he strolled down what was affectionately known as 'Vendor Street' by native Ibilians without a single merchant daring to brave his scowl. The foot traffic dwindled as he left the business district, turning down one street after another. It wasn't until his knee began to ache that he roused himself enough to wonder where he'd wandered to.

Forehead creasing, he looked up and down the street. The houses, most of them three stories tall, seemed surprisingly familiar. The corner street sign was obscured by a thriving bush, and when he moved closer to get a better look, he saw a relatively modest two-story house that he knew instantly.

Chapter 5

"I thought you said you were too busy to go out," Mardul pouted from where he'd positioned himself in the one decent chair in the tiny kitchen garden.

Leuna stepped over Mardul's outstretched legs for the twentieth time—not that she was counting—and set a bundle of fresh herbs on the small table by the door to the kitchen. She'd hoped working in the garden would encourage him to leave, as it always had in the past. Unfortunately, this afternoon he seemed filled with determination.

"I said I had obligations to my grandparents and my patient," she corrected. Again. "Attending the concert tonight will fulfill both."

"Both?" Mardul frowned. "You mean you'd rather spend your evening with a sickly old man than with me?"

He watched her closely for a reaction, but other than a slight hesitation, there was none. He'd talked to everyone he could think of in an effort to discover who her mystery patient was and come up empty handed. Rather than being discouraged, he was now further intrigued. It had to be someone wealthy. Not because she cared about money, but because only an extremely wealthy person could afford to be sick quietly. Everyone else had to make their excuses at work. He'd investigated the society matrons as well and all of them were reported in public that same week. Which left a wealthy, wealthy man.

"I think it's terribly bad form of you to put me off like this," Mardul sniffed, oblivious to how sulky he sounded. How could she keep washing those herbs when he was trying to speak to her about something serious?

"Put you off?" Leuna turned to stare at him. How she wished she could! What a relief it would be to tell him exactly what she thought of him, even if it sent him storming out the door to (hopefully) never return. Swallowing the words, she forced herself to admit that would be unkind. Also an utter waste of breath, for Mardul was satisfied that he was in the right.

Closing her eyes, Leuna counted to fifteen before picking up the mincer. Frustration and sharp objects didn't mix well. Was it her imagination or had the garden begun to shrink since Mardul followed her out there?

"I told you during your first visit that I'm very busy and on a short schedule." Expertly, she prepared the mint, scooping up little piles of it once she was finished and setting them in the bowl Dari provided. All the while, Mardul was thankfully silent.

"Arratsalde."

Leuna nearly dropped the bowl as the familiar voice reached her ears. Almost—almost—called out to Neba.

Txoko's smile slipped when she didn't immediately turn to greet him. He'd hoped to have a private moment with her, to discuss the truth of Zain's identity before she came to the embassy that evening. Or so he'd told himself.

"See here." Mardul, startled by the voice at the back gate, bounded to his feet and positioned himself before it. "On your way, man." His lip curled as he recognized the interloper. "Go tell your master that the doctor is not to be hounded like this.”

“Mardul!” Leuna couldn’t hold back the sharp rebuke this time. “You do *not* speak for me.”

“I was just trying to save you the bother,” Mardul protested, a wounded expression in his eyes. No one appreciated him.

Approaching the gate, Leuna wiped her hands on the borrowed apron. They’d had to take two folds in at the waist to make the length about right, then cinch the strings around it. It hadn’t bothered her before, but now she was acutely aware of it. Aware of the dirt under her nails, the wisps of hair that had fallen out of her hastily-made bun…she must look a fright.

Txoko abruptly realized that he was staring. “Barkamena,” he begged her pardon in Marroi, ignoring the overgrown oaf behind her. It was the sorrow in her eyes that made stringing words together a problem. “I… There is something I need to…”

“Yes, of course.” Beckoning for him to enter, Leuna swiftly removed the apron, stuffing it and the bowl of herbs into Mardul’s hands. “Take these to Dari, please. And I don’t mean to offend you, but I really don’t have time to see you this trip. Have a good day!” She made eye contact with Dari, who was kneading bread just inside the door to the kitchen, which they’d prudently left propped open while Mardul was there.

Now that it was just her and Txoko, who seemed uncharacteristically flustered, Leuna shut the door firmly in Mardul’s face. The reflection of Txoko that she saw in a pane of glass showed him as being engrossed in one of the plants, so she risked pulling out the few pins she'd used to secure her hair. Smoothing it hastily, she tied it back with a length of string she found on the table. Her feet slid a little in Dari's garden shoes when she turned to face him, but there was nothing she could do about that right now.

Txoko inhaled deeply, savoring the scents of the tiny garden. Floral, herbal, damp and earthy, to him it was the sweetest perfume in Jatorri. Here and there leafy herbs spilled out of round wooden tubs, while the narrow planters held more colorful, regal-looking plants.

"Nola lagun zaitut?" *How can I help you?* she asked, choosing Marroi since she was fairly certain that no one else in earshot spoke it. His gaze swept over her like a warm summer breeze and she reminded herself that it was just business. He was her patient. He…was coming closer.

Txoko watched her move away from him, putting a hip-high wooden sink between them. As if she needed to keep her hands busy, she filled a metal glass with water and set it down, her movements stiff and jerky. Plucking leaves from three separate plants, she began rolling them between her fingers, crushing them lightly. Her retreat matched the mysterious hunching of her shoulders from when he'd spoken earlier. Confused, he decided to stick to the reason he'd given himself for visiting the house at all.

"You speak Marroi very well." He felt a little silly saying that to her in Marroi, but assumed she had a good reason for choosing it over Lurrakian.

"Thank you." She got caught looking at him, and gestured toward the now-empty chair. "You should probably sit down. Take the weight off that knee." She held her breath for an instant, wondering if he'd remembered, if he was going to try to explain calling Zain 'brother.' Then he chuckled and settled into the chair instead.

She exhaled a little in relief as she used a long-handled metal spoon to stir the crushed leaves into the water. She'd known Txoko was hurting yesterday when he walked her home, but she hadn't said anything to protect his pride. Also, she'd assumed the embassy doctor would tend to him, forgetting that a man's pride could prevent him from doing common sense things like calling on a doctor. Wrapping a clean cloth over the top of the glass, she poured the liquid into a second glass.

"Drink this." She offered it to him. "It will help with the inflammation in your knee," she added when he eyed it suspiciously. Their fingers touched as he took it from her and she turned away under the guise of a consuming interest in tossing the spent leaves into the compost bin.

Sipping the tonic water cautiously, Txoko watched her over the glass rim as she deftly washed the first glass. "Do I taste mint?" he asked.

"Yes, of course." She smiled knowingly. "You thought it would taste like the hezur potion, didn't you?" He'd been briefly—and unjustly—jailed shortly after their arrival in Ibilia. Several of his bones were broken by his smuggler cellmates before he was freed, and she'd dosed him repeatedly with the hezur. He was squinting at her thoughtfully, so she recited his description of it back to him, "I believe you said it tasted like rotten musker fruit mixed with ground-up river rocks and swamp water." She nearly dropped her glass as she realized that they'd uttered the last two words together.

"I…the jail…" Txoko set the glass aside and pressed both hands to his head as his hazy dream memories solidified. A few more of them, anyway. These were particularly violent. Based on circumstantial evidence, he'd been thrown in an Ibilian jail. Specifically into a cell filled with known smugglers, who'd beaten him out of fear that he was a government spy. He exhaled a slow, shuddering breath, almost laughing at the irony.

Fearing a mind fever, Leuna was beside him in a flash. Dropping to her knees, she gripped his wrists. "You control your mind. No one else." The exact same words she'd repeated until she was hoarse during one of his worst mind fevers.

With a flick of his wrists, Txoko had reversed the situation so that it was him holding onto her wrists. "I control my mind," he repeated, staring into her lovely, worried brown eyes. Rising, he pulled her to her feet. Releasing her wrists, he caught her about the waist and drew her to him.

"Neba, I…" Too late, she caught herself. Bit her lip. *Neba*—the nickname she'd given him shortly after they met. In the old tongue, it meant *brother* and seemed appropriate at the time. Now, despite everything that had happened, despite her best efforts, she still thought of him as the man she'd known in Herrixka.

"I'm…not your brother," Txoko murmured, a memory stirring. He'd said that to her once in the forest, when he'd been convinced he was Jerl

Karruan, dragon soldier of the first order. She'd seen through the false memory immediately—but even so, at the time he'd sensed her reluctance as she politely refused his advances. "I'm not sure even the most devoted of sisters would've done what you did for me, though. You left everything, your home, your friends, and came with me to make sure I got my memories back." He frowned. "You could've died in Ilun."

She gaped up at him. *He remembers!*

"You loved him." He wasn't asking. He'd seen it in her eyes every day of their journey from Herrixka. Felt the ache of wondering whether his reciprocal feelings were a betrayal to an unknown someone from his mysterious past.

Unable to meet the intensity of his gaze, she looked away in confusion. That seemed to encourage him and she caught her breath as his calloused hand slid around the nape of her neck.

As he leaned closer, his fingers encountered the tie in her hair and he pulled it loose, allowing her hair to fall freely down her back and about her shoulders. How many times had he longed to run his fingers through her hair? Touching his lips to hers, he felt the shock of contact. Her eyes fluttered open, as if she, too, felt the wonderfully inexplicable sensation. More than curiosity prompted him to gather her even closer, to kiss her again. And she was warm and alive in his embrace, returning every kiss he gave.

Emotions rammed into each other in her mind, splintering and shifting and blending until the turmoil gave way to one, soul-searing realization. "I love you." She wasn't ignoring that he'd been pompous and overbearing in Ilun as the recently-returned King Txoko. However, there was a dire risk of heartbreak no matter what she did. And she sensed that, underneath the crown, he was first and foremost the man she'd come to know in the forest outside of Herrixka.

Txoko, caught between kisses, nearly froze in place. She loved him? Looking down into her eyes, the sure knowledge that he loved her, too, burst from deep within him. As Neba, certainly. Also as Txoko, king of Marroi. *What have I done?* Some of his consternation must've shown on his face, for she began to shrink away from him.

"No woman has ever said that to me before," he explained huskily, tightening his hold a little. Kissing her eyes closed again, he cradled her in his arms, his cheek against her luxuriously soft hair.

It's the truth, he told himself defensively. His wife, Nire, had gone out of her way to make it clear that she'd married him strictly out of an obligation to her father and the Marroi people. She'd never shirked any of her wifely duties, but he'd been startled and a little saddened to hear the doctor announce she was with child. Raised by loving parents of his own, Txoko naturally worried about his child's future. That only added to his guilt at their deaths.

"Txoko?" Leuna gulped as he squeezed her a little too hard. "I can't breathe." Instantly, he released her and she wobbled a little in surprise.

Running both hands through his hair, Txoko inhaled a lungful of Leuna-free air. Nothing changed. His heart still raced from their kisses. His arms still felt empty without her in them. His mind still told him he'd done the unforgivable, for he couldn't possibly marry her. When was the last time a Marroi king married outside of his own people?

Alarmed by the wild look in his eyes, Leuna took a slow step closer. Any feelings of hurt or rejection she might've felt faded at his obvious distress.

"Txoko?" Taking hold of his hands, she repeated his name. "Txoko!" As if in answer, he took another deep breath and shook his head.

"I must go."

"Go? Now?" Leuna couldn't seem to release his hands. "Why?"

"I..." He shook his head again. The pain in her eyes was like a two-bladed knife twisting in his gut. "I can't explain it."

Leuna took a deep breath of her own and forced herself to open her hands. The gate banged shut behind him so hard that the latch fell into place on its own. Dropping back onto the chair, she buried her face in her hands and wept.

Thankfully, no one disturbed her. A dozen smaller things contributed to her tearstorm, for she hadn't had a good cry since...goodness, since Gaia's triplets had all arrived safely. She'd been so worried about the dangers of a multiple birth that the relief manifested in tears. Sniffling, she wiped her cheeks, then rinsed her face at the sink.

She took several slow, deep breaths while patting her face dry. It was getting late and she needed to clean up before dressing for the concert, but instead she paused to let the sun warm her face.

The wind lifted her loose hair and draped it across her face, prompting a surprised laugh. She hadn't expected him to take her hair down. Smoothing it back, she sighed. She enjoyed kissing Txoko. There was no question of that. She enjoyed his company, too, as she'd learned yesterday at the stables. Apparently even a king could be personable when he wasn't tied up in knots over something important. She'd just have to hope he'd be able to explain his abrupt departure soon, before the uncertainty tied *her* in knots.

"Leuna?" Merezi stuck her head out the kitchen door. "There you are! I've been hunting the house over for you, child."

"Sorry." Leuna quickly picked leaves from two of the herbs and popped them into her mouth without rinsing them. "I didn't hear you calling." Hurrying over to her grandmother, she took her outstretched hand.

"Oh, it wasn't really urgent," Merezi laughed. Deciding not to ask why Leuna needed the pain relieving properties of the herbs she was chewing on, Merezi continued, "I simply wanted to ask what you were wearing to the concert."

"I haven't given it much thought," Leuna admitted.

"Excellent!" Merezi giggled like a girl and tugged Leuna up the stairs. "I had a perfectly brilliant idea this morning."

"You did?" Leuna couldn't help raising her eyebrows.

"Absolutely. Do you remember the outfits we wore to the Marroi festival?"

Leuna reached back, way back in her memory for a Marroi event big enough to call 'the' festival. Finally, she offered, "The one we attended with Liria?"

"Yes, exactly!"

"You aren't going to suggest that we wear those outfits tonight?" Leuna objected. "They're over ten years old!"

"And as beautiful as they were the day Liria gifted them to us," Merezi assured her. Hurrying over to the door to Leuna's room, she flung it open. "See?"

The freshly-pressed suit hung on the door of Leuna's wardrobe, tempting her. The grass-green trousers seemed to provide the foundation for the embroidered vines that wound their way up the knee-length bata. White flowers fairly burst from the vines, a lovely contrast to the nearly flame-orange fabric, which gradually softened to a dusty orange around the shoulders.

"Isn't it terribly out of style?" Leuna suggested warily. More importantly, what would Txoko think if she showed up at the embassy wearing traditional Marroi clothing? That she was trying to look the part of his wife? That she…what? Was somehow desperate?

"Nonsense." Merezi waved the idea away. "The palantzia is such a classic that it never goes out of style. And these colors, my dear." She stroked the wrist-length sleeve. "So perfect for you, especially now that you have that lovely tan."

Reluctantly, Leuna nodded, then laughed when her grandmother squealed and hugged her. She sort of had to agree, so that her grandmother could wear her palantzia, too.

"I had mine cleaned and pressed as well," Merezi

announced, pleased with herself for her forethought. "And Xelebre has a dashing galtzak outfit, charcoal with silver and red." She clapped her hands with excitement.

"That should match your palantzia perfectly," Leuna agreed. That was that, apparently. They were all going in traditional Marroi dress, and Txoko could think what he wanted. Stifling a sigh, she acknowledged that he would have anyway.

"Now, you better hurry and get cleaned up." Merezi made a mental note to speak with Xelebre about Mardul. Really, if he was going to make a pest of himself and put Leuna in a bad mood, something was going to have to be done. "Use the orange blossom soap," she suggested, hoping it would at least help Leuna perk up a little. "That way, you'll smell like you look," she teased.

Leuna wrinkled her nose at her grandmother, then waved her out of the room, grateful to at last hear the door click shut. Pouring herself a glass of water from the pitcher on her chest of drawers, she rinsed her mouth and swallowed. The herbs would take the edge of her tearstorm headache, but a warm soak sounded marvelous.

She wet her hair under the tap while the bath was running, and worked a thick shampoo into it until it was thoroughly coated. Tying it up so it would be out of her way, she added a few drops of scent from the vials on the bath shelf and stirred the water.

She smelled more like a flower garden than an orange grove by the time she dropped the damp towel and her dirty clothes into the hamper. Slipping into a dressing robe, she rang for a maid to come dry her hair. At home in Herrixka, she often dried its length over her supper fire, but it would hardly do to show up at the concert smelling like a narrasti steak.

"Shall I put your hair up, Miss?" asked the maid. While she loved working with Merezi's fine, silver hair, it wasn't often she got the chance to work with thick locks like these.

"Yes, thank you." Leuna was a little surprised at the offer, since she usually did her own hair. That didn't stop her from relaxing against the padded chair back, though. Having someone else brush her hair did wonders for her state of mind.

Deftly, the maid swept Leuna's hair back so that it was loose and soft on the sides, tying it off at the base of her head. From there she wound and braided and pinned and tucked until the rest of it was arranged in an ornate chignon around the original tie. Tired, but pleased, she shyly asked, "Will that do, Miss?"

Leuna blinked her eyes open and gasped. "You've outdone yourself!" Turning her head this way and that, she stared at her reflection, wondering at the stunning creature that stared back at her.

"Do you really like it, Miss?"

"Like it?" On second thought, Leuna wasn't quite sure she looked like herself with her hair done so intricately. Already tired of trying to figure out how it might affect Txoko, she brushed that thought aside. However, she couldn't disappoint the eager maid. "It's exquisite!"

Later, as they entered the embassy, she caught a glimpse of herself in one of the large mirrors that hung on the wall, strategically placed a few feet into the entranceway. Like most of the women passing by it, she paused an instant to assess herself for anything that needed to be smoothed or straightened. It hadn't been especially windy on the ride over, but it was a sensible precaution.

One tail of the long, white sash…um, gerri…that completed the palantzia hung down from her waist on her left side, not quite to her knees. From where she'd wound it once about her waist, it looped up, over her right shoulder, then draped down her back, again not quite to her knees. A tie on the bata's right shoulder kept it all from falling forward and tripping her.

"Now or never," she murmured to herself as she turned to join her grandparents.

Chapter 6

The concert had barely ended before a pair of servants began moving through the hall, removing the coverings from the firestones. Personally, Txoko couldn't care less about seeing the rest of the guests. Leuna hadn't come and she was the only one who mattered to him.

"Don't forget to give the Argian ambassador a moment," Zain cautioned in a low voice. "She insists that she pay her respects."

Txoko nodded automatically and rose, straightening his bata and gerri. They had a tendency to skew to one side or the other, depending on which way he leaned while sitting. While scanning the room for the Argian party, his attention was drawn to a lovely brunette. Dressed in traditional Marroi clothes, she still sat and stared at the orchestra's chairs. Did she expect to see young Peldu—the subject of the night's paeans—rise from the floor in full armor? Or perhaps, ride in on his gallant dragon, Ausart? She turned away, presumably to speak to someone in her party, and he continued searching the crowd.

The firestones were all uncovered by now, which made it easy. While many of the women present wore gaily colored clothing, the entire Argian party was attired in their standard earth tones. A highly intellectual society, their research and engineering had done much to advance the fabric industry in terms of dyes and process simplification via machinery, but their citizens seemed to have no use for the fancy clothing they helped to produce. All they wanted was sturdy clothing that required a minimum of care.

Smiling, Txoko made his way over to them. His journey was interrupted a dozen times by those gushing over the performance—whose praise he redirected to the chief musician, situated near the refreshment table; and by those seeking audience—whom he redirected to his aide. At long last...

"Counselor Bardin." Txoko bowed, not because she required it but because his own culture did. Likewise, her culture requiring nothing but a welcoming smile from her, he was not offended by her omitting a curtsy or any other form of deference to his title. "I trust you found the performance satisfactory."

"Quite." She nodded. "The music particularly had an interesting effect on myself and some others of my party. I wonder if you could direct us on how to acquire a copy of the notations so that we might study it further?"

Txoko bowed again. "It would be my pleasure to have a copy of the notations sent to your consul in the morning."

"You are too kind." Bardin turned slowly at the waist, then took a step. Satisfied that Txoko was following her lead, she began walking toward the exit. "I presume your cousin relayed my message."

Typical Argian. To the point and no messing about with titles, Txoko thought wryly.

"He informed me you wished to speak with me, yes. How may I be of service?"

"Ah, but my message is on how we can better serve you." She allowed herself a small, satisfied smile. "Innovations in crop production and processing have allowed us to prepare your annual order of lekale beans early. We must arrange transport."

Txoko nearly sighed. He understood, he supposed, why she'd believed it necessary to discuss the transportation of lekale beans with him, personally. Argian pride was tied up in everything they undertook, and this was as close to boasting as he'd ever heard Bardin come. It was also a pretty good trading strategy. Apprise the king that they were ahead of schedule in the hopes that he'd praise them when speaking to others, that sort of thing.

"I'll speak with my minister of trade," he promised smoothly. She gave him a parting nod and he bowed in turn. He was seriously considering slipping out into the hallway with the Argian party when he caught sight of the brunette again. *Leuna!*

As if she'd felt his gaze on her, she looked in his direction. Their gazes met. Locked. He took a step toward her, then thought better of it. If he plunged back into the mass of guests, he'd never get out again, not until the last chatterbox had been politely herded out the door. Barely controlling a scowl, he caught the attention of a passing server.

Leuna tried to watch without appearing to watch as Txoko murmured something to a server. Did he want to speak with her? What would they say? Something in the way he was looking at her made her wonder if he had more kissing in mind.

At that thought, she dropped her gaze and caught hold of her grandfather's hand. She wasn't sure what was about to happen, but she knew she couldn't just disappear and leave them wondering. She smiled reassuringly up at him, then glanced nonchalantly around. Her agitation grew with every inquisitive gaze that she met. It felt as though everyone in the room had noticed how Txoko was staring at her.

"Doctor?"

She jumped. She'd forgotten about the server. Tongue-tied, she just nodded.

"Would you come with me, please?"

Her grandfather tightened his grip on her hand. "Come where?" he asked.

"It's alright." Leuna squeezed his hand. "I'll meet you back at the house." Startled by her own bold declaration, she hastily turned to follow the servant.

Xelebre kept a firm hold on her hand. "Are you sure that's wise?" He'd been a young man in love and was fairly confident that Txoko could be trusted where Leuna's true happiness was concerned. Still, he wanted to be sure she gave herself a moment to think.

Leuna looked up at him, startled by the question. She didn't have to look very far up, not quite so far as she would've had her own father been the one asking the question. She imagined the look in his eyes would've been a perfect match, though. Xelebre's wise gray eyes seemed to be cautioning her, warning her not to reach for a vine without checking for thorns first. She took a slow, deep breath, and nodded.

"Thank you, Grandpa." She kissed him gently on the cheek. Then, finding her hand free, she turned to follow the server through the maze of chatting guests.

The press of people thinned as they moved into the hallway. A few Marroi dignitaries had escaped as far as the entryway, where they chatted with other dignitaries, some of whom were already slipping into jackets and hats. After they turned a corner, even the noise began to fade.

"M'lady." The server stopped before a glass door and bowed.

Puzzled, she watched the server hurry back to the party. If Txoko wanted to talk with her, why bring her out here? Or, rather, why have someone else bring her out here and leave her? Rubbing her forehead to stop the scowl she could feel coming on, she sighed. Guessing games were not her favorite pastime.

A cool breeze struck her and she looked up. Txoko stood, framed in the doorway, one hand extended toward her. Slipping her hand into his, she allowed him to draw her outside.

"Oh." She inhaled deeply. The fragrance of the night-blooming lurrin flower called to her from deeper in the garden. As sweet as any perfume, it was a soft, alluring scent.

Txoko eased the door shut behind her, hoping against hope that they would have a few minutes of privacy. Except…now that they were alone, he found himself tongue-tied. He'd always found her attractive, but this was a completely different look for her. Half of him wanted to pull out all the pins holding her hair up in that dignified style and kiss her until they'd both forgotten he was king of anything. The other, more sensible half, grown strong through years of training, insisted that he speak to her first.

"Leuna."

"Hmm?" She hadn't been in this garden in ages!

Stepping forward, she looked down the path to her right. So much had changed! "There used to be a statue of your great-grandfather over there." She pointed.

"Oh?" Taking a deep breath, he reached for her hand, but she moved just quickly enough that he missed.

"And over there," she turned to her left, "was a berry bush big enough to hide in." Laughing, she walked toward the memory. A small stone basin perched on the back of a…a wingless dragon—she wasn't quite sure—where the bush used to be. It was the sort of thing that birds might bathe in, though quite a bit deeper and bigger around than she was accustomed to seeing. "Not that we ever did," she clarified. "Hide in it, I mean."

"We?" Txoko was confused. "You've been here before?"

"Oh yes, years ago." She answered the second question first. "My friend, Liria, used to invite me over after classes at university. She specialized in children's medicine, but we still had classes together for a while."

"I had no idea." Nor did he have even a glimmer of an idea how he was going to broach the subject of her… Wait, that was it! Opening his mouth to speak, he was preempted by her walking off, in the direction of…well, how should he know? He'd hardly spent any time in the gardens this trip and the blasted gardener kept changing things and… He hurried to follow her before she moved out of sight.

"Here they are." Leuna dropped to her knees beside the lurrin patch. Too late, she remembered her outfit and jumped to her feet with a gasp of dismay.

"What?" Txoko was beside her instantly, his arm closing about her waist as he lifted her clear of any lurking danger. He saw nothing. Still holding her against his side, he looked at her. "Are you alright?"

"I…" Leuna managed a small smile. It was the oddest thing, to be dangling there with her feet a few inches off the ground. "Just a little breathless."

Txoko smiled back, unable to hold onto his annoyance with how things had worked out thus far. "If I set you down, will you promise to stay in one spot?" he asked, arching an eyebrow.

Leuna nodded quickly.

"Good." Lowering her gently so that her feet were again on the path, he kept his hand on her waist, just in case. "There's something I want to…need to ask you." Her eyebrows rose slightly and he found himself wanted to kiss her delicately colored eyelids. In his experience, though, women's powders left a terrible taste on one's lips. That made it easier for him to focus and he continued, "Please come to the dragon festival in Marroi."

He considered kissing her when she didn't respond right away. Her lips were their usual tempting shade of healthy red, so there was probably no artificial coloring on them. He liked that.

"You want me to come to Marroi?" she whispered. Her lungs had tightened so badly that she could barely get a breath of air, let alone enough to speak at a normal level.

"Please." He thought looking her in the eyes might help, and it did, a little. Something in them made him want to explain his purpose in inviting her, to reassure her. "It would be unfair of me to ask more of you than that right now. I believe, however, that after you've spent some time in Marroi, gotten to know the people..." He felt her pulling away from him and his heart rate shot to panic speed. "Then, I could ask for what I really want. What I hope you want, too."

Leuna stilled. It shouldn't be possible to detect someone else's heartbeat through their chest muscles like this, but she could've sworn she could feel his heart pounding under her palms. *What I hope you want, too.*

"Before I could possibly decide about your invitation," she struggled for a breath, "I would need to know exactly what you're getting me into."

So, he kissed her. Softly. Just once. "Stealing kisses is fun," he admitted, "but I want so much more with you." Taking one of her hands, he lifted it to his bowed forehead, an unspoken pledge of devotion. "If I could do as I pleased, I'd be on my knees right now, asking you to share my life."

I want so much more with you—not 'from you.' His choice of words didn't escape her notice. There was no longer any doubting his meaning or intent. But could she leave Herrixka? She closed her eyes to block out the powerful longing in his, which threatened to pull her heart into her throat. And then what could she say but yes?

"I need to think about it." A barebones statement if ever she'd made one. She rested her head against his chest and closed her eyes.

"Of course." Resting his cheek against the crown of her head, Txoko kept his arms wrapped loosely around her. A night bird chirped somewhere in one of the carefully sculpted hedges and he smiled.

"What would I do about Herrixka?" she asked.

"Herrixka?" He remembered many places, so many. He hadn't just spent his summers chasing adventure; he'd done a good bit of traveling, too. But it was never the *places* that he really missed. It was the people. "Jartz. Rakin, the butcher. Your friend, Ama." He hugged her gently. "Do you suppose there is somewhere in Lurrak a doctor who could take good care of them for you?"

Leuna sniffled a little and leaned back before she got his fancy jacket wet. His fingers came up to wipe away her tears, and he kissed her damp eyes softly. Rising on her tiptoes, she brushed her lips against his. She liked stealing kisses, too. Especially his. They lingered in that pose until a bell tower somewhere nearby began sounding the hour.

Reluctantly, she drew away from him. "I should go."

Txoko quickly compromised by taking her warm hand in his and holding it while they walked toward the nearest exit.

"How long is the dragon festival?" she asked, suddenly curious. The stories she'd heard defied her imagination, and it seemed that the festival must last for weeks, or even a month.

"People begin to gather a few days before it starts," he admitted, nearly grimacing at the thought of the work that lay ahead of him, "but officially, the event only lasts five days."

"Really?"

"Unfortunately." Txoko smiled down at her even

as he waved away a guard who was coming to check on them. He'd have to speak to the head of embassy security about instructing the guards at these events to be more discreet. Barring an emergency, couples usually came to the garden so they wouldn't be disturbed.

He hesitated at the exit, eyeing the street traffic beyond. Many of the evening's guests had arrived in private carriages, but there were plenty of public carriages lined up along the curb.

Turning to Leuna, he suggested impulsively, "How would you like to fly home?"

"On a dragon?" She immediately felt silly for asking, even though dragons were still relatively new to her. "I mean…you just happen to have a dragon at the embassy right now?"

"Always." He grinned at her. "It can be very handy, having a dragon about."

"Well, in that case…"

They were giggling like children by the time Txoko pulled her up the last flight of stairs to the roof.

"I can't believe the steward didn't see us," Leuna gasped, clinging to his hand.

"I think he did," Txoko laughed. "He was just polite enough to pretend not to!"

She stopped suddenly when a sleek shadow moved in the center of the roof. "Is that the dragon you want me to ride?" she half-asked, half-squeaked. The rooftop was fairly well lit by firestones, but somehow the dragon's scales were absorbing that light. Even the light from Jatorri's three moons produced only the faintest reflection, allowing Leuna to see that the dragon was much narrower than the Sparks, much longer.

"Yes." Txoko squeezed her hand reassuringly. "She's beautifully tempered, I promise you." He maintained contact with Leuna even as he motioned for a guard to cinch up the girth on the long, lightweight saddle. Leading Leuna to the dragon's head, he introduced, "This is Aldia, a gauean dragon." Aldia blinked, recognizing her name, and shoved her head into Txoko's chest. "Easy there." He cuddled her head affectionately.

Leuna watched as he ran the knuckles of his free hand up and down what looked like the bridge of Aldia's inky black nose. She almost laughed out loud when the dragon's ears began fluttering.

"That means she likes it," he explained. "Here." Coaxing Leuna closer, he showed her where to stroke Aldia under the chin. "This is probably her second favorite spot," he confided.

Smooth, warm dragon scales slid underneath Leuna's fingertips as she mimicked Txoko's demonstration. Aldia's eyes locked on Leuna's face, but somehow she wasn't afraid. Suddenly, Aldia sighed and shifted herself forward, planting her head in Leuna's arms.

Txoko laughed as he gripped her shoulders and steadied her. "I think she likes you."

"She's so…beautiful." Awed, Leuna glanced down the considerable length of the lean dragon to the tip of her tail. As Txoko prepared to step into the saddle, Leuna sensed a shift in Aldia's mood. A slight tensing of the muscles. A small spreading of her wings. The tiniest of back-and-forth flicks of her slender tail as it rasped along the stone beneath her feet. "Does she enjoy flying?" Leuna wondered aloud, unable to help the nervous catch in her voice.

"All dragons enjoy flying," announced the guard as he finished adjusting the second set of stirrups. Leaning in, he patted Aldia's rump with pride. "This one more than most, though. That's part of why she was chosen for emergency duty."

"Come."

At that single word, Leuna's eyes, which had been straining to see the tail movements that she could so easily hear, lifted to meet Txoko's. His shoulders were relaxed, his hand extended invitingly. Setting aside her trepidation, Leuna put her hand in his and set her foot in the empty stirrup. The saddle, which she'd noted for its length, had no pommel, just a slightly raised lip in front. To her relief, Txoko had taken the front position.

"By your leave, Miss." The guard clumsily interrupted her bravery. "It's best that you put your left foot in. Lever yourself up, then lift your right foot up over her hips." Embarrassed by her ineptitude, he gripped his belt a bit more tightly than necessary. "Otherwise, you'll…you'll wind up watching where you been."

Red-cheeked, Leuna did as he'd suggested. Granted, she could've just as easily gotten her hands on the jarlekua and swung her right leg back and over as she'd planned, but she didn't want to embarrass the guard further. Then she was in the soft, leather jarlekua with Txoko's back looming large before her. Instinctively, she wrapped both arms about his middle. And resisted the urge to hide her face when Aldia pranced a few steps forward.

"Aldia, ireki," Txoko commanded. Her muscles bunched, her wings spread, and they were aloft! Rooftops slipped along beneath them, different shapes and sizes, but growing smaller and smaller as they went.

"We're climbing."

Txoko tried not to wince as her fingers dug into his sides. Holding the reins with one hand, he laced the fingers of his free hand through hers, willing her to feel the steady rate of his breathing. Anxious for a diversion, he looked out over the city.

"Look." He pointed, leaving plenty of slack in the reins that streamed over the back of his hand. "There's the railway station where we arrived. And over there." He pointed to another building, one that stood out by its sheer size and height. "The stables."

She did her best to laugh. "If we get much higher, we're going to be able to see Auzo, too. It's a much smaller city," she admitted, "so it might be difficult to spot."

"Hmm, not a bad idea," he chuckled. "Shall we fly over and visit Afaria? Perhaps have a late supper?"

She couldn't help herself. She laughed despite her fear. "We'd freeze before we got there."

"Can't have that." Signaling to Aldia with a nudge of his boot and a shift in his bodyweight, Txoko urged her still higher. "Let's visit somewhere a little nearer instead."

Looking up, Leuna gasped in awe.

Chapter 7

The darkness of the night gave way to brilliant light as they broke through the lower layer of the star expanse. Dozens of colors flashed past, Aldia's wings scattering puffs of loose stardust about them as she winged her way along.

Txoko craned his neck around so that he could see Leuna. Eyes wide with wonder, lips parted in delight as she half-uttered words that seemed to fall short of what she was seeing. It was as if…no, it was even better than his memories of seeing it for the first time himself.

"Never in my wildest dreams…" Reaching out, she trailed her fingers through a particularly thick cloud of pale pink stardust. A few glowing particles clung to her skin, then were absorbed in a rush of tickly, tingly sensation.

He bit back a promise to bring her there as often as she liked. He'd promise her anything to win her, so he'd better not get started. Not even with something this simple. Discreetly applied cues guided Aldia through a leisurely circle of stars, bringing them into contact with the outer edge of several different hues.

"It's so warm here." She paused, listening. "And so quiet."

"Yes," he agreed. "That's one of many reasons I love coming here." Her hand squeezed his encouragingly when he lapsed into silence. He appreciated that she didn't immediately jump into the conversational gap, that she wanted to hear what he hadn't yet said. "There've been times in my life when I didn't know what to do or how to do it. I've…made some of my most difficult decisions up here, where I could hear myself think." He'd never told that to anyone before and now he waited somewhat anxiously for her response.

"Is it very hard to be a king?" As foolish as the question sounded, even to Leuna, it was what she needed to know if she was to seriously consider marrying him. Her heart declared itself every time their eyes met, and had he asked her to marry him that very night, she probably would've said yes. How grateful she was that his own prudence granted her the time she needed to at least try to think things through!

Txoko took his time answering. If nothing else, the innocence of her question proved to him that it was wiser not to rush her, however insistent his heart might be. "I suppose, given the proper preparation, it is no more difficult to be a king than it is to be a doctor. For example, I imagine you experience some distress as you face each new situation?"

"Like the first time I set a broken leg?" she offered, trembling slightly at the memory. Resting her cheek against his back, she felt him nod.

"Yes, exactly. No matter how hard we've tried or how prepared we think we are, there's almost always something unexpected, something that strips away our complacency and forces us to face down our fears." Biting his tongue to stop himself, he wondered what he was thinking, giving voice to such thoughts! She was going to bid him goodnight and mean goodbye—or good riddance!

"Hmmm." Leaning back slightly, she ran her hand down his back, noting the bunched muscles. Under other circumstances, she'd say he was bracing for a blow. Wrapping both arms tightly around his waist again, she offered, "I think I know what you mean. There's no such thing as a routine broken bone. A routine surgery. Even a 'simple' fever must be treated with respect." The tension left him as suddenly as it had come, giving her the sense that she'd said the right thing. Never before had she felt so much a part of someone else. It frightened her, a little.

Lifting her hand to his lips, he pressed a kiss to her fingers. "It's getting late." Reluctantly, he signaled to Aldia. He watched Leuna capture a handful of eggshell blue stardust, as they glided smoothly down from the star layer. "Will your grandparents be waiting up?"

"Probably." Her lips twitched in amusement. "I'm so used to keeping my own hours that I'd quite forgotten about them." She'd forgotten everything, except as it related to Txoko.

Txoko directed Aldia first toward the glow of Ibilia's lights, then took a sighting on three known buildings as they drew closer. Aldia's wings ruffled the tops of the trees in the park, folding in further and further until she gracefully landed in the street before Xelebre's home.

"I can't seem to let go," Leuna teased after failing to extricate her hand from his.

Swinging his leg over Aldia's neck, Txoko released Leuna's hand before sliding down.

"Remember," she braced her hands on his biceps as his hands settled around her waist, "it was your idea to come back."

The jacket she was wearing bunched beneath his hands as he held her above the walkway for an instant. For the first time that evening he really noticed the fact that she was too small for the jacket she wore. Thinking ahead to the dragon festival, he observed, "You look very lovely in that outfit. Where did you get it?" Breathing deeply, he inhaled the fragrance of her floral shampoo and the warm scent that was hers alone. It stirred him on a deep, instinctual level, one that made it much more difficult not to pledge whatever little bit of the world was his to give.

Blushing, she ventured a casual shrug. She couldn't fail to sense something of his change of mood. "It was a gift from my friend, Liria." A smile began tugging at the corners of her mouth when he moved nearer. "I mentioned her earlier."

"I love you," he murmured, resting his forehead against hers.

"I love you, too." That last was more of a breath than a word, for his lips were already settling on hers. Her senses were filled with him then—his warmth that seemed to envelope her; the tickle of his fingers in her hair; the whisper-soft kisses he was scattering across her face.

A shrill whistle startled her from his arms. For the next several seconds, she could do nothing but stand where she was, her hand pressed firm over her rapidly beating heart. At length, the whistle sounded again. A tremulous laugh bubbled up from inside her. "It's just a goiz bird," she announced in relief. Sure enough, the edges of the sky were turning from black to a dull gray.

Txoko smiled and nodded even as his conscience pricked him. "Here." Slipping an arm about her shoulders, he walked with her to the front door of her grandparents' home. "I've kept you up all night. I'm sorry."

She smiled when he pressed a light kiss to her temple. "Something tells me you're not all *that* sorry."

"Probably not," he agreed huskily, moving to open the door for her.

Halfway through the open door, she hesitated. "I had a wonderful time tonight. I wish I could say yes or no, but…"

"I'm glad you're taking time to think before deciding about the festival," he offered when her words trailed off. "And I assure you, the next question will be much more important."

Blushing, she stepped inside and closed the door behind her. Leaning against it, she closed her eyes. *What am I going to do?*

"Welcome home." Xelebre eyed his granddaughter with concern. Unless he was very much mistaken, he'd seen that look before. On his own daughter's face.

"Hello, Grandpa." Glancing at the clock, Leuna bit her lip. "I'm sorry to keep you up so late."

"Oh, no matter." He waved her apology away. "This makes up for all of the times that you didn't stay out late while you were attending university."

She laughed and hugged him. His padded dressing robe was soft against her cheek and she wondered if she didn't have to reach quite so far up to kiss his forehead as she used to. Her grandparents were ageless in her eyes before, yet now she couldn't help noticing that the fine lines around his eyes had deepened since the last time she'd noticed them. Yes, and there was more silver in his hair than she remembered.

"Come now," he chided her lightly. "You mustn't look at me like that."

"Like what, Grandpa?" she asked, tucking her arm through his as they turned toward the stairs.

"Oh…" He blustered briefly, then came right out and said it. "Like you've suddenly realized I'm an old man." He'd no sooner spoken than a muscle in his right leg cramped, probably the result of spending the night trying to get comfortable on the couch. How had he never before realized the sorry state of its cushions? If this courtship kept up much longer, he was going to have to speak to Merezi about redecorating their sitting room.

Leuna blushed lightly. "I don't know if that's what I realized just now. Not exactly."

"Well, then what, exactly?" He winked at her cheekily.

"I think…I think I realized how old *I* am." She paused at the door to her bedroom. "I've been so busy these past ten years. Being and doing and learning." She shook her head. "Shouldn't I be too old to be swept off my feet?"

"My dear child," Xelebre chuckled softly and squeezed her hand, "I make it a point to sweep your grandmother off her feet at least once a month."

"You do?" Leuna had often witnessed her grandfather's thoughtfulness and certainly she'd happened upon them sharing kisses over the years, but she hadn't associated that with the romantic love that was still swirling in her veins.

"Indeed. I know I hope I never grow too old to be swept off my feet!" His brows lowered thoughtfully. "Though I do think it's a tad easier for your grandmother." He nodded in answer to the surprised tilt of her head. "Yes, in fact, it's much easier. Most days, she just has to walk into the room, as lovely and warm as a fine summer's day." His voice lowered to a soft, almost reverent tone, and a far-off look came into his eyes as he spoke of his wife, the woman he adored.

Impulsively, Leuna kissed his cheek, giggling a little at the scruff that tickled her lips. "I love you, Grandpa."

"I love you, too." He kissed her cheek, then began making shooing motions with his hands. "Now get to bed, you crazy youngster. You'd think a doctor would know enough to get a decent night's rest."

That brought her giggles back, even as she closed the door between them and began taking her hair down. How many times had her sleep been interrupted by someone who needed a doctor? Opting for a pared-down version of her nightly routine, she slipped into her comfy pajamas, splashed water on her face, and closed the drapes against the inevitable sunshine. She fully expected to have difficulty sleeping, but she barely had time for one good yawn before her eyes fluttered closed.

That was how Merezi found her a few hours later, a sweet, peaceful expression on her face as she snored faintly. Shaking her head indulgently, Merezi retrieved last night's outfit for the waiting maid and softly closed the door again.

She drew the line, however, at sleeping past the midday meal. "Thank you, Dari." Picking up the prepared tray, Merezi proceeded up the stairs to Leuna's room. Balancing the tray on one hand, she knocked with the other. Much to her surprise, the door opened almost immediately, revealing a fully-dressed Leuna.

"Well!" Merezi entered the room without waiting for permission. "And how long have you been up?"

Leuna closed the door and came over to join her grandmother at the desk where she'd placed the tray. The smells rising from the covered dishes hinted at food, but her body just wasn't responding like it should. "An hour or two, I guess." Leaving the desk chair for her grandmother, Leuna sank back onto the end of her bed, where she'd been sitting for most of those two hours. Bracing the balls of her stockinged feet on the side of the desk, she looked out the open window.

"Hmmm." Merezi glanced at the untouched tray, then seated herself. "I hear you got home late last night."

"Yes. I was with Txoko." Leuna left off staring at the sky and looked at her grandmother. "He wants me to go to Marroi for their dragon festival."

"That sounds lovely." Merezi smiled and patted Leuna's knee. "A vacation will do you good, I think."

Leuna offered her a wry smile. "Oh, it's a little more complicated than that. If I like it, and if his people like me, I think he's going to ask me to marry him."

Merezi's chest constricted painfully. It was hard enough having Leuna in Herrixka, where they were at least able to pretend they could visit if the fancy struck them. How many times had she inadvertently dissuaded herself from a visit because of her local obligations? Or the difficulty of the journey? Or the inconvenience of closing the house? Silly excuses, all of them. But what would they do if their only grandchild moved to Marroi?

Leuna fiddled with the utensils on the breakfast tray without any real intent. The enormity of the decision—and the even bigger decision that might follow—weighed on her, robbing her of hunger.

"I remember when you had an important examination or project coming up." Merezi patted Leuna's knees. "You couldn't eat then, either." As much as she would've liked to excuse herself and go have a good cry, that wasn't an option. "Do you want to marry him?"

Leuna tried to shrug and wound up wrapping her arms protectively around herself. "I don't know. I think so."

"I think you must," Merezi agreed softly. Meeting Leuna's wide-eyed gaze with a smile, Merezi pointed out, "If you did not, this would be a much easier decision."

Leuna smiled wryly. "Good point." Tilting her head to the side, she asked, "How did you know you wanted to marry Grandpa?"

"Mmmm, well." For the second time since sitting down, Merezi blinked back tears. "I seem to recall having a very similar discussion with my mother, for one thing."

Leuna extended a hand to her grandmother and they sat in silence for a moment. She missed her mother, too; more than she had in years. During her childhood, she'd been quick to recognize the disparity between her life and the lives of her friends. Knowing that most of her friends already shared their mothers with their own siblings made her feel worse about the times she needed them, prompting her to rely on her father or herself whenever possible. The only relief lay in the lessons her father arranged for her in exchange for his services as a doctor. She'd learned everything from how to stuff a mattress with sweet grass to how to can meat at the elbows of those same, cheerful village mothers. This, though. This was different.

"Grandma?" she prompted hopefully. "I've never done this before."

Merezi perked up at that. "Haven't you? Oh, perhaps nothing of this magnitude, but I've seen you make dozens of difficult decisions. Now, I assume you wouldn't want to marry him if you didn't love him." Taking Leuna's blush as confirmation, she pressed on. "What exactly is so important that you'd allow it to come between you and the man you love?"

Slack-jawed, Leuna stared at her grandmother. "I wouldn't…I," she sputtered. The directness of the question had hit her smack in the middle of the obstacles she'd been pondering before her grandmother arrived. "Why…" Leaping to her feet, she folded her arms across her chest and paced the length of the room, then back. "Herrixka. I'm the only doctor in Herrixka."

Merezi dismissed that with a wave of her hand.

"You are hardly the only doctor in all of Lurrak, my dear. There must be a dozen who would be thrilled to learn of a chance to work in a small, out of the way town like Herrixka. Perhaps *two* dozen."

"But…but they wouldn't *know* Herrixka the way I do," Leuna protested. "They wouldn't know about Gaia's allergies. Or that Ama positively won't come in on her own, that they have to seek her out before her arthritis gets her bound up. Or when and where to harvest herbs. And what about Zaharre?" She threw up both hands. "He relies on me to help him make the difficult village decisions." Her objections faded before Merezi's knowing smile. Dropping to her knees before her grandmother, she whispered, "They'd have to learn it for themselves, wouldn't they? Just like my father did."

"Yes." Merezi smoothed her hair and kissed it. "That's right." Slipping her fingers under Leuna's chin, she tilted her head back so they were looking at each other. "Darling, every bride leaves who and what she knows to make her own life, at least to some degree, so let's not hide behind your affection for Herrixka, hmm?"

Resting her chin on her grandmother's knee, Leuna reconsidered the rest of the 'obstacles' she'd been worrying over. "I'm scared."

"That's perfectly normal," Merezi assured her. Joining Leuna on the floor, she slipped her arms around her. "You've been scared before, haven't you?"

Thinking back to the conversation she'd had with Txoko just a few hours ago, Leuna nodded slowly. "I love him or I don't. The rest of it is just…stuff, isn't it?"

"It's a bit more complicated than that," Merezi countered. "Though I think in this case, you can be fairly certain your intended will be able to provide for you materially." They chuckled together at that. "And from what I've seen of him, I'm fairly confident he would never knowingly hurt you."

Leuna sobered instantly. There was very little domestic abuse in Lurrak, thankfully, but as a medical student and then as a doctor, she'd seen things she'd never be able to forget.

"No, he wouldn't," she agreed firmly.

"And you would love him even if he grew old and bald and fat?" Merezi persisted, thinking of a few of her schoolgirl friends who'd been startled to learn that there were no exceptions to aging.

Leuna rolled her eyes. "Well, I doubt he'll go bald, if his father's and grandfather's portraits are any indication."

"What about fat?" Merezi held her hand out in front of her own, slender waistline, indicating a pretend paunch.

"I'm more worried about growing fat myself," Leuna gave in to a laugh. "I know you and Mother didn't," her grandmother's figure was *still* the envy of many society women here in Ibilia, "but what if I have several children and…and…" Her smile faded. "Grandma…what do you think it would be like, to grow up as the half-blood heir?" Her voice trembled a little.

Merezi didn't know what to say to that. When was the last time a Marroi king had married outside of his own people? Hmm. When was the *first* time? Knowing that Leuna expected an answer, she shook her head.

"That is a concern you must discuss with Txoko."

"Yes." Her arms wrapped protectively around herself again, Leuna nodded jerkily. "Yes, you're right, of course." A dozen thoughts tumbled about her brain. Not the least of which was *how*, exactly, she was supposed to broach such a subject.

Rising, Merezi took Leuna's face in her hands. "That only leaves one, terribly important thing," she announced. "Asking Grandpa's permission." They both laughed a little, but Leuna's distress was still plain on her face. Unable to lift the burden from her granddaughter's shoulders, Merezi hugged her instead.

Chapter 8

Txoko shook the last ambassador's hand warmly and ushered him into the hallway, where a liveried servant waited to guide him to the main exit. Closing the door to his office between them, Txoko sagged against it.

"You look terrible," Zain announced from where he was straightening things up. "Like you stayed out all night or something."

Txoko shook his head and came over to help. "I can't look any worse than you did while Katxa was teething. And before that Alak. And before that, Deko…" His teasing grin died upon his noticing the solemn expression on Zain's face.

"Yes, but that was different." Zain finished shuffling a pile of papers into an orderly stack and set it on the desk. "I was doing my duty."

"Yes, of course you were. Truthfully, I've always respected your dedication to your role as father." Abruptly, he registered the faint note of reprimand in Zain's words. Startled, he almost dropped the glasses he was carrying to the serving tray. "Are you rebuking me?" he asked.

"Yes." Zain fluffed a pillow with unnecessary force. The cleaning staff would come by later and give the room a proper going over, but tidying up was a habit he'd learned early on. Besides, it gave him an excuse to stay and discuss this with Txoko. "I think I am."

"For what?" Txoko demanded, suddenly irritated. Slamming the glasses onto the tray, he took a deep, calming breath. So this was why Zain had been acting strangely the whole morning, distant and disapproving. Spurred on by a need to defend his actions, Txoko repeated, "For what? I have attended every meeting, every dinner, every *event* since my return. I will not be accused of shirking my duty because I spent one evening wooing the woman I love."

Zain froze in place, arm half-extended to place another pillow. Slowly, he completed the action, then turned to face his slightly-older brother. "I am happy that you have found a woman to love." He acknowledged his personal feelings first. "And yet I must ask what you think will come of it?" It was a terrible thing to do, to dash his brother's hopes. He hated watching the light fade from Txoko's eyes, but it was better for him to hear it here and from someone he could trust.

"The law says nothing about the nationality of the queen." Txoko's rebuttal came too late to carry any force. Even though he knew it was true—hadn't he spent what was left of the night poring over the copy of the law books in the embassy library?—he also dreaded offending his people.

An uprising over the nationality of his second queen seemed absurd. Especially here, in the calm, cool office of the embassy generously provided by the Lurrakians. Yes, here they were as much kanpotarrak, or 'outsiders,' as the officials with which they met. But in Marroi, where her milk-colored skin would stand out amongst the shades of browns, where her floral scent would clash with the aromas of sand and spice…would it seem too impossible?

"There are many who will perceive that fact as evidence that our ancestors believed only a Marroi woman should rule," Zain pointed out. "We both know the bias against kanpotarrak runs deep, despite Lady Adeita's influence." He rolled his eyes. "Shall I tell you the joke I overheard the guards laughing at this morning?"

"No." Txoko shook his head. It had never been his policy to encourage rude behavior, including jokes told at the expense of others. "I know it won't be easy. But…I have to try."

Zain nodded. "Yes, I understand." His lips twisted wryly at the dubious arch to Txoko's eyebrow. "Have you forgotten so quickly the reluctance with which Min was given to me, an untitled aditua?" Somewhere between noble and soldier, a Marroi aditua was afforded great respect but few privileges in their culture. Many had considered him a fool for publicly professing his love for Min, the daughter of a wealthy dragon breeder.

Txoko hardly thought the last eight years to have passed 'quickly,' but said simply, "I remember."

Zain could've appealed to the crown, as Txoko's supposed cousin, to intervene on his behalf with Min's stubborn father. Instead, he'd nearly died leading a flight in the lustrum, the quinquennial wild dragon chase. Then he'd smashed all the rules by petitioning her father in public on the following night, at the feast the crown threw to honor his flight.

"I will help you however I can," Zain promised, reaching out to clasp his brother's hand. "However, I do not anticipate a simple resolution to the problem."

"Thank you." Txoko cleared his throat of the emotions crowding in on him. Under his father's rule, Zain had become an integral part of the king's court, and was almost as popular as Txoko himself. "Your support may make the difference."

"If you will permit me an observation?" Zain couldn't resist a guilty grin at Txoko's amused shake of his head. Bluntness served him well at times, but tact had its place, too. "You shouldn't be here, in Lurrak. Not now, while our people prepare for the dragon festival. I'm sure Queen Ema, for example, is beyond exasperated at having to consult you by letter." One of their mother's many roles, resumed since Nire's death, was arranging royal Marroi festivals, feasts, and holidays.

"I agree." Txoko took a deep breath and let it out. "And I've invited Leuna to return with me to Koroa."

Slack-jawed, Zain stared at him. He hadn't expected such a bold move. Though he probably should have. Wasn't he preparing to go to Herrixka? "When do we leave?"

Txoko hesitated. "It's only been a few hours since I asked her." Of course, it might be better if she arrived in Marroi after he did. That would give him time to begin preparing the minds of his peers. They were presently a mix of those appointed by his father and those few worthies he had appointed himself. *Assuming she chooses to come*, he reminded himself.

"Then let me tell the staff we depart in five days. That will be little enough time for them to close the embassy properly, but plenty of time for you to obtain her answer."

Txoko laughed aloud. "Will I ever understand women the way you do?"

"I doubt it," Zain returned without hesitation. Slapping Txoko on the back, he advised, "Now, you must think of her as well. She needs to understand that her duties as your queen will be very different from those of the typical Lurrakian wife."

Txoko's heart sank. Zain was right. His wife would be many things besides his helpmeet. Hostess to Marroi's guests. Overseer of celebrations. Administrator of the crown's benevolence. And that was only the beginning.

"A fine situation," he groaned. "How can I persuade her to marry me when there are so many disadvantages?"

Zain laughed, caught himself, then laughed again. "Forgive me," he chuckled. "Jatorri is full of so-called 'ordinary' people who spend their lives envying you."

Txoko gave in and laughed with him. With a little friendly prodding from Zain, he left the room as it was and caught a bicycle carriage to Leuna's grandparents' house. *Awkward conversations are part of married life*, he reminded himself as he approached the door and raised his hand to knock. The door opened before he was able to complete the action.

"Jaurla Izan." Taken by surprise, he was late to bow. He hadn't expected her to answer the door personally.

"Your Majesty." She stepped back from the door and curtsied in the same, graceful motion. "Won't you come in?"

"Thank you." Possessed of a sudden urge to fidget, he placed both hands behind his back as he entered the house. "How are you this fine day?"

"We're all quite well, thank you." As lady of the house, she took the liberty of answering for all in her household. As Leuna's grandmother, she took the direct route to what she thought was on his mind. "Though we were all up rather late last night." She carefully maintained her demure expression while his chin jerked up and to the right, as if his collar had suddenly grown uncomfortably tight.

This…wasn't the uncomfortable conversation he'd been preparing for. With an effort, Txoko maintained a neutral expression. Leuna's grandmother had every right to be concerned.

"I apologize if I caused you any distress." He bowed again.

Merezi turned and led the way into the sitting room, where she motioned for him to take the room's only straight-backed wooden chair. She'd learned a long time ago that having a decoratively turned chair spindle digging into one's back had a way of encouraging guests to spill their secrets.

"Leuna will be down shortly," she promised, then took for herself the plushest, most comfortable seating.

Once she was seated, Txoko eased himself onto the wooden chair. In a matter of moments, he'd learned that there simply was no comfortable position. Resting his back against the excessively knobby spindles brought to mind the old fable about a man who slept on a bed of nails. Sliding forward for relief brought the unpadded front edge of the seat digging into the backs of his thighs. Compromising, he leaned forward slightly, keeping his back straight. It felt remarkably like he was preparing to share something confidential with his hostess, who was watching him expectantly. *How much does she already know?* he wondered.

"I hope you've had a pleasant morning." It was a weak conversational offer, but he felt the need to say *something*.

"Yes, thank you." She debated briefly. Ordinarily, she would let him sit and squirm until she thought he was ready to unburden himself. However, as she'd said, Leuna would be down soon. While the man may someday soon be her grandson-by-law, he wasn't yet… And it was a delicate subject, even without his title.

"Jaurla Izan," Txoko began, having made up his mind to tell her what she had every right to know.

"King Txoko," she said at the same time, determined that she wouldn't allow herself to be intimidated by his title.

They stopped and stared at each other. A tiny smile tugged at his lips.

"I would be honored if you would call me Txoko," he said softly.

"And if I understand my granddaughter correctly, perhaps you should call me Merezi."

He ducked his head, made shy by her gentle tone and the warm light in her eyes. Clearly, his future would have nothing in common with his past. Tipo Baden, his former father-by-law, was buru of Deleku, the jeweled city of Marroi's southern reaches. He regulated all trade for a day's flight in every direction around his city. He commanded the city's feared fighting forces, and at over two hundred pounds, was feared himself. And he'd welcomed Txoko into his family by arranging a bout with the local champion. Called it an honor, dressed it up as part of the wedding festivities and presented it in such a way that he couldn't possibly refuse.

Clearing his throat, Txoko huskily murmured, "Thank you, Merezi."

A mischievous gleam in her eyes, Merezi leaned forward herself. "Then you do intend to offer a betrothal?"

Squarely caught, Txoko couldn't help chuckling. "Yes, Merezi." He nodded. "If all goes well in Marroi," his smile faded slightly, "I will ask her to share my life."

Merezi clasped her hands in her lap. "Why does that make you sad?"

He blinked. Was he so transparent? He looked into her keen hazel-green eyes a moment, then reflected that there must be very little she had not seen in her time.

"A woman may love a man," he began carefully, "without wishing to assume the duties uniting herself with him would bring."

"Young man," Merezi narrowed her eyes at him. "Are you seriously implying that Leuna might be afraid of taking on marriage?"

"No, not as you put it." He bit his tongue to keep himself from speaking without thinking. He could feel his forehead creasing as he struggled to find the right words. "But the woman who chooses to marry me will not have the luxury most women do, needing to primarily please only her own husband and family. She will also take upon her the title and crown of Marroi queen." Remembering the white hairs that had begun to streak his mother's onyx hair, he exhaled slowly. "And heavy rides the crown of a mindful queen."

Abashed, Merezi held her peace while she mentally regrouped. "Heavy rides the crown of a mindful queen," she echoed. "That sounds like a proverb."

"Yes," he nodded. "Our historians attribute it to the third Marroi queen, Itsua. Her people suffered from an entire season of savage gorakas, massive storms of sand and dust that choke the air, killing man and beast. That year they blotted out the sun so completely and for so long that even the hardy desert plants refused to grow. They eventually had to follow the dragons to their far mountains just to survive." Rubbing his palms together slowly, he finished, "It was her husband, King Durek, who began shaping Koroa out of the limestone there."

From the corner of his eye, he spotted Leuna standing in the doorway. Her plain outfit of loose brown slacks and twilight purple blouse made him feel overdressed, but then he *had* come directly from official business.

"There you are." Merezi rose as lightly as a grass blade springing up after a heavy dew. "I believe this gentleman wishes to speak with you, my dear." She offered Leuna a tiny nod of approval as she slipped past, then took herself to the kitchen, where she could close a door against the temptation to eavesdrop.

Rising, Txoko said the first thing that came to mind. "You look lovely."

Blushing despite herself, Leuna entered the room. She'd almost made it past him when his fingers curled about her wrist, and he gently tugged her down onto the smaller couch, where he joined her. Finding herself knee to knee with him, she hardly knew what to do.

"I suppose you've come to see what I've decided," she hazarded.

"Have you decided so soon?" he asked, leaning in a little closer than was strictly necessary.

Her pulse picked up and she tugged her hand free before her pulse point could betray her. "I have."

"Oh." He stared down at where her hands were demurely clasped in her lap. What would he see if he raised his eyes to hers? Pity? Kind concern? The thought of her trying to soothe his 'bruised' ego provoked a visceral response, bringing him to his feet. He couldn't breathe. He had to get out of there. Glancing around the daintily appointed room, he expanded his plans to getting out of Ibilia. Out of Lurrak. "If…"

"Txoko?" Leuna rose, too. His hands were behind his back, so she caught hold of jacket front instead. Why wouldn't he look at her? "Txoko, you sit back down. I mean it," she added when he tried to turn away. "This instant." At last, his eyes met hers. "Please?"

Perplexed, Txoko allowed her to coax him back onto the couch.

"Now, I don't know what that was all about," she admitted, still clinging to the front of his jacket even though his fists were now resting stiffly beside his legs. "But I've been through a lot this morning and you're going to hear all about it. Understand?"

Further puzzled by her tone and manner—neither

of which matched his preconceptions of the situation—he nodded.

"All right, then." Releasing his jacket, she tried to smooth the crumpled spots. "I spent hours in the university's hall of records this morning. I only got back about an hour ago." Puffing out her cheeks, she expelled a breath that was mostly disbelief as she announced, "I found five suitable replacement doctors and asked the university curator to draft offer letters to them for the position at Herrixka." Suddenly, his hands were gripping her shoulders, turning her to face him directly. There was such joy in his eyes that it hurt to look into them.

"For me?" he asked huskily. "You'd give up Herrixka for me?"

Shyly, she dropped her eyes and rested her forehead against his jaw. "For us."

He held her for a moment, then came to his feet. Pacing away from her, he found that a mere three strides took him almost to the entryway. Pivoting to pace back, he saw her hands twisting in her lap, her forehead creased with lines of concern.

"Telling you I love you may be the most single most selfish act of my life," he confessed abruptly. "For I am not as other men. I cannot offer you the hope of a peaceful private life." He took a deep breath, trying to keep his hands from shaking with the excess energy coursing through him. "I cannot even offer you the certainty of a life together, the promise of marriage. I must speak in terms of what *may* lie ahead for us."

"I know. You're the Marroi king," she interrupted.

She flung up a hand to keep him from speaking until she'd forced out her own concern. "And I'm a Lurrakian doctor who may or may not be welcomed by your people. Whose children may or…may not be accepted." She lifted her hands helplessly when he didn't respond. "Anyway. I could never go back to Herrixka. It's all my past, where I've already been. I'm looking forward now. Either a new life with you in Marroi, or in a new medical position." Warming to the subject, she expounded, "Why, I might even return to university. Get a second degree…"

Suddenly he was standing before her, his hands closing around her waist. She gasped as he lifted her to her feet, where she sort of hung, her heels not quite on the ground, as he looked down at her.

"My wife will be the Marroi queen." Exhaling raggedly, he eased his grip. If her wide eyes were any indication, he'd just frightened the wits out of her. "As my counterpart, her duties will be comparable to mine."

"You mean," she interrupted again, "that she'll be your partner in creating and preserving peace, both near and far?"

"Ummm…yes." He squinted suspiciously down at her. "Were you listening earlier?"

"Well." She looked to the side and lifted her shoulders slightly. "I may have overheard something as I was coming down the stairs."

Chuckling, he cupped her face in his palm. "Something tells me you're going to make a fabulous queen."

Chapter 9

Txoko eased the girth around Presa's middle and cinched it into place. He'd scrounged up an hour each day for the last six days to come to the stables and help prepare Leuna's dragons for the journey to Koroa. The stable hands did most of the work, but they wouldn't be there to help out en route. The last step in securing the leather riding jarlekua was the chest strap, which he buckled whilst ignoring Presa's glare. The less fuss he made, the sooner this would become a routine matter for her. He grinned a little when her disgruntled shake set the stirrups to dancing.

"We'll have to cover over five hundred miles today," Zain reminded him, eyeing the untested dragon doubtfully. "Are you sure you wouldn't rather ride Abutzu?"

Txoko's personal mount heard his name and rattled his gleaming gold and black scales in response. A fabulous creature half again as long and broad as Presa, Abutzu had made many such flights. Why, at ten years old, he was just entering his prime. His attitude toward the new dragons was relatively good-natured, though his interest in Presa had gotten Txoko thinking it might be time to start thinking about finding him a mate.

"I'm sure." Txoko reached out to caress Abutzu's soft ears. "No offense, fella. She needs the experience, alright?"

"So does Sparks," Zain pointed out, unable to shake the idea that Presa was going to take off and never come back. Sparks looked up from where he was sniffing Presa's jarlekua. Earlier, he'd been as bad as Presa, darting back as if in fear of his life each time the stirrups moved.

"Leuna wants to ride him." Txoko answered Zain's look of surprise with a slight shrug. "She rode him from Ilun to Ibilia."

"Not even half the distance of our ride," Zain objected. "She'd be safer riding in the howrah with her grandparents." Howrah's were partially enclosed carriages, with curtains that could be lowered in case of gorakas or a wish for privacy. Made of strong but light-weight izei wood, which had the bonus of resembling gold when kept at a high polish, a howrah could be set up by a single man. And strapped to the back of an enormous zaldiz dragon, they could carry up to six passengers at a time.

"Now I told you," Txoko groaned. "I didn't intend to invite them."

"What?" Zain shook his head. "I remembered, I just couldn't believe your lack of foresight."

"What?" Txoko asked in turn, thoroughly confused. While he was personally rather glad they'd be accompanying Leuna, he'd assumed Zain would see them only as an inconvenience. Two more mouths to feed, two more sets of bedding, two more…of everything.

"I can't believe you didn't include her only family in your plans for her future." Zain spelled it out for him. "Were you just going to sweep her through a Marroi wedding ceremony after the festival?"

"No, I…" Txoko scrubbed his hands across his face. "Alright, I give up. It was stupid of me not to think through every detail of my hypothetical wedding to its logical conclusion."

"Yes." Zain maintained a perfectly straight face. "Exactly."

Txoko promptly grabbed him and threw him to the ground with a simple wrestling move. He made the mistake of trying to ease the fall, and wound up on the ground beside him.

"No you don't!" Twisting sharply, Txoko managed to roll clear.

Unbeknownst to the brothers, Leuna had arrived and was watching from the edge of the meadow as they scuffled in the shin-high grass. Shaking her head, she leaned back against Sparks, who'd come the moment he scented her.

"Boys. Don't you ever grow up?" she asked the dragon. He sneezed and shook his head, making her laugh. "I think you're right." Throwing her leg over his shoulder, she held on while he took off, giving her an aerial view of the match. The toes of her soft-soled boots rested firmly on the small ledge of the larger scales that covered his sides. Her fingers clung to a ridge in his neck scales, and her knees pressed against his sides just enough to stay on. Experience indicated that Sparks flew differently when she was aboard, almost carefully, but she didn't want to accidentally squeeze more speed out of him. Their gentle glide right now was just right.

"They're playing, right?" she muttered, as much to herself as Sparks this time. Txoko was slightly taller, but Zain's thick, muscular body gave him a distinct advantage. He barely had to get a hand on Txoko to change the other man's angle of motion. The match would've been over almost as soon as it began if Txoko hadn't been so blindingly fast on his feet.

Suddenly, Zain's right hand shot out. Txoko swerved and ran directly into Zain's left hand, which got a firm grip on his shirt. Txoko was flat on the ground before Leuna had quite realized what was happening. Gasping, she urged Sparks to land.

"Are you alright?" she called, almost tripping in her haste to dismount.

"Leuna." Txoko wheezed and tried to glare up at his brother. It was a difficult thing to manage, considering that Zain had flipped him onto his stomach and planted a knee in the middle of his back. "When did you get here?"

Zain hauled him unceremoniously to his feet and dusted him off. "He's fine," he informed Leuna, not unkindly. "We've been knocking each other down since we learned to stand up." More importantly, wrestling was a harmless part of Marroi life. Semi-serious arguments often escalated to friendly matches when the heat wasn't bad.

Leuna stopped a few feet away, eyeing them warily. Both men were much older than the athletes she'd dealt with while attending university, yet that was what immediately sprang to mind. Zain's shoulders were thrown back unnaturally far, as if to compensate for any remorse he might feel. Meanwhile, Txoko was lounging casually—too casually—against Zain's side. Actually, he seemed to be sagging there, still out of breath and upright only because Zain had maintained an arm about his waist.

"Alright, you two." She brought her hands to waist height, palms forward in partial surrender. "If this is how you do things, just say so." Something about Zain's answering smile, the way it made the skin crinkle around his eyes, made her feel like she'd just passed a test.

Txoko relaxed and started to laugh, wincing at the same time. "I told you she was smart." Straightening away from Zain, he walked over to her and wrapped her in a hug. "You look beautiful," he murmured.

"I'm glad you think so." She allowed him to step back, holding her out at arm's length while he took a long look at her. "You picked it out, after all." She turned a little to one side, then the other, making the lightweight bata swirl about her boots. The wide gerri wrapped about her waist was the same tan color as the bata, setting off both the near-crimson trousers and the sky-blue, short-sleeved shirt she wore underneath.

"I like it very much," he acknowledged. His forehead creased thoughtfully. "Will you mind wearing Marroi clothes all the time?" To his way of thinking, the loose, flowing batas with trousers and lightweight, button-less shirts were vastly superior to the stiffer, tighter clothing preferred by the average Lurrakian.

"Oh, I don't think so." She slipped her arm through his. "The climate in Marroi is much drier and hotter than what I'm used to, after all. Although…" She wrinkled her nose as she thought of one item she'd left back at her grandparents'. "I do wonder if wearing the zapia is strictly necessary, though?"

Txoko smiled, pleased that she'd asked. Zapias were large, rectangular pieces of cotton worn to protect the neck and head from both the sun and sand of his homeland. "I suppose it does seem bulky," he admitted first. "But yes, I recommend wearing one whenever you go outside in Marroi. A goraka, a wall of sand driven before the wind, can blow up out of nowhere. And while the wind is often calm, the sun has no compassion for either light or dark skin."

Leuna shivered slightly. "I guess I have a lot to learn. Even more than I realized."

"We will help you." He squeezed her hand gently. "We all had to learn these things, too."

"Yes, but you learned them as a child," she pointed out. "I'm going to look pretty foolish asking questions like that of your courtiers."

"Then they are the fools for not recognizing your willingness to learn. Nevertheless," he winked at her, "I will make sure your mirabe will take good care of you."

"My what?" she asked after trying vainly to remember the word.

"Your mirabe." He began leading her over to where Presa was consoling herself with fresh-caught fish from the artificial stream. "A lady's maid assigned to assist you during your stay at Koroa."

"Oh." She nodded and smiled her understanding. While he went to coax Presa into letting him remove the jarlekua, she tried again to grasp the magnitude of the role of queen. She'd learned quite a bit from her grandmother about being the lady of a house. Though her grandmother had servants to help, she ultimately held herself responsible for keeping the house clean, the larder stocked, and offering a healthy, appealing menu to all who sat at her table. All of which she was determined to accomplish without exceeding her husband's budget.

With all she'd learned from her grandmother, it still staggered her to think of the possibilities. Receiving finicky guests from all over Jatorri. Supervising details for local and national celebrations. Reviewing requests for aid from the crown. Being herself without giving offense.

"Hmm?" She looked up at the sound of her name. Txoko and Zain were both watching her. "What?"

"May I send over a cart for your baggage before supper?" Zain repeated himself politely.

"Oh. Yes. Yes, of course."

Txoko handed the jarlekua he'd just taken off Presa to a stable boy, then motioned for Leuna to join him. "She did well today," he smiled. "How shall we reward her?"

Leuna glanced at the buckets of dragon treats stacked over by the main door, but decided against them. "She'd probably appreciate a good belly buffing."

"Excellent idea." Txoko nodded to the waiting stable boy, who ran to get the stones for them. "I think she's got a few she'd like to cast, actually."

Leuna interpreted that as a few scales that were stubbornly hanging on despite Presa's attempts to shed them. Dragons seemed to always be in the process of shedding scales or teeth. She rather wished humans could shed their teeth and grow a new crop of them. It would certainly help out Zaharre, Herrixka's village elder. Their old friend, Ama, too. Shaking off thoughts of her friends, Leuna accepted a buffing stone and slipped the strap over her wrist.

"Look!" Txoko shook his head as Sparks immediately

dropped and rolled onto his back, begging for a rub. "I'm afraid he's pretty spoiled."

Leuna laughed. "No arguments there." Presa at least pretended not to be interested, if only for a minute or two. "Would Abutzu enjoy a rub?"

"I'm sure he would." Txoko put his hip against Presa's shoulder and shoved her over a bit farther so they wouldn't wind up on their knees trying to reach her belly. "I only wish we had time."

Time. That was the key word these days. Leuna's mind darted back to her grandmother, who was making final arrangements for closing the house that day. Dari had kindly volunteered to carry letters to Herrixka for Leuna, though her mind seemed to be more on spending time with Jartz than anything else.

"What?" Txoko paused in his buffing to cock an inquisitive eyebrow at her. "You giggled."

"I was just thinking about Dari, my grandmother's cook."

"Ah, the amazing Dari." Txoko nodded, though his memories were from his time as Neba. "If not for her using her cooking as a bribe, I'd never have taken all the hezur potion you prescribed."

Leuna chuckled. "And you'd still have been nursing a broken bone or two." She resumed her own buffing. "Anyway. Grandmother has warned me that she's not sure Dari will return from Herrixka."

"No?" Txoko was a little surprised. From what he'd seen, Dari loved the Izan's, and her job.

"Hm-mm." Leuna shook her head. "Dari's offered to take my letters to Herrixka, and if Jartz is smart, he'll ask her to stay."

"That's unlikely." He shifted uneasily under Leuna's

startled stare, then reached over with his free hand to gently close her mouth, which had fallen open in surprise. "It's different for a man than a woman." Leuna's lips began to tighten and he quickly continued, "However much he may *want* to ask her to marry him, he'll first ask himself what he can offer her."

Leuna felt a little guilty for not having a ready retort for that. Like she was being a bad friend to Jartz somehow.

"I can almost guarantee that when he got back to Herrixka and saw his cabin, the first thing he did was compare it to your grandparents' home." He carefully worked over a loose scale. "It's a snug cabin. Well-built. And roughly the same size as the kitchen Dari is accustomed to."

Leuna grimaced. He was right. That didn't mean she had to admit it, did she?'

"In short," Txoko eased the stubborn scale loose and set it aside, "his present home is perfect for a single man who is often gone for days at a time. But significantly less than ideal for a new family."

She liked the way he referred to Jartz and Dari as a family, just the two of them. And yet, she could guarantee that Jartz' cabin wasn't large enough to hold Dari's dreams of children. During her courses on women's health, which included spending most of a semester on duty at the local maternity hospital, Dari had once shared a precious list of potential baby names. Precious because, despite Dari's hopes, she was still unmarried at thirty-six. Precious because Dari intended to adore every baby she was ever blessed to have.

Twelve children? Leuna had asked in amazement. *That's a very large family!*

Twelve names, Dari had laughed. *Six for boys and six for girls. I probably won't have that many,* there'd been a wistful note in her admission, *but I chose a few extra in case my husband doesn't like my favorites.*

Txoko took her gently by the shoulder and turned her to face him. Shaking his cuff down over his arm, he dried the tears he saw, then hugged her. He'd known she was friends with Dari—and Jartz, for that matter—but hadn't realized she was so emotionally invested in their story's outcome. Thinking of the potential for a spectacular failure of his own hopes and dreams, he gathered her even closer.

"You mustn't assume I'm right," he told her. "Why, Jartz owns a huge parcel of land. He showed it to me one day. There's plenty of good timber on it, too. More than enough for him to add onto his home as needed." Herrixka, already a colorful village given its use of the local hardwoods, had many homes originally built with one color of wood, then expanded with another. The pragmatic approach of expanding as needed lent the village a curiously haphazard look, and took a little getting used to.

Leuna snuggled closer, enjoying his attention. They probably wouldn't have a lot of private moments once they got to Marroi, where Txoko would need to be everywhere at once, at least until after the festival, so she closed her eyes and tried to store up all the details of this memory. Dragon scale dust wasn't her favorite thing—it made her sneeze—so she tried to concentrate on the smell of bruised grass that clung to him from his wrestling match. The fainter scents of sage and cedar that always accompanied him. The way his breath stirred her hair.

Txoko could've stood there like that all day, his arms wrapped about his hope for the future. But Presa had other ideas. She rolled to her feet, bumping them so hard that they nearly fell over. Shook herself, and took off.

"Presa!" Txoko was about to call her again when Leuna kissed his cheek.

"Let her go, darling," she advised. "She didn't mean anything by it."

"Hmm. No, I suppose she didn't," he agreed.

"Anyway, I should probably go home now." She didn't move.

"Probably." He lowered his head slightly.

"I promised to help Grandma make supper."

"Really?" He leaned still closer. "I'm surprised she still has food in the house." Part of the chore of closing a house or an embassy for an extended period was making sure that there was nothing left to spoil during one's absence. His lips grazed her cheek, her forehead.

"Mmm. Well," Leuna inhaled shallowly, "that's why we're having supper at home tonight." They'd eaten supper at the embassy twice that week, and ordered in once. "To finish off the last of the odds and ends and…" She kissed him back, keeping their surroundings in mind. Any and all of the stable boys, grooms, clients, people off the street, and so forth could look around and see them.

Txoko rested his forehead against hers, wondering

what had possessed him to kiss her in public? Timing was a critical part of his plans, and this wasn't supposed to happen until *after* she was presented in Marroi. Judging by her reserve in returning the kiss, even she'd known it was a poor idea. Not that she'd stopped him, come to think of it.

"I have to go." Uncurling her fingers from where she'd gripped his shirt front during their short kiss, she stepped back. "I just remembered, Zain is sending a cart for our baggage."

Txoko nodded and said nothing. If he opened his mouth, he'd volunteer to go with her. To help them make supper. To help them eat it. Anything to prolong his time with her. He expelled a frustrated breath as he let her leave, alone. He really had it bad.

"Getting ahead of ourselves, aren't we?" Zain asked from beside him.

"You might say that," Txoko agreed. "Does it get any easier?" He turned to face his brother. "I mean, how did you wait to kiss Min when you were courting?"

Zain considered the question and its implications. "You're going to have to do better than just not kissing her in public," he warned. As beautiful as Nire had been, he'd never seen Txoko watch her with such longing in his eyes.

Surprised, Txoko looked at his brother directly. "What do you mean?"

"I mean that the statue of our great-grandmother is going to start singing a wedding processional and an entire clowder of dortoka dragons will roost in the throne room if you don't learn to control your expression." Several species of diminutive dragons shared Koroa with them, including an occasional dortoka pair, with their so-called love songs and affectionate behavior.

Txoko rubbed the back of his neck, embarrassed. He had it worse than he'd known. "I guess I really need your help this time."

"You certainly do," Zain agreed. Slapping Txoko on the back, he jerked his head toward the exit. "Come on. You can practice keeping a straight face on the way back to the embassy."

"A straight face?" Txoko tossed his buffing stone and a small tip to the stable boy who'd been helping that day. "I do that all day long during petition days!" He opened his court to all comers on petition days, regardless of age, station, or gender.

Zain snorted softly. "I'll grant that you have seen and heard almost everything at those."

"Ha. Like the time the woman wanted me to declare her pet dragon her sole heir?" Txoko would never forget. The querulous woman had bullied her son into leaving his family and farm to transport her clear across the country to see the king because the buru had laughed her out of his court. Txoko had nearly laughed as well when he heard that the 'inheritance' would amount to the paltry sum of seven gold arranos.

"Of course." Zain shook his head. What an abuse of her offspring, causing him to waste dozens of hard-earned arranos on her selfishness! Eyeing the handful of available carriages, he chose the cleanest and beckoned to the driver. "The Marroi embassy," he instructed as Txoko climbed in. Following suit a moment later, he settled in for the ride. "Now. Don't think of something funny or sad or infuriating. Think of her." He slapped Txoko on the arm. "Not like that. Keep a straight face."

Txoko's arm bore a few new bruises by the time they reached the embassy, but he flattered himself that he'd made progress. At least, Zain had stopped punching him a few streets back. Though that might've had something to do with the odd looks the cyclists were giving them.

"Practice every spare moment," Zain advised as they entered the embassy. "And try to get her to practice, too. The court will accept her readily enough as Doctor Oneko."

Txoko nodded. "Yes, you're right. I'll speak to her about it."

Chapter 10

Leuna laughed as Txoko settled his goggles into place, then tried to hide her amusement behind her fingers when he turned to look at her. Light from the strategically placed firestones turned the amber lenses gold in the darkness, making him look like a huge insect. The slow grin on his face had her narrowing her eyes suspiciously. Then she noticed that he was holding a second pair.

"For you." Txoko enjoyed watching the consternation flit across her face as she realized that she was to wear goggles, too. What had she expected? Goggles were as necessary to their safety as bridles. Even now Zain was helping her grandparents into theirs.

"I…" Reaching up to intercept his hand as he held them out to her, she ducked away. "I don't really wear goggles."

He caught her arm as she tried to slip past him. "You do today." Deftly, he slipped them into place. "There."

Taken by surprise, she slapped at his hands, but it was too late. The goggles were on. Mortified, she pulled them off and looked away. Goggles had been mandatory at university and the memories of some of the jokes at her expense still made her cringe.

"Hey." Catching her other arm, he turned her to face him. Taking the goggles back, he frowned at her. "Look at me." He put the goggles back on her despite the strange expression on her face. The colored lenses of his goggles allowed him to see every worry crease on her forehead without giving him a clue as to why she was upset. "We have a long flight ahead of us," he reminded firmly. "We can't risk an eye injury." As hard as he tried to focus on the process of adjusting the straps, he was acutely aware of her proximity. This wasn't how he wanted their journey to start. Glancing quickly around to see if anyone was watching, he stole a kiss from her pouting lips. "There." Tugging gently on her braid, he asked, "Do they feel alright?"

Stunned, she stared up at him. "What?"

"The goggles." He touched the strap. "Are they too tight?"

"Oh." Stiffening, she pulled away, she ran a fingertip under the strap. "No. They're…" She shoved her hands into her slacks' pockets. "Yeah, they're fine." Jerking her head in the direction of the enormous zaldiz dragon that would be carrying the howrah, she said, "I'm going to go check on my grandparents."

Puzzled, Txoko watched her leave, ripping off her goggles before she'd gone two steps. Zain, who was coming the opposite direction, offered her a slight bow as they passed each other.

"The Izan's are settled comfortably. And I just spoke with the chief gidari," Zain offered. "He says we're ready." He discreetly omitted the man's muttering about how much he hated travelling with kanpotarrak. Apparently, they were all in for a long day of extra bathroom stops and general complaints from the howrah. Personally, Zain hoped that Leuna and her grandparents proved the man wrong. It would go a long way toward smoothing the path ahead if they had a group of fifty Marroi already on

Leuna's side when they arrived at Koroa.

"Good. The scouting party left an hour ago." Clapping his hands for attention, he shouted, "Hegalak gora!"

Those near him passed the call along even as they moved to tighten cinches, adjust goggles, and so forth.

"Are you sure you don't want to ride with us, dear?" Merezi asked anxiously. She wasn't at all sure she liked the idea of riding inside the flimsy-looking howrah, but at least a dragon the size of a house could bear their weight easily. Sparks and Presa, whom she'd just met, barely seemed large enough to carry themselves!

"I'm sure, Grandma." Smiling, Leuna kissed their cheeks. "Maybe tomorrow." Waving, she slid down the surprisingly smooth dragon side and patted the beast. "Take good care of them, alright?" The weird thing about looking this dragon in the eye was that she could see her head and shoulders reflected there, even when she was standing right beside it!

"We go," announced the gidari assigned to the zaldiz she was addressing. "Wings up."

"Yes." She tried not to take offense at his blank-faced response to her smile. "We go." She almost ran into Zain when she turned to rejoin Txoko. "Morning!"

Zain, his eyes mostly hidden by his goggles, smiled back at her. "Morning. Are you ready?"

"As I'll ever be." Taking a deep breath, she slipped her goggles into place.

"Good." Staying right with her, Zain escorted her back to Txoko. It was on the tip of his tongue to advise her not to mingle with the staff, but he couldn't quite bring himself to say it.

"There you are." Txoko scooped her up and placed her atop Sparks. "Now, take this strap," he offered her the safety strap from the training jarlekua, "and buckle it onto your harness."

"Right." Her fingers shook a little as she threaded the leather through the buckle's frame. Try as she might, she couldn't quite get the prong through the hole.

"Here." Txoko took it from her. Backing the strap out a bit, he explained as he finished the job, "You had it too short. You'll want to be able to turn and look at things, probably even stretch your back." Handing it back to her, he squeezed her fingers gently. "Nervous?" Her short, jerky head nod was all the answer he needed. "Don't be. We know the dangers and take every precaution to keep ourselves safe."

"Yes. I think it's the safety equipment that's making me so nervous." Her fingers gripping his, she laughed weakly. "I mean, I always knew flying involved being high up in the air, but every new piece of equipment makes me more aware of how many different ways I could accidentally die up there." She hadn't breathed a word of that to her grandparents, of course.

"It would actually be pretty difficult," he assured her, settling his free hand on her near knee. "These precautions are exactly that—steps taken in case something goes wrong. On shorter flights, we don't even use harnesses. Or," thinking back to earlier, "goggles."

She laughed and looked up, then away. "I'd almost managed to forget I was wearing goggles."

Chuckling, Txoko hurried over to mount Presa. Urging her upward, he listened to the great whisper of wings behind him as they started their journey. Shadows appeared on the rooftops beneath him, then they were past the city walls and free! Higher and higher they soared, leaving behind the dust and dirt stirred up by the wings of the magnificent creatures.

Looking over to check on Leuna, he was puzzled to see Sparks humping his back and pulling his neck in. Studying the situation a moment longer, he directed Presa to fly closer.

"Something's wrong with Sparks!" she shouted. "I don't think he likes flying with so many dragons!"

"Relax!" Txoko called back. She shook her head at him, but he shouted again. "Relax your legs a bit! You're squeezing him!" He stayed there while she worked it through in her head. "That's it!" he encouraged, detecting a subtle change in Sparks. "He's better now, you see?"

Nodding, Leuna continued to work at it, ordering her fear-strengthened muscles to loosen their grip. She was delighted to find that she wasn't flung from the saddle as a result—and, yes, Sparks was behaving more like himself. Swallowing hard, she transferred her anxiety to a white-knuckled grip on the jarlekua's edge.

"Good job," he called, irritated with himself for not preparing her better. She'd only flown a few times, and only…twice at any real height. "You're doing fine." Just then, they hit an airbump that bounced them upwards a couple of inches. She screeched and compressed herself against the jarlekua. "It's alright!" he shouted. "Perfectly normal!"

Leuna forced herself to slow her breathing. She'd instinctively tightened her legs to keep from falling off and Sparks was already acting out his disapproval, each twist and turn of his body sending a message screaming from her brain to her legs to tighten still further. Closing her eyes, she overrode the panicked message. The wind whipped sweat from her face as she mentally worked through calming steps her father taught her so many years ago.

Again, Sparks' flight smoothed out. Focusing her mind, Leuna felt his muscles moving under a thin section of the jarlekua. Moving. Pumping his wings up and down. Up and down. His lungs expanded and contracted effortlessly and she matched her breathing to his. In and out. In and out.

"Leuna?" Pleased as he was that she seemed to have relaxed, Txoko didn't know what to make of her scrunched-up facial expression.

"I'm alright," she called back. *For now.* She reminded herself of that declaration repeatedly until it slowly became the truth. When they paused for lunch, Txoko tried to persuade her to ride in the howrah with her grandparents, but she stubbornly refused. For the next three days, she refused. By the end of the fourth day, she was even able to dismount and untack Sparks without assistance.

Covering a yawn with her hand, she snuck a look in Txoko's direction. As usual, he was busy talking with Zain and another man. Judging by the maroon accents and weaponry, the third man was a guard.

Her stomach clenched unhappily at the memory of watching a pair of the guards playing at being daredevils today. Only they weren't defying each other to eat various gross things or trying to see who could stay in the ice cold creek near Herrixka the longest. *They were cavorting about on dragons hundreds of feet up in the air!* Txoko told her it was called 'aerobatics,' with such a note of pride in his voice in that she'd swallowed her disapproval. Nevertheless, she'd nearly been sick all over Sparks when they leapt from one dragon to another.

Shoving the memories to one side, she focused on polishing the bugs and dust off of her goggles as she walked over to check on her grandparents.

"Leuna!" Merezi slid down to the ground. "You looked very natural up there today." Smiling, she kissed her granddaughter's dusty cheek. The closer they got to Marroi, the more she appreciated the zapia, which could be unfolded to cover her mouth and nose.

"Thank you." Leuna smiled back. "It's getting easier." They joined Xelebre on the ground, stretching tired muscles. Leuna had felt sheepish about the stretches at first, then realized that everyone in the party did at least a few before moving on to the business of setting up camp.

"I feel twenty years younger," Xelebre announced. Leaning forward so that his nose touched the knees of his outstretched legs, he counted to fifteen before sitting up. "And such a beautiful view!"

"It is," Leuna nodded and struggled to hold back

her laughter. His hair stuck up at odd angles where the wind had run it fingers through. Even her own hair, which she carefully brushed and braided each morning, looked comical by the time they landed each evening.

"I think if I could travel everywhere by dragon, I'd want to tour the whole of Jatorri."

Merezi, knowing how much he liked his own chair and his own bed at the end of a long day, was understandably skeptical, but said nothing. Anyway, it was time to start putting up their tent.

The work around the camp moved at a slower pace than Leuna might've expected of such veteran travelers. The dragons came first, naturally. After receiving their water ration, they flew off to hunt, leaving their handlers to set up tents while others began preparing supper. Fuel was already growing scarce as the land changed, and most of the cook fires consisted of a little indar fluid from the dragons spilled on the ground, then ignited. Last night had been stew made with dried auroch and vegetables, served in bowls with a roll on top.

"Looks like we're having stew again," Merezi observed, nodding at where kettles were already being hung over the small fires.

Leuna nodded as she began untying the poles they would use for their shared tent. Her mouth watered at the thought of the fresh untxi she'd enjoyed on the trip from Herrixka. After a lifetime of being able to pick fruit off a tree, would she be able to adjust to eating dried fruit? She shook her head. Of course she would. If she truly loved Txoko.

"Leuna." Xelebre called from where he was draping

the roof cloth over the top of one of the poles. "Leuna?" This had to be done just so or it would collapse on them when they moved on to the next step.

Coming out of her reverie, Leuna hastily began matching his movements. Centering the roof cloth on her end pole, she double-checked the line and stake before nodding that she was ready. Merezi went quickly along one side once the end poles were up, setting the side poles in place. Staking the end poles quickly, they helped her with staking the side poles, then hung a long, heavy cloth as a wall on the side where it would protect them from the setting sun. The rest of the camp did the same, radiating out from the cook fires in a half-circle.

Leuna dropped her bedroll and night bag in her corner of the tent. "I better refill our canteens," she suggested.

"Right," Xelebre agreed. Taking a long pull from his, he handed it over.

"Did I hear that gidari correctly?" Merezi asked, following suit. Since stopping for her to get more water during the day meant stopping the entire party…well, she'd learned quickly that her canteen was of prime importance. "We're flying straight through tomorrow?"

"Yes, I heard the same thing." Xelebre frowned. "I suppose the dragons can handle it, but I'm not sure I can."

"Good evening." Txoko stepped around the side of the tent and bowed.

"Good evening." Xelebre reflected that this was one part of traveling he didn't much care for. The cloth-sided tent afforded almost no real privacy.

"If I may answer your question," Txoko had long ago grown accustomed to the public-private conversations of a dragonflight camp, "we fly in different formation tomorrow. So far, we have travelled as a single, very large group." He smiled and took the canteens from Leuna. "Since we will arrive at Koroa tomorrow, however, the party will separate. The servants will take the baggage ahead of us, flying almost straight through the day."

"That sounds like a terrible hardship," Merezi dared to observe aloud.

"They are at liberty to make the necessary stops to rest and refresh themselves," Txoko reassured her amiably. "And once they arrive in Koroa, their work for the day is done."

"Oh." Merezi colored slightly under her light sunburn. "Forgive me, I didn't realize."

Txoko smiled despite the concern swirling in his gut. This was one very small, very mild example of the kind of misunderstandings that lay ahead. While Merezi's question voiced a reasonable concern, even an admirable one, yet there were those whose pride would cause them to take offense.

"I am happy to help," he bowed slightly. "It is the work of a diplomat to represent their people and encourage understanding." Taking Leuna lightly by the elbow, he led her away.

"Xelebre?" Merezi stepped closer to her frowning husband, lowered her voice. "What is it?"

"It sounded like advice to me." Moving even closer to his wife, he murmured, "The work of a *diplomat*. I think he was telling us to be careful what we ask of whom."

Merezi paled. "You don't think I offended him?"

"No." He shook his head. "I believe that was his point. He's travelled widely and interacts with other cultures on an almost daily basis. *He* knows there's more than one way to do things." Xelebre lifted one shoulder. "Perhaps the same cannot be said for his entire court."

Merezi bit her lip. "And anything we do or say would reflect on Leuna." She turned to look after them, but the couple had already moved out of sight.

"I see what you mean," Leuna was saying. "I just didn't realize we were going to be under such scrutiny." She paused, looking up at him. "What I can't understand is why you waited until now to tell me that this visit to Koroa was to see if your precious court can stomach the idea of me." That was more vitriolic than she'd intended, but her skin was already crawling with the urge to look around and see if anyone in camp was watching them.

Txoko frowned, disturbed by the anger and bitterness in her voice. It was too late to change his mind, however, so he took a deep breath and admitted the rest of it. "I wasn't going to tell you at all." Shifting his grip on her arm, he held her there beside him when she would've stormed away. "I know it hurts, but it's the truth. I thought that it would be easier for you to be yourself if you didn't know."

"Let go of me." She kept her voice down for the same reason that she didn't forcibly remove his hand. She was on trial now. An unofficial jury of thousands waited at Koroa to tell her whether she was good enough to marry the man she loved.

The second his hold on her arm loosened, she shook off his hand and strode away from him. Walking to the edge of camp, she stared out over the bare, arid land. Barrel-shaped plants stuck up here and there from the dusty, rocky ground, their flaming orange flowers standing out like beacons.

"The belaki plant has saved many an unfortunate traveler," Zain observed from where he stood, a cautious foot or so away. He'd tried to dissuade Txoko from trying to explain their delicate situation to her, arguing that it would do more harm than good. Now, as always, he was here to support his decision. "Others have been fooled by its poisonous cousin, victims of their own ignorance."

Closing her eyes, Leuna counted to twenty before responding. "Ignorance is the root cause of a great many tragedies."

Amused, Zain moved a little closer. "You are glad he told you."

She flicked a glance at him, surprised at her own surprise that he knew exactly what had just happened. Txoko told him everything. Something else she would need to get used to if she intended to marry the Marroi king.

"Yes, I suppose I am," she conceded.

"Even though it makes you angry?" Zain probed.

She shrugged. "Anger is a powerful and dangerous emotion, able to flood its host like a fast-acting poison. Thankfully, my father taught me at a very young age that the antidote to anger is reason." And reason told her that Txoko couldn't just change hundreds of years of tradition with a snap of his fingers. No matter how much he wished her could.

"I am impressed." Zain scanned the landscape before them for movement, something that *he* had been taught to do at a very young age. It gave him an idea.

"Did Txoko send you?" she asked, turning to look at him.

"He didn't have to." Zain studied her briefly. "Each night of this journey, a story has been told. Do you remember them?"

Leuna blinked, thrown by the change of subject. "Why…yes, I think so."

"Good. We teach our children with stories," he explained. "Teach them of the dangers of the desert. How to handle dragons."

"And to fear strangers." She met his gaze unflinchingly. "In every story so far, the stranger visiting Marroi has brought trouble of some sort."

It was Zain's turn to blink. "I never thought of it that way." A wry smile tugged at his lips. "Perhaps because I am not a kanpotarrak." Insulting her was a calculated risk, one where he hoped the benefit would outweigh the cost.

Leuna struggled to control her exasperation. She *was* a kanpotarrak, an outsider. It hurt to hear Zain, whom she considered an ally, say it aloud, but that hurt didn't make it any less true.

Chapter 11

Smoke from a thousand fires swirled up to greet them as they flew into Koroa. Txoko, astride his gold and black gailen, swept low over the crowds, eliciting cheers from his people as he dropped gifts from twin bags draped over Abutzu's shoulders. Zain, astride his fearsome red and black gailen, received an identical reaction from where he performed the same pleasant task on the other side of the festival camp. Today, they wore no harnesses.

Leuna, mindful of her flying lessons, had a white-knuckled grip on the jarlekua as she waited for the stunt they'd warned her about. Bile rose in her throat as Txoko moved to a kneeling position. The crowds went wild when Zain skipped that and leapt straight into a low crouch, as she supposed befitted a legendary aditua.

Txoko lunged to his feet, running straight forward along his gailen's neck. He and Zain became airborne at precisely the same instant. Felt the familiar slap of his arm striking Zain's, fingers digging into his forearm and holding on for dear life. Their momentum carried them in a pivot around the central point of their joined arms. Halfway through a circle, they let go. Adrenalin surged through Txoko as he reached out to grab the safety line on Zain's performing jarlekua.

It was over in a heartbeat, leaving Leuna limp as a wrung-out rag. The roar of the crowds chased her all the way to the broad ledge where they landed. She tumbled off Sparks and ran to the edge, where she vomited. There wasn't much. Having been warned as to what was coming, she'd barely been able to choke down a few bites of lunch. Sagging against the wall, she waited for someone to come check on the kanpotarrak. Humiliating, really, to throw up on the castle, even if it was technically on the mountainous outside of the castle.

Merezi was beside her in an instant. "There, there," she murmured, splashing water from her canteen onto a handkerchief so she could wipe Leuna's face. She felt like passing out, personally, and was proud of Leuna for her self-control.

Leuna snorted and, lifting her own canteen, rinsed her mouth out, then spat. "I doubt he'd think so."

Merezi sighed. The look on Txoko's face certainly had spoken of exhilaration and pride. "Come on. Let's get you inside." She straightened slowly, still stiff from the long ride.

"I'm alright." Leuna shrugged off her grandmother's helping hands and got to her feet on her own. Tears stung her eyes when she realized that Sparks had been taken away with the other dragons. She could've used the familiarity of untacking him. "Or at least, I will be." As he'd explained, Txoko and Zain landed on a different ledge, where they would be greeted by his family.

"Welcome to Koroa," said a pleasant, alto voice. It belonged to a middle-aged woman standing nearby. "Doctor Oneko." It was less question than statement, but Leuna nodded anyway. "Jaurle and Jaurla Izan." They nodded also. "My name is Fiantza. Follow me, please, and I will show you to your rooms."

Still a little dazed, Leuna fell into step behind the woman. Automatically she noticed that while Fiantza had a slight limp in her left leg, it didn't seem to trouble her. The ledge was smooth, but dusty, and a shadow fell over them as they stepped through a doorway into the mountain. King Durek, the third Marroi monarch, had begun hewing a shelter out of this mountain hundreds of years ago after sandstorms nearly scoured their land clean of man and beast. Each generation since had dug their capitol deeper into the mountain, using the fierce heat of dragonfire to transform it into marble.

When they stepped through a second doorway, Leuna stopped abruptly. To her immediate right, the walls fell away and down, revealing a massive domed room lit by firestones of all shapes and colors. Even squinting against the brightness of their light, she couldn't see the far wall. Vividly colored tapestries, battle standards, even full suits of armor hung suspended from the ceiling.

"That is our gallery," Fiantza announced patiently. She was used to this reaction from kanpotarraks. Though this lot was special. She'd sensed that from the way the queen spoke of them. "Currently the life of our fifth king, Garren the Bold, is being displayed. If you wish, I can arrange a tour."

"We would love a tour." Merezi smiled even as she clutched the railing and inwardly questioned the wisdom of riding a dragon in an enclosed space. There didn't seem to be any other way to reach the display items.

"What are those?" Leuna asked, pointing at a darting shadow.

Fiantza smiled, pleasantly surprised at the girl's quick eye. "That's just a gezi dragon. They patrol the castle proper."

"Patrol it?" Xelebre lifted a quizzical eyebrow.

"Yes." Fiantza gestured toward the long hallway before resuming the walk to their rooms. "They keep the castle free from insects and the like."

"Wonderful." Leuna meant it, too. "I could have used a few of those at my last position." She mentally crossed her fingers that Dari was enjoying her time in Herrixka.

"Yes, I think every household in Lurrak would benefit," Merezi agreed.

"They're not pets," Fiantza cautioned. Nevertheless, she tucked the idea away as something to mention to the queen. It would be a simple, inexpensive way to win friends. "Though they are without fire, should you happen across one, I recommend standing away from the doors and windows so it can escape." A handful of the small gezis swooped past, their wings glittering. "They look cute, but have very sharp teeth."

"Understood." Xelebre took his girls by the arms and ushered them along after Fiantza. A proper introduction to Queen Ema would go better, he thought, after a wash and a bite to eat, but it was late enough that he wasn't sure what to expect in the way of formalities.

Firestones, which Leuna'd believed to be growing scarce, lit their way through hallway after room after hallway. White, pink, and yellow walls glistened around them, with an occasional blue and gray.

Nearly every hallway boasted an intricate carving along one wall. Each of the larger rooms had sculptures, most of them depicting man or beast caught mid-motion and all of them so lifelike Leuna hardly dared blink for fear they would come alive. Patches of delicate pink flowers jutted out of the floor in one room. In another, a group of men burst from the walls, swords and axes in hand, locked in eternal combat. Yet another room featured a storm of gailens descending from the ceilings.

"I could spend a lifetime examining these," she sighed, running her fingers along the scales of a life-size gailen dragon as they passed it.

"Two lifetimes," asserted a voice dryly.

Whipping about, Leuna found herself face to face with a tall, well-built man. Approximately her own age, his face was dark from the sun but his hair blond and his eyes gray. He looked so comfortable in his Marroi clothing that she looked at his face again to confirm his Lurrakian ancestry. The skin around his eyes crinkled as the corners of his mouth lifted and she realized he was taking stock of her as well.

Unaccountably flustered, she took a half-step back. The heel of her riding boot caught on the lip of a carving and she fell, only to be scooped up by the stranger.

"If I'd known you would be here," he grinned down at her, "I would've arrived days ago."

Wanting nothing more than space between them, she reached out and pinched his shoulder muscle, causing him to drop her feet. The hand on her waist pulled her tightly against the muscular stranger. Gritting her teeth, she dug one of his fingers free and peeled his hand off, not really caring that it made him flinch.

"Really, Latz." A blond woman leaned lazily against

the statue Leuna had been admiring. "Don't be such a boor." Her pouty lips curved in a cold smile while hooded eyes assessed Leuna. "Apologize."

Leuna's mind leapt ahead to the assumption that they were siblings. The startling similarity in the blues and shapes of their eyes. The woman was a few inches shorter than her brother, but carried herself in the same apparently languid manner—though judging by the way he'd tried to hold her against her will, there was nothing soft about him. So most likely nothing soft about her, either. They were like narrasti's sunning themselves, yet ready to strike should one stupidly get too close.

"Come now, Katti." Latz leaned toward Leuna, his eyes daring her to contradict him. "She knows I was only having a little fun."

Fiantza materialized between Leuna and Latz. Turning her back on the man, she motioned for Leuna to continue down the next hallway. They went several steps in silence before Fiantza murmured, "Latz and Katti are the children of Lady Adeita, childhood teacher of King Txoko. Best to avoid them."

Leuna bristled at the idea that Latz' behavior would go unreproved. What kind of woman was this Lady Adeita to have raised such adults? She recognized the name as being Lurrakian, which made even less sense.

Are all Lurrakians perfect now? her conscience jabbed her. Guiltily, she admitted that was definitely not the case. So perhaps Lady Adeita was a bully like her children? No, that didn't make sense. The one time she'd heard Txoko speak of her, there'd been genuine fondness in his voice. What did that leave? Vain and self-absorbed? Weak-willed and easily ignored? She gave up trying to puzzle it out and resolved to tell Txoko exactly what had happened.

"These will be your accommodations during your stay in Koroa." Fiantza opened double doors and stood aside to reveal an open, airy sitting room.

Three windows, each large enough to fly a gailen through, were evenly spaced along the outside wall. Thin, cheerfully-colored drapes were tied down over the openings, keeping the dust out while allowing fresh air to circulate. In the center of the room, two low couches were angled to face an equally low table. They were just about the right height for barking a shin on, actually.

Each of the six walls held at least one work of art. Intricate carvings that would take hours to study filled two walls. A giant kinetic sculpture—that appeared to double as a clock?—dominated one corner, with three fist-sized balls in a cup at the bottom, waiting to be put back into play. Personally, Leuna felt immediately drawn to a landscape painting with a horizon that seemed to stretch away, so very far away that she knew she could get lost in it.

"Please find your room," Fiantza nodded to Leuna, "to your right. And your room, to your left." She motioned for Merezi and Xelebre to come through. "The servants have tended to your baggage. Let me know if you find that anything is missing and a search will be made." Thievery was almost non-existent in the royal household, but Fiantza had seen too much to rule it out absolutely. "Each room has a private bath as well as a rain booth." Beckoning for them to follow her, Fiantza led the Izan's to theirs and demonstrated how the taps worked.

Drawn by the rhythmic sounds coming from below, Leuna walked over to the windows. Bright, cheerful musical notes leapt over the windowsill to dance about her. *Come and play!* the instruments seemed to call. Through the finely-woven drapes she could just barely see as far below, dancers moved in a long, graceful line to the energetic drumbeats. Sitting on the windowsill, she leaned back against the frame, listening.

Fiantza, returning from the Izan's room, hesitated upon finding the girl so engrossed in the festival music. Daylight was fading swiftly and she wrestled with herself to know what to do, for their audience with Queen Ema was scheduled for before dawn on the morrow. She exhaled in relief when the music became softer, softer, then stopped.

"Thank you for letting me listen." Leuna, feeling more relaxed than she had in days, rose with a smile. "I don't think I've ever heard such lovely music."

Fiantza twitched, then nodded sharply. "Follow me, please." Her experience with Lurrakians and Marroi music involved terms such as 'racket' and 'din' and other uncomplimentary words. Opening the door to Leuna's room, she stepped back to allow her to enter.

The first thing Leuna saw was that her bed was literally in a hole in the wall. Filmy white drapes hung suspended from the top of the hole, held back by ties for now. A small stack of lightweight blankets waited patiently at the foot of the bed while a huge stack of pillows at the other end made her long to lie down. Two screened windows, slightly smaller than those in the sitting room, provided some light, while the rest came from firestones embedded in the walls.

"There is your bed." Fiantza pointed. It was easier than waiting for her to ask, as kanpotarrak usually did. "The lehorra bags will be topped off each morning."

"Topped off?" Leuna echoed, confused. "With what?"

"With water." Fiantza smiled and walked over to lift the thick sleeping rug. "See? The bags are laid end to end, three layers deep. Very comfortable."

Leuna wasn't so sure, but she kept that to herself. "Do the bags ever break?" she asked hesitantly.

Fiantza shrugged. "They are changed routinely to prevent such occurrences."

"Oh." Feeling foolish, Leuna shrugged back. "Of course they are. That makes perfect sense."

Amused, Fiantza led her over to a folding wooden wall. "This is for privacy while bathing and changing." She demonstrated how easy it was to open and close the hinged wall, then showed the girl how to use the taps in the rain booth.

"This is amazing." Leuna stared up at the metal orbs that protruded from the walls, water still dripping from them after the display. "I can see why you call it a rain booth! It must be just like getting caught in a spring storm."

Fiantza paused to observe the wistful expression on the girl's face. "You enjoy getting caught in the rain?" She was truly curious. Rain was rare in her land, and often violent.

Leuna giggled. "Well, not so much getting my clothes wet, that's a nuisance. But feeling the water drops on my hands and face while I work in the garden or while I'm walking somewhere…yes, I do rather enjoy that. It can be quite pleasant."

Fiantza glanced up at the orbs as well, an entirely new concept of rain dawning on her. Force of habit carried her on to say, "The royal family will be eating privately this evening. Supper will be delivered to your rooms at six. I will come by to wake you at five tomorrow morning and help you prepare for your presentation to Queen Ema." She gestured to the waist-high chest of double drawers and companion armoire on the far wall. "At her son's request, Queen Ema has graciously provided a few outfits for each of you."

Apprehensively, Leuna walked over to the armoire and opened the doors. A dozen outfits swayed lightly on their hangers, whispering to her from wherever they touched. She saw silk, cotton, linen, and fabrics she didn't even recognize. Bold colors, muted oranges, heavy embroidery, and a single, plain shirt. Something for every occasion, she supposed.

"Will there be anything else?" Fiantza asked, puzzled by the slump in the girl's shoulders. Was she disappointed by the queen's generous gifts? But no, there was no haughty tilt to the girl's chin. Nothing dismissive about the way she was running her fingers along the sleeves of the green silk shirt.

"Hmm? Oh." Leuna closed the doors. "No, thank you."

Fiantza excused herself with a bow, then hurried off to report to the queen.

Leuna allowed herself a long, soothing soak in jasmine-scented water. The towels were thin, but absorbent, and she hung hers to dry on a rack near a screened window. Even her hair dried quickly in the moisture-free air, though the thick marble walls kept things cool.

There was a knock on her door and her grandmother's voice called, "Supper's here."

"Coming." They were already seating themselves when she entered the common area and she joined them quickly. "This looks delicious!"

"The servant who brought it told me that they have kitchen dragons here," Xelebre explained, taking a generous helping of the seasoned ground meat. "Something about how cooking with their fire makes the food taste better?"

"Yes, it does," Leuna agreed, thinking back to the few days she'd spent visiting Txoko and Sparks in the forest outside of Herrixka. "I was disappointed when they didn't cook with dragonfire on our way here." Tearing a piece of flat bread, she overlapped the halves on the bottom of her plate.

"I'm just glad they didn't bring any more food," Merezi admitted cheerfully. "If I ate as much as I wanted to, I would need an entirely new wardrobe."

Leuna laughed along with them, even as her mind drifted back to something Merezi had said days ago, about growing old and fat with Txoko. Where was he right now? What was he doing? She hadn't seen him all that day, not to talk with him. He hadn't even come over to talk with her before breaking camp that morning, though he *had* made sure someone warned her about the aerial stunt. Hmm… That stunt, combined with the revelation from the night before, made her think that it might be best if she didn't see him that evening after all.

Chapter 12

"I don't understand." Txoko frowned at his advisors. "How can the distira be missing?" Every year for the dragon festival, a plumed distira dragon was brought to Koroa and presented to the king. He, in turn, released it to beautify Marroi. As traditions went, it held no practical value, but was meant to show that the king had the best interests of his people at heart.

"We're not sure." While it pained the older man to admit that, it was the sad truth. "We coaxed one in weeks ago, and she seemed happy in the upper caves. Then, she vanished." Koroa's upper caves were open to wild dragons, who came and went as they pleased. "We have flights out now, scouring the land for a new distira."

Txoko hesitated, his brain already staggering under the weight of festival details they'd shared. "How will it impact the people if another one cannot be found?" Txoko asked. The silence that finally fell over the group underscored the gravity of the situation.

"My king." An advisor bowed respectfully. "This was the third distira to be found."

Txoko's headache increased exponentially. "What?" He hated to sound dull, but he couldn't have heard that correctly.

"It is true." The other advisors exchanged unhappy glances.

One of them stepped forward, spreading his hands in a conciliatory gesture. "We have been pondering an alternative." All but one of the others leaned forward eagerly. "A statue."

"A great statue, atop Koroa."

"Yes, a distira made of the same mountain as the castle!" They kept adding to the project, speaking over each other in their excitement, until Txoko raised a hand to stop them.

"You've given me a great deal to think about." That at least was true. "We will meet again in the morning." Dismissing them with a wave of his hand, he turned to look out of the nearest window. He'd hoped to find time to visit with Leuna tonight. Even for a few moments. Tonight, though, he doubted he'd be fit company.

"You have something else to say?" Wearily, he turned to face the oldest, and arguably, wisest, peer. The door had already closed behind the others, leaving them in relative peace. Unfortunately, the expression on Kintsu's lined face gave him no hope for a solution to the distira problem.

"It is good to have you home." His leg aching where he'd broken it twice during his last lustrum, he shuffled over to a chair and seated himself. Appointed to the position by Txoko's father for turning back a rogue dragon that was decimating the smaller villages, Kintsu was growing weary of the court's tendency to try to solve problems with distractions.

Txoko almost laughed. "It is good to be home. Even if it means having every unsolvable problem laid on my back." He took a chair for himself. "My mother will expect me for the evening meal soon," he prompted.

"I believe the distiras are being taken."

"Why?" Txoko had learned never to reject Kintsu's assertions without testing them for himself first. The man didn't speak carelessly.

"Why are they being taken?" Kintsu lifted a shaggy white eyebrow. "Or why do I believe this?"

"Both." Txoko grinned despite the gravity of the situation.

"Not in two hundred years has a distira left once it was coaxed in." Kintsu shifted to a more comfortable position. "Also, there are rumors of people on Koroa's high peaks."

"Rumors." Txoko shoved his fingers through his hair. True, it didn't make sense for things to change so drastically without a good reason. "What would anyone have to gain by…" He stopped as something occurred to him.

Kintsu leaned toward him, recognizing the expression on his king's face. "You have just thought of something important."

"Yes." Scowling, Txoko rose. "You may be right. There is a poacher who…" He broke off abruptly as the doors began to open. His face already set in a scowl, Txoko let it remain so when he saw who was entering.

"Your Majesty." Latz mock-bowed. "Your mother has asked me to fetch you."

Txoko managed a sardonic smile as he made his apologies to Kintsu. "You'll forgive me, old friend." He rose. "Mustn't keep the queen waiting. Join me for breakfast," he patted Kintsu's shoulder on his way past. "And I'll finish telling you that story."

"Your Majesty." Kintsu kept his seat, one of many benefits of his age, but inclined his head in acknowledgement.

"Regaling old chums with tall tales?" Latz snorted.

She could've sent anyone, Txoko gritted his teeth, *and she chose him.*

Forcing a smile, he changed the subject. "I understand that your mother was not well enough to join us this year. I'm very sorry." And yet, relieved. One of his primary concerns about exposing the head poacher's identity was that Lady Adeita would be present to see it take place.

Latz shrugged diffidently. "She likes her own home best these days." Which simplified his life significantly. "Katti was able to come, though." He jabbed Txoko with his elbow. "She still has an eye for you, you know."

Several embarrassing incidents from their youth spun through Txoko's mind, leaving him feeling slightly ill. "Surely not," he objected mildly. "I was under the impression that a wealthy merchant had caught her attention. Um…Teus, wasn't it?" Maintaining an innocent expression, he glanced at Latz, who'd broken step. Teus was the name of one of the smugglers they'd recently arrested for his connection to the poaching ring.

"I don't know anyone named Teus." Latz did his best to bury the fear that had lanced through him at the carelessly dropped name. Of course he knew Teus. The man was bold, arrogant, and currently in prison. Here. That was part of the reason he'd come to this stupid festival. It was his only chance to get at Teus, who knew far too much.

"Oh?" Txoko kept his tone breezy while inwardly

gloating. Latz knew exactly who he was talking about. "My mistake."

Latz tapped the extravagant silver studs on his belt, then smiled as though he'd thought of a private joke. "Forget it. If there ever was a Teus, I'm sure Katti already has." He waved his hand dismissively. "Even our most interesting acquaintances never hold her interest for long."

"You make her sound quite the heartbreaker," Txoko observed as casually as he could. Katti was pretty enough, but held no attraction for him with her languid, pouting ways. "Pity the poor conquests." He congratulated himself as they entered the dining room. That had gone rather well, he thought. Yes, his one regret as he greeted his mother and Zain's family was that Leuna wasn't present. Not that he wanted her exposed to Latz if it could be helped.

"Queen Ema." Latz grinned from ear to ear. "Seeing you again is like waking up to a mountain sunrise." He bent over her hand in Lurrakian fashion before taking his seat.

"Isn't that the line you were saving for your mystery girl?" Katti dug a spoon into the serving dish and her claws into her brother simultaneously.

Latz flushed, irritated with his sister for giving him away. "The only mystery, my dear sister," he resisted the urge to dump the pitcher of chilled juice over her head, "is how you can be so childish."

"Mystery woman?" Min intervened, helping her youngest with some soft bread. She tried every day to help her children get along and this bickering was setting a bad example. "Whomever do you mean?" Her dark, mahogany-colored skin glistened in the light of the firestones, and she avoided the queen's curious eyes. The physician thought twins were likely this time and she was just too tired to think about it, let alone discuss it.

"We were on our way to our rooms this afternoon," Katti pursued the topic with relish, "when we bumped into a fairly pretty Lurrakian girl." Smirking at her brother she added, "He hasn't stopped talking about her since."

Txoko took a bite of his food, unwilling to trust himself to speak. Zain, who was seated directly across from him, at their mother's left, cleared his throat.

"She must be more than fairly pretty if Latz is interested in her." Reaching over his daughter, he lifted a half-full glass clear of his son's innocently swinging elbow. Patiently, he put the glass back where it had been at the head of the boy's place setting. Table manners, like everything else worth learning, took time to learn.

"Sorry, Papa," Erdiko murmured, wiping his hands on his napkin.

Zain smiled and accepted the apology with a nod. Latz was already talking, but he was only saying the expected.

"…better than you do." Latz shook his head at his sister. "He knows that I never settle for 'fairly' anything."

Txoko politely cut his meat into bite-sized chunks and stabbed one. Latz could only be referring to Leuna. There were only a handful of ambassadors at Koroa right now, and none of them were accompanied by their children.

"She will be formally introduced at my court

tomorrow." Queen Ema tasted her juice and set her glass aside. She tried to anticipate the lumps and bumps life would throw at her sons, but somehow she'd overlooked Latz'…incorrigible nature. Unable to resist what he didn't already have, he would inevitably pursue Leuna. "However, I doubt we'll see much of her once she discovers our medical library."

"A scholar?" Katti wrinkled her nose in disdain. "That would be a first, brother."

Min tried again to divert the siblings. "I understand that there will be a number of historical displays at this year's festival."

"Yes." Txoko gratefully seized the conversational offering. "There will be several booths featuring reproductions of famous items. Also theatrical reenactments of a number of important events." Noticing the gloomy expressions on the faces of Zain's children, he cleared his throat. "Including aerial reenactments."

Zain's daughter, Rena, brightened at once. "Will you be participating, Papa?"

"Will there be battles?" Erdiko asked at almost the same moment. He was going to be a dragon soldier when he grew up and was terribly proud of his father's prowess.

"There won't be any real fighting, no." Zain looked his son in eyes. "Thankfully. But I am part of a dragon flight that will be helping recreate the Battle of Katurrik."

"We'll be there to watch, won't we, Momma?" Erdiko swung his attention to his mother. "We'll cheer loudest, won't we?"

Min managed to smile and wink at her son. "If you both behave at the junior dragon show, then yes, we can go to the reenactment." She took a long drink of her chilled juice to counter the memories of standing out in the heat of the day during years past. Why the reenactments couldn't happen in the cool morning hours was beyond her.

"The junior dragon show?" Erdiko cried. "That's for babies!"

"I think you'll find," Zain admonished his son sternly, "that those 'babies' are all many years older than you."

Sensing an impending collapse in discipline, Queen Ema signaled for the servants to remove the empty dishes. "I had the cook save an especially juicy melon for us tonight," she announced. Clasping her hands in feigned concern, she looked at Rena and Erdiko. "I hope you like melon."

Zain smiled fondly at his children, who leapt verbally to reassure her, then dropped some bait for Latz. "I almost forgot." He looked at Txoko. "If you have time in the morning, one of the dragon goods smugglers has asked to speak with you."

Txoko frowned. "I'll be very busy tomorrow with festival preparations. I'm afraid he'll have to settle for my chief deputy." Latz, who'd been lounging in a most disrespectful fashion, had suddenly moved to sit upright. He wasn't looking over at them, but clearly he was listening.

"It was the deputy who brought it to my attention," Zain countered. "Apparently the prisoner claims to have information that he'll only give to you."

Txoko grumbled something unintelligible and bit into a slice of melon, the juice streaming down his fingers and face. "I suppose I'll have to meet with him then. This poaching business is nearly in hand, but if we can get it taken care of even a day sooner, it will be worth it." He took another bite while Zain nodded agreement. "What's the prisoner's name?"

"It's…" Zain screwed up his face in profound thought. "Teus." He smiled, then turned a worried gaze on Latz, who was unaccountably choking on his melon.

"I'm alright," Latz coughed, holding up a hand. "Just," he wheezed, water beginning to come from the corners of his eyes, "swallowed wrong."

Katti showed her first real concern for her brother's well-being that evening by pounding him on the back until he waved her off.

"Alright," he gasped. "I'm alright." Before he'd begun choking, he'd been watching Zain and Txoko closely. Neither of them seemed overly interested in the name of Teus, yet it was the second time it had just 'come up' in Latz' presence that evening. How much did they really know? "Queen Ema." Rising, Latz bowed. "Thank you for a lovely meal. If you would be so kind as to excuse me?" He had to get Teus. Tonight.

"And me." Katti dropped a brief curtsy.

"Of course." Ema waved them away and was relieved when the door closed behind them. Usually she felt it best to get obligatory associations over and done with as soon as possible. Tonight, though, she wondered if she hadn't erred in choosing to have them in company with Zain's children. Not to mention Txoko's odd behavior. If the Lurrakian girl—Leuna, was it?—loved him, she wouldn't be swayed by Latz' overbearing approach.

Zain pointed at the pitcher of water and said softly, "I already have an agent assigned to follow Latz."

Txoko handed him the pitcher. "Was he followed this afternoon?"

"Yes, but by a different agent." Zain checked with each of his children before turning his attention to his own glass. "His brush with Leuna was short and she handled it well enough."

Txoko would've liked to know exactly what 'well enough' meant, but his mother claimed his attention. The festival, which would begin the following evening, was essentially already underway. They agreed on which families should be invited to join them in their tent for the opening ceremonies, then concentrated on their guests.

During his attempts at entertaining the older children, Txoko felt a pang of sorrow at knowing he would never be able to tell them he was their uncle. His mind immediately leapt from there to Leuna, who was most likely already asleep. The children reacted with glee to an error he made with a simple hand trick and he had to agree to teach them how it was done to restore peace.

"Alright. Time to go." Min rose from her seat at the table. "It's nearly bed time and you two haven't even had your baths."

Erdiko scowled and opened his mouth to protest. Fortunately for him, his father had also risen and was in the process of slipping his arm around his wife. Seeing the love in his father's face as he looked down at his wife, Erdiko bit his tongue instead of arguing.

Rena curtsied prettily to Txoko and reminded Erdiko to bow. Then, the baby safely tucked in Zain's arms, the little family took itself off to their rooms.

"You will have a family of your own," Ema promised her forlorn-looking son.

Txoko permitted himself a heartfelt sigh. "I hope you are right, Mother."

Knowing that servants were waiting nearby to clean up, Ema joined her son, tucking her hand through the crook of his elbow. "It is good to have you home."

"I am glad to be here." Txoko smiled down at her, then led her into the hall. They might still be overheard on their walk to her rooms, but it was less likely.

"And the woman you brought?" Ema quirked an eyebrow at him. "Is she glad?"

"I don't know. I haven't spoken with her today." Txoko shrugged unhappily. "I don't think she quite realized how much I need the approval of the peers and my people before I remarry…not until I explained it to her last night."

Inwardly, Ema shook her head, amazed at her son's confession. "You didn't think to tell her before?"

"I…" Groaning, he scrubbed one hand across his face. "Not as plainly as last night."

Ema squeezed his arm gently. Her son's letters had explained his misadventure, how he lost and regained his memories. Leuna's part in it all. That he was attracted to her was as plain as the colorful ruffle on a distira dragon. But that was of secondary importance. "You must think she will make a good queen."

Txoko absent-mindedly reached up to stroke the sapphire-eyed carving of his grandfather's gailen dragon as they passed it. He'd been great friends with that carving as a youngster. Such marvelous quests and exploits they'd shared. He longed to see his own children playing on and about the statues of Koroa.

"She's warm and kind. Sweetly-tempered, yet strong. This," he gestured at the marble halls they were passing through, "is all new to her. If she will make Koroa her home, then yes." He paused to open the door to his mother's rooms. "I believe she will make a fine queen."

She studied her son's face, admiring his willingness to try to see Leuna objectively. "Good night, my son." She offered her cheek, which he kissed, then stepped into her rooms and closed the door behind her. It was a pity that she couldn't solve this situation for him. Only time and learning the will of their people could do that.

"Your Majesty." Fiantza stepped out of the shadows.

Ema waved her to a chair. "Tell me."

Chapter 13

Latz dropped his expensive, tailored shirt into the laundry and slipped into the cheap button-up he'd hidden in the depths of his luggage. His blond hair would make him a little too memorable, but his skin was sun-browned and the rough clothing would help him blend in. Anyway, the plan was simple. Get to Teus. End Teus.

"What *are* you wearing?" Katti lounged against the door jamb.

"A disguise." He didn't mind her jeering at him in private. He'd had years to get used to it. "I've got a little business to take care of."

"Here?" She frowned. "You been holding out on me?"

"Nothing like that, dear sister," he laughed coldly. "You've more than proven yourself these last two years." Sure, he'd been skeptical about including her in his business ventures. Hadn't figured she'd the nerve to deal with the kind of people that were part and parcel of his life.

Katti smirked. She knew better than he did how important she was to his organization. Someday, she'd have to tell him. For now, though, she was content to let him think what he wanted.

"You stay in this evening," he instructed, tugging on the scuffed boots he'd borrowed from his valet. "If anyone asks for me, I'm having dinner with a friend."

Katti scowled. She'd had interesting plans for that evening with the Tariek ambassador. Knowing that business came first, she nodded anyway. No real loss. After all, she knew perfectly well how to turn the ambassador's irritation to her advantage.

Just as I suspected. While Latz didn't interfere with his sister's habit of finding a new plaything—or two or three—everywhere they went, he wished she'd exercise a little more restraint. The festival lasted an entire week and there would be plenty of time for such things after he'd taken care of business. With a short nod, he let himself out of their rooms.

As soon as he was out of sight, Katti eased over to his case. Most of what she found there was old news, stuff they could easily explain to any official who happened to find it; though, as usual one or two things hadn't been 'shared' as fully as Latz claimed. With one eye on the door, she investigated the hidden compartment in his tresna. It took two men to carry the tall, multi-stringed instrument, which Latz only played passably well. Yet somehow, nobody ever questioned his decision to take it with him everywhere he went.

Hmmm. Straightening, she examined the unmarked bottle she'd found. Shook it. It was less than half full, but *what* was it? She started to open it, then changed her mind. There was something menacing about the thick, dark glass the bottle was made of. Instead, she turned the bottle, studying each of its eight sides. She was only halfway done when her sensitive fingertips detected barely raised lines. Carrying it over to the nearest firestone, she let the light play over those lines—one straight line cut through by three diagonals. A warning symbol any poacher would recognize. Her eyes narrowed. How delightfully interesting. And convenient. She was getting awfully tired of her brother's over-cautious methods.

Blissfully ignorant of his sister's prying, Latz was halfway to his destination. He'd already left the plush guest suites behind and was entering the section of Koroa that *wasn't* on the public tours. Ornate carvings gave way to bare rooms where unrefined firestones glared at him from every angle.

"Halt!" A brace of guards blocked his path. "State your business."

Latz dropped his eyes and shuffled his feet as if they made him nervous. "I've cum ta see me uncle." Cautiously, he observed them exchange a glance. Ordinarily, Koroa's prison didn't see much use. Despite the normal ebb and flow of traffic in and around the palace, only a special few were foolish enough to break the laws here. Even fewer were colossally stupid enough to get caught. However, this was festival week. Travelers had traversed the length and breadth of Marroi to be here, disrupting the usual way of things.

"Your uncle's name?" barked the shorter guard.

Surprised, Latz gulped and scrounged through his memory for a Lurrakian name common enough to go unnoticed. "Arru," he said at last. Shuffling his feet again, he let his shoulders slump. "Kin I see him? Please?" He added a bit of a whine as he pretended to blurt, "Me aunt, she ain't gonna like it iff'n I don't."

"You're afraid of your aunt?" The taller guard had been observing him carefully and Latz just hoped he'd struck the right balance between looking poor and clean.

"Yessir!" He nodded vigorously. "She gonna whup me iff'n I don't tell Uncle Arru she mad at him." Again the guards exchanged glances.

"Well, we wouldn't want that," the taller guard said soothingly. Assuming the uncle wasn't a vicious killer, he'd be in with the other petty criminals they were always plagued with during festivals. Pickpockets, cutpurses, the occasional brawler… He pointed at the tunnel on his left. "Follow this till you reach the next guard. They'll show you the way from there."

"Thankee, thankee." Latz bobbed his head

and made a show of hurrying off.

"Pretty convincing," the short guard muttered darkly.

"I dunno." The taller guard scratched his cheek as they resumed their patrol. Aware how voices carried, he kept his low. "Did you see that haircut? And how about his hands?" If they hadn't been tipped off to expect a blond Lurrakian male *and* to let him pass, he'd have hauled him in for questioning.

"True," his companion agreed. "But I was talking about your performance." They laughed and continued on their way, their job done.

Latz, hearing their voices fade, did an abrupt about face. Finding the other tunnel empty again, he pulled a pair of false cuffs from his pocket and fastened them about his wrists. He hadn't expected to run into guards this soon, and it worried him. The cuffs, embroidered with the royal crest and worn by all the servants here, would help him blend in.

He dodged the next two sets of guards, which did nothing to ease his mind as he drew nearer to his destination—the kartz. Repeat offenders and violent criminals were kept there, in individual cells. Apprehensive, he paused at the last opening and peered inside. If it was possible, the firestones were even brighter here, eliminating any soothing shadow. There were no guards stationed here, though they patrolled on an erratic schedule that only they and their superiors knew. No guards were necessary.

Stepping between two rows of cells, Latz took a deep breath—and nearly gagged. The air was stale at best this deep in Koroa, so the odors pooled and mixed, going from unsavory to intolerable. Retreating hastily, he stood in the cross corridor for several seconds while he fought for control over his stomach. The scent was there, too, just not nearly as powerful.

Irritated with his own weakness, Latz returned to the tunnel. There was absolutely nowhere to hide but plain sight, so he did his best to stride along as though he belonged there. While breathing shallowly. And looking from side to side to see who occupied each cell. He didn't stop, not even when he recognized three in a row as poachers he'd been told were dead. Killed in skirmishes with the soldiers.

At the end of the second row of cells, he savagely wiped the sweat off his face and leaned against the cold marble wall. It felt good against his forehead. How long had they been collecting poachers and holding them here? How much did they already know? Would killing Teus even help?

Hearing the *thump* of a hard boot heel on stone, Latz scurried around a convenient corner. What if this was the corner they came around? He couldn't explain his presence here, this deep in the kartz. Not even as a servant. Sure, he could claim he'd gotten lost, turned around in the never-ending tunnels that were Koroa, but if he hadn't begun dodging the patrols, he'd have been found and sent back long ago. Escorted back, most likely. His plan to claim that he served in his own retinue seemed very, very thin as he listened to the footsteps coming nearer.

Still as a statue he stood until the guards passed, then gasped for air. He had to get this over with! Find Teus and eliminate him. The other poachers he'd seen were just the brutes who trapped and killed the dragons, the nobodies he sent to die when the soldiers got too close. They had no idea who he was or that he existed.

Latz straightened his shirt and smoothed his hair. Alright. Time to finish this. Ignoring the next few rows of cells, he moved deeper into the kartz. Teus wasn't a nobody. He was certain now that Txoko knew of or suspected a connection, that he and Zain were baiting him when they mentioned Teus at supper. Well, somebodies weren't kept with nobodies, so he pressed on until…

"Hssst!" A hoarse whisper caught his attention. "Latz!"

"Shut up, you fool," he growled, springing over to grip the bars of Teus' cell. Set twelve feet back from the wall, it was in a deep pool of shadow, the first he'd seen in an hour. "Don't say my name." He could barely see Teus in the weak light from the firestone in the cell's ceiling. Usually clean-shaven and dapper, Teus now had a scraggly beard and wore dirty clothes that were probably the finest money could buy at one point.

Teus bared his teeth. "I'll say plenty," he threatened. "I'm not going to be left here to die, not even of old age!"

Latz allowed his shoulders to droop. "You've said plenty already, I'm sure." He was elated at being so close to his goal, but first he had to know. Was he going to kill Teus for betraying him? Or because he could?

"You know better than that." Teus lurched off his bed and wobbled up to the bars. "Anyway, these idiots haven't asked me an intelligent question yet."

"No?" Latz hesitated. Perhaps things weren't as bad as he'd thought. Perhaps he wouldn't have to flee to the islands of Ihes after all.

"No." Teus licked his lips and looked longingly at the barrel of water that served this corridor. While they gave him enough to keep him alive, it wasn't nearly enough to satisfy a man with nothing to do but stare at bare surroundings. "Now quit stalling. I've seen the keys they use on these doors." He ran his hand over the narrow bars that splayed out from the lock, preventing him reaching it. "It's embarrassing to be kept here by a lock a baby could pick!"

Latz grunted. "I guess they don't expect anyone to get this far."

"Yeah." Teus scratched his unkempt beard. "How'd you manage?"

"Dumb luck, I guess." Stooping, he pretended to examine the lock. He shook his head as he straightened. "Nothing I can do with it right now. Left my knife in my room in case I was caught and searched."

"What about your boot knife?" Teus demanded, unwittingly sealing his own fate.

"How could I explain a boot knife?" Latz snorted with irritation. Teus definitely knew too much, more than Latz had even realized. "I'll have to come back." Looking around as if to make sure they were still alone, he spotted the water barrel.

"Alright." Teus wiped the back of his hand across his lips. "Get me a drink of water before you go."

"Huh?" Latz stared at him, unable to believe his good fortune. "Yeah. Sure." Eyes and ears open, he hustled over to the water barrel and lifted the lid. There were no cups, so he filled the dipper and began counting out drops of inky black liquid from the dark bottle he was carrying.

"Hurry up!"

Latz twitched and cursed as the water sloshed over the side of the dipper and down his fingertips. He'd lost track of how many drops he'd added, but he was pretty sure it was enough to do the job. Not as quickly as a larger dose, but… Stuffing the bottle back into his pocket, he decided it would be rather poetic for Teus to die a slower death because of his own impatience. Wiping his fingers off on the damp wall, he returned to the cell.

"Here, take it you, you greedy, stupid…" Latz bit his tongue to keep from saying more. Anyway, he needn't have worried. Teus was draining it far too quickly to taste the poison.

"Thanks." Teus grinned, then glared. "Now you be back before breakfast, or I'll make sure you have a nice, comfy cell just like mine."

"I heard you the first time." Latz had to work hard to inject bitterness into his tone when triumph was all he felt. Teus' couldn't hurt him now. Taking the dipper back, he ducked into the corridor. Pausing, he splashed a little water into the dipper, rinsing it haphazardly before returning it to the peg where he'd gotten it. One mysterious death would go overlooked. More so if it was accompanied by a dozen mysterious illnesses. However, he imagined a dozen or more mysterious deaths would bring on an investigation and he couldn't have that.

A shadow he hadn't noticed followed him all the way from the kartz back to the guest wing, where a second shadow took over.

Without breaking stride, the first shadow pressed a note into the palm of the second, warning them to be on the alert for a midnight trip to the kartz. Continuing on his way to report to Zain, he pondered what he'd overheard. Teus hadn't actually said anything they could use in a trial. Would they wait to catch Latz in the act of freeing the known poacher? Or would both men be dragged from their sleep to answer questions?

His fingers tapped idly against his knife hilt as he walked, reflecting that the truly puzzling part was the fact that Teus was still alive after threatening Latz.

Chapter 14

Ema's audience room had one chair. It discouraged lingering, which meant she got a lot more work done. People came, stated their business, got an answer, and left. Truth be told, it was an especially useful tactic at times like this, when events such as the festival drew citizens from the furthest reaches of Marroi. And, while these twice weekly morning audiences were primarily intended for Marroi citizens, the fact that the Marroi peers and their spouses who took an active interest in the throne's benevolent works were patiently *standing* to her right, prevented visiting dignitaries from taking offense at the arrangement.

"Yes, I see." Ema nodded at the map the young, slightly sweating councilman held up before her. More than that, she was impressed. His city had gone to great pains to recheck their boundaries, then to reconcile with their neighbors peacefully. "All city charters are copied and kept on record in our legal library. Leave the map with me and I will have it confirmed with our records."

He surrendered the map, but hesitated. "And then, my queen?"

"And then I will send land surveyors to place boundary stones." Apparently intent on rolling the map, she added, "Along with a small military detachment to protect and assist as necessary." The relief on the young man's face only added to her concern that the neighboring city had already begun making threats. Why was it that, in times of peace and plenty, people *chose* violence?

"Thank you." He bowed. Bowed again. Hurried over to take a young woman from the gallery by the hand, speaking excitedly to her as they left the room.

Ema passed the map to a servant. "I want this report by the lunch hour," she told the woman quietly. Acting swiftly, decisively, would send a clear message to the rest of Marroi.

"Your Majesty," her steward, whose chief responsibility lay in keeping the line of audience seekers in order, bowed and announced, "Visiting from the land of Lurrak, Jaurle and Jaurla Izan of Ibilia. Doctor Oneko of Herrixka."

Ema had been anticipating this moment all morning. Debating it, actually. For better or worse, her actions in the next four to five minutes would have a great impact on her son's future. Given Fiantza's favorable report last night, she was willing to take a chance. A low murmur swept the room as she rose to greet them, something she almost never did.

"Welcome to Koroa."

Merezi and Leuna curtsied while Xelebre bowed over the hand Ema offered him.

"Thank you, Your Majesty." The accepted diplomat of the group, Xelebre answered for them all.

Taking her hand back, Ema motioned for the lovely, graying-haired woman to rise. Their eyes met, and she liked what she saw. Poise without arrogance. She wore her Lurrakian clothes with simple grace, the soft heather purples and muted oranges creating an attractive color scheme without screaming for attention. Reserved, but not weak.

Uncomfortably aware of the whispers and scrutiny from the elegantly attired group standing near the room's lonely chair, Leuna tried to calm her wildly floundering heart. She almost wobbled when the queen finally beckoned for her to rise. And she absolutely wasn't expecting the queen to step closer. So close that she could see that the queen's nearly gold irises had flecks of greens and browns scattered throughout. That they weren't quite as perfectly oval as some others Leuna had seen. That they were…tired. Yes. Her eyes flicked over the queen, noting other telltale marks of fatigue.

Ema, amused at finding herself being as closely inspected by Leuna as she was inspecting her, noticed a subtle change in the younger woman's expression. A slight drawing in of the nicely shaped brows. Faint narrowing of the eyes. Tiniest parting of the lips, as if she had something to say. Which was only natural. No doubt she had a lot to say, in fact. Unfortunately, this was hardly the time or the place.

"I hope you enjoy your stay." Ema turned slightly, angling her body so that a glance past her would show them the exit. "And that you'll join me for luncheon?"

Leuna glanced at her grandparents, unsure if the invitation included all of them? Or just herself? Would it include Txoko? She'd already caught herself looking around for him a few times that day, when she saw something she wanted to share or had a question to ask.

"Fiantza knows when and where." Ema patted Leuna's arm softly, alert to the impatience of those still waiting for an audience.

Accepting the queen's gesture toward the exit as a dismissal, Xelebre bowed and ushered his girls out of the room.

"I think that went rather well," he observed quietly, winking at Merezi.

"Yes." Merezi looked past her husband to where Leuna walked silently on his other side. "Yes, quite well." In the absence of solid evidence to share on the matter, she decided to change the subject. "Do you suppose we have time for that tour?"

"Hmm, good question." Xelebre was looking around for a familiar object by which to regain his bearing and his gaze landed upon a patiently waiting Fiantza. "We can certainly ask."

"I'll need to visit our rooms before lunch," Leuna inserted. "I have something I want to give to the queen."

Fiantza's quick ears caught their words and she couldn't help wondering what sort of a gift the Lurrakian had in mind. It couldn't be large. The maids would've discovered it while unpacking their things. Smiling pleasantly at her charges, she answered Merezi's question. "We can begin the tour, if you wish."

"Begin?" Xelebre echoed.

"A full tour would take the better part of a day," Fiantza clarified. Sensing hesitation on their parts, she offered a compromise. "If you would prefer it, we could instead visit the hallways of Koroa's first and second rulers."

"Oh." Merezi beamed at her. "That sounds lovely."

"This way." Fiantza indicated the hallway to their left. "Your rooms are en route, if you wish to stop?"

"Yes, thank you." Leuna pounced on the offer. "I'll only need a moment." While there was no instant cure for fatigue, so far as she knew, she did have a few things that could help. As promised, it took her less than a minute to locate the desired items in her medical case and rejoin the others.

Fiantza's curiosity doubled when Leuna emerged

emerged from her room empty-handed. There was only time for a cursory scrutiny of the girl's clothing, and it hardly seemed likely that the small bulge in Leuna's pink gerri could hold a gift fit for a queen. Perhaps it was tucked in the folds of the alabaster bata, disguised by the swirling cream-colored pattern? Still smiling, Fiantza directed them to the halls of rulers.

"Are these halls dedicated to the first and second Marroi rulers?" Leuna asked, squinting at one of the wall carvings. "Or the third and fourth rulers, who would've been the first and second to inhabit Koroa?"

Startled, Fiantza just stared at her for a moment. "The third and fourth rulers," she confirmed at last. This girl was more than just a pretty face! "Durek the mighty, and his daughter, Queen Gina the fearless."

"The fearless?" Xelebre moved to examine the carving Fiantza nodded to when speaking of her. "She must have lived in turbulent times."

Fiantza had braced herself for the behavior she'd come to expect from kanpotarrak. The ignorant declarations about how absolutely 'inappropriate' it was to use a word like 'fearless' to describe a *woman*. The insulting questions about her 'grand' achievements—*I suppose she got fifty people seated at a table built for forty?* Now, hearing Xelebre's words and gentle, respectful tone, she was silent for several seconds, trying to decide how to respond.

"She outlived her husband and three of her children," Fiantza explained quietly. "The peers appointed by her father schemed to wrest the kingdom from her."

"But why?" Merezi frowned and laced her fingers through her husband's.

"Because they could." Leuna pointed at a carving of a woman kneeling before three, heavily armed men. "Bullies and cowards will do whatever no one stops them from doing."

"They were stopped." Txoko hadn't meant to eavesdrop on them. Their interest in the carvings, however, had allowed him to approach unnoticed. "The generals rallied to their queen in defiance of the peers and drove them from the land."

"Her reign is remembered as one of peace and plenty," Fiantza finished. "Koroa doubled in size and trade flourished."

"Fearless indeed." Leuna met Txoko's eyes and saw fatigue there as well. He must've been working very hard since his return to Koroa. He didn't smile, but he did offer her his arm, which she took.

"Most of the laws she enacted are still in force today." Txoko smiled at the final image of Queen Gina, crowning her son before a cheering crowd. "She never forgot the struggles that brought our people to Koroa. Never allowed the injustices she endured to harden her."

Leuna felt more than admiration for the woman he was describing. She felt fear. The future of an entire people—how did anyone shoulder such a burden without breaking under the load? Certainly she couldn't be expected to. Could she?

Txoko remained, watching her, while the others moved on to another hallway. "Leuna?"

Blinking, she looked up at him. "Is this what you expect of me?" Removing her hand from his arm, she backed away from him. "You think I'm some kind of paragon who can build up a whole nation?"

He started to reach for her, then stopped when she took yet another step back. "I am a king who needs a queen, yes. But I'm no paragon." He leaned back against the wall, still mostly facing her. "Being perfect would most likely make ruling easier to bear." He smiled playfully at her.

Leuna glowered at him, irritated by the ease with which he'd dismissed her question. "I'm glad you think it's funny."

Confused, Txoko stopped smiling. He'd missed something. He felt sure of it, though several seconds of silent mental scrambling left him none the wiser. "You knew I was a king back in Ibilia," he pointed out uncertainly.

"Oh yes, I knew." She threw up her hands. "I

knew you had lots of meetings. I knew you had…responsibilities." Vexed that that was the best she could come up with, she began to pace.

"Are you upset with me because I haven't been able to spend time with you?" he guessed. The exasperated look she gave him in response had him raising his hands in self-defense. "That's good, because I can't always do what I want to." Gesturing at the world in general, he exclaimed, "Do you know what it means to be a ruler? It means doing what nobody else wants to do. And yes, sometimes that includes making laws. It includes enforcing laws. It includes spending hours, day and night, searching for solutions to impossible problems when you'd rather be..." Realizing that she'd stopped pacing and was staring at him, he shook his head. "Power, prestige? They're just illusions. I'm at the mercy of my people."

She took a step toward him. "How can you even think of asking me to risk subjecting my children to that kind of future?"

Stunned, he gaped at her. "Your children?" Taking her by the arms, he drew her close. So close that he could count the freckles on her pert little nose. "*Our* children. It will be *my* son or *my* daughter who will reign after me and I want you for their mother." Easing his grip, he exhaled raggedly. "Your ignorance is betraying you, my love. A ruler is not allowed merely to be born, then tumble up to the throne in a haphazard fashion, granted fealty simply because their parent served well. A ruler is trained up from childhood, taught with love and great care. Loyalty and respect are theirs because they've been proven worthy."

She blinked furiously against the tears until they overran her defenses and spilled down her cheeks. "Even a half-blood?"

He had to lean down to hear her barely audible question. The fear in her voice cut him to the quick and he gathered her close. "There are always bullies," he whispered. "Gina faced them. I faced them." Pulling back, he cupped her face in his hands, thankful to see that her tears had stopped. "I can't promise an easy life, not for us and certainly not for our children. They'll have to live their lives as best as they can, the same as every other child on Jatorri." Her arms tightened around his waist. Resting his forehead lightly against hers, he confided, "No one truly rules alone. Not king or queen. I will help you learn your role, as will my mother."

Inhaling sharply, she straightened away from him. "Your mother!"

"Lunch!" He was only an instant behind her in recalling where they were supposed to be. "We're late!" Catching her hand, he led the way through a bewildering series of turns that brought them to his mother's favorite dining area.

"Wait!" Leuna tugged on his hand, bringing him to a halt. Through the open double doors, she was able to see some of the luncheon party. "That man." She nodded at the Lurrakian man she'd encountered the day before. "I bumped into him yesterday and he…"

"Yes." Txoko interrupted, glaring at Latz. What was he even doing there? "He mentioned it."

"He did?" Leuna hadn't expected that! "And…" How could she say this? "What did he say about it?"

"He said you were pretty." Txoko's eyes narrowed. "Why? What happened, exactly?"

Leuna bit her lip, suddenly unsure it was worth repeating. She glanced up at Txoko, looked again. The frustration and concern in his eyes drew the truth from her. "We were on our way to our rooms. Fiantza was there. My grandparents. His sister."

"And?" Txoko needed to know before his imagination drove him crazy.

"And he caught me when I tripped on one of the carvings. I wanted him to let me go, but I had to make him do it."

Txoko hesitated, torn between a surge of relief and surprise. "You *made* him let you go?"

Leuna straightened a little huffily. "Shall I demonstrate?"

Grinning, Txoko obliged her. Putting his

hands on her waist, he lifted her off her feet and carried her a few steps into the connecting hallway, where they wouldn't be casually seen by those in the dining area. Setting her gently back on the ground, he cupped her face in his hands and kissed her.

"No fair," she whispered against his lips. She felt his deep, answering chuckle rumble in his chest, making her smile, too.

"No?" He kissed her again, loving how she followed him up on her toes to prolong it a little.

"Hmm-mm." She shook her head, the tip of her nose barely touching his. "This is nothing like what happened with—whatshisname." She wrinkled her nose teasingly at him, but his smile had vanished.

"If he so much as looks at you," Txoko murmured, "I'll banish him." Latz had dared to flirt with Nire, who'd dismissed him as weak, which Txoko hadn't found overly comforting as a new husband. The mere thought of him harassing Leuna made his blood boil. When he kissed her again, he wasn't teasing.

"I," she cleared her throat, "um, I believe you." With an effort, she forced her eyes open. Saw him nod once, felt the chill as he stepped back. She wasn't ready for the moment to end, but already the voices from the dining area were nibbling at her conscious, making it impossible to linger.

"I'm sure you're right." Merezi's voice held a hint of uncertainty that belied her words.

"You must watch them with me, from the royal observation deck," agreed Ema's voice. "No festival experience is complete without the aerobatics. We'll be able to see every detail!"

Merezi, her appetite lost to the idea of watching people cavorting about between dragons while in mid-air, was relieved to look up and see Leuna. And looking happier than she had in days. Excellent. They'd needed either a good talk or a good talking to, those two.

Ema, following Merezi's gaze to where Txoko was entering the room, noted that he was unabashedly holding hands with the girl. That wasn't too surprising under the circumstances. She just hoped they had the good sense not to rush things. Signaling the servants to begin bringing out the food, she patted Merezi's arm and excused herself.

"There you are." Smiling up at Txoko, she held her hand out to Leuna. "I'm so glad you could join us as well."

"Thank you." Leuna looked around the dining area, appreciating the live plants. One in particular she recognized from her medical classes—daketa. Its flowers were known to soothe frayed nerves. "This is a lovely room."

Several small serving tables were strategically positioned around the room, encouraging mingling amongst the small group of people. It would probably take some strategy on her own part to avoid Latz, she sighed inwardly. She certainly didn't plan to hold Txoko to banishing him.

"It's one of my favorites," Ema admitted, flattered by the girl's sincere tone. Winking at Txoko, she looped her arm through Leuna's. Deliberately walking away from Txoko, she asked, "How are you enjoying Koroa so far?"

Leuna shot Txoko a look, but went along with his mother, who was aiming them at the nearest food table. "I haven't had time to see very much of it yet." She accepted a sort of flat bowl from the queen. "Fiantza showed us the hallways of the first and second rulers. Very impressive."

"Thank you." Ema beamed at her. "What impressed you about them?"

Leuna took up a pair of tongs and set two pieces of bread in her plate. "The history. I mean." She hesitated between two bowls of shredded, spiced meat. "I love how available your history is. In Lurrak, we have books about history. Some paintings and tapestries." She shrugged and added a pile of tart, whipped cream to the top of her plate like a snowdrift on a small hill. "Here history surrounds you, reminding you of those who went before, everything they've done to make your life possible. Sort of gives you something to live up to, while reminding you that nothing is impossible." Looking up to find the queen staring at her, Leuna retreated a half step. "Me. I mean, it makes me feel like that. You, well," she swallowed, "you've lived here all of your life, you already know all of that."

Ema touched Leuna lightly on the arm, smiled. "What a charming perspective." Leaving her hand on Leuna's arm, Ema guided her to the beverage table next. "And though I have lived here for several years, I do not think I could have said it better."

Relieved, Leuna smiled back. Willing herself to breathe, she looked at her choices for a drink. "I was wondering," she spoke quickly when the queen began reaching for a pale orange juice. "If I might be allowed to make you a flavored water?"

Ema blinked and lowered her hand back to her side. What an odd request. "But of course."

Stuck somewhere between anxious and determined, Leuna's hands were trembling slightly as she set her plate down to pour two glasses of water. Producing two finger-length bottles from where she'd tucked them in her sash…um, gerri…earlier, she held them up. "I thought I'd bring two, in case you liked one of them better than the other." Shaking a little of the powder from one bottle into one glass and a little of the other into the next glass, she quickly stirred them. "Please." She gestured for the queen to take her pick.

Ema was intrigued by Leuna's odd behavior. She'd known many Lurrakians over the years and none of them had ever offered to make a flavored water for her. Especially not at her own luncheon. Still, she was inclined to humor the girl who spoke with such admiration of their traditions. Her hand hovered over the glass with bright yellow, yet translucent, water, then veered to her right, selecting the lovely pink liquid instead. Raising the glass, she sniffed, tasted, and puckered.

"Too tart?" Leuna dove back into her gerri for a third bottle. "Sorry. Let me…" Two taps of the bottle of sweetener. "I hope you'll be willing to try it again." She ducked her head sheepishly as the queen stirred the glass to mix it in. The powder was marginally more effective taken plain, but she'd never yet met anyone who could just gulp it down that way.

Warily, Ema took a much smaller sip. "Mmm." She eyed the glass, then nodded. "That is much improved."

"I'm glad." Leuna felt her shoulders sag a little in relief and quickly called them back to order.

"Shall we?" Ema indicated an empty window

perch.

Taking up her things, Leuna obediently followed the queen away from the others. Two small, portable shelves waited for their plates and they settled themselves comfortably.

"I was just inviting your grandparents to join me for the aerobatics display tomorrow." Ema stirred her meat, sauce, and vegetables together. "I hope you will be there as well."

Chapter 15

Leuna laughed hollowly. She wished she could find even a scrap of enthusiasm for the event, but somehow, waiting for someone to jump and miss and then—almost inevitably—die, simply did not appeal to her.

Ema chuckled softly at Leuna's distress. Kanpotarrak, even the nice ones, were too predictable. "Would it ease your concern if I told you that only the best are permitted to participate?" Leaning closer, she added, "And that we haven't had so much as an injury in the last one hundred years?"

Leuna, taken off guard by Ema's confiding air, gasped in surprise. "That…seems impossible!"

"It's only logical." Ema rolled a bit of meat inside a thin slice of bread. "We could hardly continue the tradition if it meant sacrificing our best for mere entertainment."

Leuna's gaze dropped to her own food. It didn't get more obvious than that, and even though Ema had spoken kindly, she felt…stupid. "Will Txoko be participating?"

Smiling proudly, Ema turned to search for her son. "He always participates."

Leuna looked up, a forkful of food halfway to her mouth, and saw Ema's smile slip. Reflexively, she turned to look. She came to her feet like there was an invisible rope tied around her waist and someone had just jerked on it—hard. Her fork hit the floor about the same time that Txoko's knees did, and she was only halfway to him.

"Your Majesty!" Leuna skidded to a halt to keep from colliding with the tall, thin Marroi man who'd leapt forward. "Quickly!" The royal physician helped Txoko lie down on his back. "Someone fetch my case!"

Leuna wiped damp palms on her slacks, fear crawling up and down her spine as she debated what to do. Based on her previous experience with the physician, offering to help would be met with irritation and disdain. She was about to rejoin the queen, who at least would be sure to have instant access to Txoko, when someone else started to collapse!

Katti screamed as Latz lurched forward, then fell flat on his face. The Marroi physician barely looked up from where he was examining Txoko, though he began working more urgently.

Darting forward, Leuna grabbed Latz by the shoulder and rolled him onto his back. His eyes, still wide open, stared lifelessly at her from his reddening face. There was no pulse when she put her hand to his neck artery to check, just to be sure. *He's so warm!* Examining his lips more closely, she saw tiny blisters beginning to form.

"Leuna." She looked up in answer to her

grandfather's voice. "What's that on his hands?"

Looking, she sucked in a breath. His fingertips were gray! Taking him gingerly by the edge of his hand, she lifted it so she could study his fingers.

"Is he dead?" Leuna shook off Katti's shrill question and vaguely heard her grandmother's soothing voice.

Frowning, Leuna compared his fingers against each other. The discoloration was splotchy, extending on one finger past the first joint, not at all the smooth spread she would've expected. Unless…picking up the napkin he'd dropped, she dipped it in the puddle of spilled drink. Taking great care not to actually touch his fingers to her own skin, she dragged his fingertips across the damp napkin. Grimly, she set his hand down and raised the napkin. There was just a trace of gray, but it left no doubt in her mind that he'd gotten the substance—whatever it was—on his fingers by *handling* it.

The facts of her inspection clicked into place in her mind: hot, flushed skin; the irritation on the tender skin of his mouth; his discolored skin. His abrupt death. As much as she'd wanted to be wrong… "He was poisoned," she announced quietly.

Reaching up to close his eyes, an unexpected mark on his chest caught her attention. Unbuttoning his shirt, she opened it to reveal dozens of small, faded scars on his left pectoral muscle, none of them larger than a teardrop. Their spacing, size, and shape were so uniform. So…intentional.

In truth, the scars were more puzzling than the thin trails of black winding across his chest, just under his skin. Taken all together, they formed a pattern that reminded her of a weirdly-shaped root-system, covering the surface of his chest above his heart and lungs. His skin bulged with whatever it was, the lines already beginning to bleed into each other to form a single, almost bruise-like, massive shadow. It was as if…as if there was *too much* poison. His body wasn't able to absorb it rapidly enough, so it was pooling there, just under his skin.

Leaning back, she took a deep breath. For the first time, she saw the syringe the physician had used to treat Txoko. "Do you know what poison was used?" When he didn't respond, she warned loudly, "If you used the wrong treatment, it could make it worse."

The physician flicked a smug glance in her direction. "This antidote will counteract any poison." Kanpotarrak were so backward.

Xelebre went to one knee beside Leuna. "What is it, darling?"

"It doesn't make sense." She put her hand over her violently twisting stomach. Tasted bile. How was she even supposed to say this? "Why is he dead," she nodded at Latz' still form, "and Txoko isn't?" Not a question she'd imagined herself asking when she got up that morning!

Xelebre squeezed her shoulder comfortingly. "Are you sure it's the same cause?"

"It's the same symptoms." She held back the bit about the difference in the appearance of their fingertips. Txoko's brown fingertips were uniformly discolored and it only rose as far as his cuticles. "*Very* fast acting."

"Fast acting?" Xelebre barely held back his scowl. "Are you sure?"

"Positive." Despite the circumstances, she almost laughed at the repetition of the question. "They both dropped within seconds of each other. Latz was dead before he hit the ground. No poison that I know of will wait any length of time, then strike this hard."

"They were poisoned here?" Katti's voice broke in on them, loud enough to call the attention of others. "We've all been poisoned!"

Leuna shot to her feet. "Be quiet!" she snapped at Katti. Holding up her hands, she addressed the shocked crowd. "Look around. We all ate from the same dishes, drank from the same pitchers. The utensils were dispersed at random." In her effort to make eye contact with as many of them as possible, she saw that there were guards blocking the doors. It made sense, she just hadn't thought that far ahead. "These men were specifically targeted."

"Leuna!" Ema's voice cut through the subsequent silence like a piece of jagged glass. "Leuna, come quickly." She caught Leuna's hand as the girl joined her by Txoko's still prone body. "It should've worked by now."

Leuna wrapped her fingers around Ema's ice-cold ones. "Fiantza!"

"Yes?"

"Get my case."

"Now really!" The Marroi physician glared at her. "There's nothing…"

"Doctor," Ema interrupted. "Why is my son still lying here?"

The man's eyes dropped to his king's shallowly rising and falling chest. Having no answer, he beckoned to a servant. "Bring me some damp cloths." Reluctantly, he met Leuna's eyes. "If there's anything in my case that you can use…"

"Thank you." Reaching over, Leuna took out a pair of scissors. "I asked before if you knew what poison was used?" He shook his head. "I haven't made a close study of poisons, but my father had a detailed book on the subject. The blistered lips, the discolored fingers." Pinching Txoko's shirt, she cut it open from the collar down the front. "And…this." Tracing the pattern spreading out across his chest to engulf his lungs and heart, she exhaled shakily.

"I've never seen anything like that," he breathed.

"If I'm right, it's a rare poison. After this is over," she flashed a smile at Ema, "I would like you to tell me what was in that antidote. It clearly had a delaying effect on the poison. Latz' chest is covered with this pattern." Seeing Ema's face growing even paler, she wished she'd kept that to herself.

"Your case." Fiantza was suddenly at her side, sliding her case into place at her elbow.

Leuna tossed the case's lid aside and drew out two vials. "Find a clean bowl," she instructed Fiantza.

"Let me." Ema reached for the vials. "Please."

Leuna nodded. Past experience told her that having something to do would be good for Ema. "Mix these together." She handed the vials over. "Help her," she instructed Fiantza.

As they left, Leuna removed a third vial. "Please apply this to his chest," she told the physician. Gripping the hard wooden sides of her medical case, she took a slow, deep breath, then reached inside. The scalpel's wooden handle was smooth. Familiar. She'd used it hundreds of times before, she reminded herself.

"Ready." He almost offered to do it for her, but something held him back.

Placing the razor-sharp blade against Txoko's

skin, she began her incision. By the time Ema and Fiantza returned, she'd laid back a large flap of skin, exposing the raised, poisonous pattern. His exposed muscles moved in sympathy with his weakening heartbeat. Hearing Ema's gasp, she shot a look at the physician, who hastily rescued the bowl. From the corner of her eye, Leuna saw Fiantza wrap an arm about Ema and lead her away.

"Alright." Leuna held the skin back. She'd concentrated on exposing the thickest lines and hoped it would work. "Pour a little of that on, lengthwise."

"I'm not familiar with these substances." He obeyed promptly, then jerked back as it instantly began to foam up out of the wound.

Leuna bit back a scream as the foam grew to a height of almost six inches. Almost completely black, with streaks of ugly yellow, it stiffened and hardened in seconds.

"I've never seen it do anything like that," she whispered.

Shaking himself, the physician prodded her, "What now?"

"Forceps."

Setting the glass aside, he took out his own forceps. Hesitated. "What will it do to his tissue?"

"Nothing compared with what the poison is doing," she retorted brusquely.

Seeing her white lips, he set himself and proceeded, twisting and pulling at the hardened foam until he was able to wrench it free.

"Again."

Wiping sweat from his forehead, he obeyed. Three more times he treated Txoko's bared muscles with the mixture, then removed the contaminated foam. "It's changed color," he noted hoarsely. "Much lighter now."

"Yes," she nodded. Weak with relief, she felt the flap of skin beginning to slip from between her bloody fingers. "It's done its job. Now we need water. Flush the wound thoroughly."

Fiantza materialized beside him with a pitcher of water. Taking it, he spilled it across the wound until the water was gone. Txoko's body shuddered and Ema cried out.

"Son!"

Txoko's eyelids twitched. Opened to slits. "Mot...Mother?" He sounded as weak as a newborn kaleko.

"Shhhh." Leuna caught Ema's eye and motioned with her head for the woman to come over. "She's right here."

"Leuna." Txoko smiled feebly. "Wha...happ...?"

"Shhhh," she repeated. "Hold your mother's hands, alright? You'll feel better soon. I promise." While Ema took her son's hands, Leuna looked at Fiantza. "There's a blue vial in my case. Please get it out and open it for me."

"Garbi oil?" The physician took the vial from Fiantza. "I am at least familiar with this medicine." Adroitly, he applied the healing oil to the exposed subcutaneous tissue. "Will you stitch the wound?" he asked.

"It should be stitched," she agreed. She rolled her neck and shoulders, feeling the knotted muscles. "But if you wouldn't mind?"

"I would be honored." For the first time since they'd met several weeks ago, he smiled at her.

"Thank you." Releasing her patient to the physician, she slumped back and found her grandfather beside her.

"Let me help you." Gently, Xelebre took her cramping fingers and massaged them clean with what was left of the antiseptic she'd had the physician use prior to cutting into Txoko. "You did marvelously," he murmured to her.

"Leuna?" Looking around, Leuna found Ema smiling at her. "Thank you."

"I recommend at least one more dose of that antidote," she told the physician. Looking back at Ema, she licked her lips. "Don't thank me yet. You're not going to like what I have to tell you."

"What do you mean?" Ema braced herself for the answer.

"As I said earlier, the poisoner targeted Txoko and Latz." Leuna gratefully accepted the glass of refreshing citrus juice that her grandmother offered her. It cut through the dryness of her mouth and throat, making her feel a little better. "I know who it was."

"Who?" Katti stepped forward, blue eyes blazing. "Tell me who did this!" she demanded.

Puzzled, Leuna took another swallow. "You did." Getting to her feet with her grandfather's help, she moved away from Txoko. She'd just saved his life and didn't like the idea of putting him in the line of fire.

"I?" Katti's voice broke on the highest note she'd hit that afternoon. "You say that *I* did this?" She pointed dramatically at her brother's fallen body.

"Fiantza." Leuna was terribly embarrassed to see that the body remained uncovered. "Could you fetch a blanket or a large towel, please?"

Katti's eyes narrowed as she watched Leuna finish off her drink and set the empty glass on a handy table. She drew herself up, preparing to defend herself.

"You're the only one who could've done it." Leuna's gaze lowered to where Katti's gloved fists rested on her hips. "Oh, your brother poisoned Txoko. But you poisoned Latz."

Katti sneered at her. "I can't believe what I'm hearing. You don't know a single person in this room, yet you have the temerity to assert that I am the only one who could possibly have wanted my brother dead."

Noticing a few gazes falter, Leuna shook her head slowly. "I'm afraid that's an optimistic estimation of your brother's standing in this group." Before Katti could splutter out an answer about defaming the dead, she continued, "Honestly? I haven't got a clue what your motive was. But I can tell from here that your gloves have trace amounts of the poison on them."

"I know why she did it." Fiantza, tablecloth in hand, stood over Lantz' body. Leuna had been careful to close his shirt, but she hadn't buttoned it, and the left side had fallen open. "He was a poacher."

"A poacher?" Leuna echoed.

"Of dragons." Fiantza looked narrowly at Katti. "The scars on his chest, they're called a poacher's tally. One for each dragon he personally killed."

"That's ridiculous!" Katti huffed. "He got very sick a few years ago and the only treatment was a barbaric practice involving a white hot poker."

"Apparently I'm going to learn a lot about medicine today," Leuna retorted flippantly. Looking back at Fiantza, she asked, "Would she kill her own brother for being a poacher?"

"If he was a poacher," Katti snarled, "I would've turned him over to the authorities."

"King Txoko is the authority here." Leuna's heart constricted as she looked over at where he was being loaded onto a canvas stretcher. "Strange, don't you think?" She tilted her head to one side. "That your brother and the king just happen to be poisoned at the same time, the same place, and with the exact same poison?"

"You can't prove that." Katti tugged at her collar, inadvertently brushing her neck with the fingertips of her glove.

"Well, well." Leuna folded her arms across her chest. "In a little while, we should have all the evidence we need." She didn't have to understand Katti's motive to know what the dark streak on her neck meant. Or what it would mean for her once it was absorbed.

"What're you talking about?" Katti asked irritably. "You have no evidence at all. I came here with my brother," she began breathing rapidly to help force tears, "who is now *dead*. And you're accusing me of killing him." Dramatically, she pointed at herself.

The whisperers in the room remarked audibly on the horror in her expression when she saw her glove. She'd worn the gloves to protect herself and now…the fingertips were damp with poison from where she'd wiped it off the bottle and glass.

"Doesn't look innocent to me," muttered one voice.

"Help." Katti pinned Leuna with a stare. "You have to help me!"

"Tell me what poison you used." When Katti glared at her stubbornly, Leuna lost her temper. "TELL ME!" Pointing at her case, she continued at a barely suppressed shout, "It's gone, alright? The hautsa dust and konpon oil that I used to help Txoko? I don't have anymore. So you're going to have to tell me *exactly* what poison you used."

Katti's eyes, wide with panic, darted to where the empty syringe had lain.

Fiantza's lips curled. "We wouldn't waste a drop of that on something like you." As if to emphasize her disgust, she let go of the tablecloth so that it fell where it would over Latz.

Leuna took a step toward Katti, recapturing her attention. "It's not too late." She held up her scissors, letting Katti see the poison slowly crawling down her throat. "I will help you."

Katti's lips moved, but no words came out. Swallowing hard, she tried again. "Heir's oil."

"Are you insane?" Dropping the scissors, Leuna scrambled for her case. Katti didn't answer. She couldn't. The poison had paralyzed her throat muscles the same way it had paralyzed her brother's heart and lungs. If Leuna didn't find a solution quickly, Katti was going to asphyxiate. "How did you even get any?"

"What's heir's oil?" ventured a voice.

"A murderous liquid compound." Emptying the contents of her case onto the nearest table, Leuna hastily checked and discarded vials. "Quite possibly the single most deadly poison known to the Lurrakian medical society. Its proper name is oleum scriptor, but the newssheets invented its grisly nickname." She stopped sorting. Held a vial up to the light. "I need a chair!" she announced to the room at large. "Fiantza, bring her here."

Xelebre, sensing a mounting anger in the room, quickly brought a chair over. "Fiantza please," he implored the glowering mirabe. "She has to have useful information."

Muttering darkly, Fiantza propelled Katti over and sat her down.

"Open her mouth." Leaning over Katti, Leuna instructed, "Do your best to swallow this." And poured the thick ziropa in, aiming as best as she could for the back of Katti's tongue. Katti's throat remained still. Leuna wiped sweat off her forehead impatiently. "Try harder!" she insisted. Under other circumstances, she would've massaged the other woman's throat muscles. Now, however, she wasn't sure if that would help the remedy or the poison more.

"What's going on here?" Alarmed, Zain stepped between the guards and entered the room. "Where's the queen?" He'd just come from the kartz, where Teus lay dead, and was in no mood for this. Without Teus they were going to have to abandon their plan and come at Latz from a whole new angle. If they could find one.

"She went to rest," someone explained helpfully. "After the king was poisoned."

Zain staggered back into the arms of one of the guards. "The king was poisoned?" For the first time, he noticed the draped body on the ground. He found himself wishing for a drink of…*anything* so long as it washed the taste of fear out of his mouth. He couldn't become king. He wasn't ready. He didn't have time. He was already a husband and a father. How could he possibly—?

Fiantza clapped her hands for silence as everyone in the room started talking at once. "The king will recover," she announced fiercely. Jerking her chin toward Latz' haphazardly covered body, she concluded, "That's Latz, the poacher."

"Back it up!" Leuna held Katti's shoulders as the woman twisted in agony, then vomited violently. Thick, black globs of muck hit the ground at their feet with sickening splatting sounds. Leuna winced as she heard several of the others beginning to vomit sympathetically. *Ooops.*

Zain covered his nose with his shirt. This was worse than the time both of his children got goragale at the same time last spring! On the other hand…things were beginning to make sense.

"All right now." Leuna rubbed Katti's back, glad the woman's hair was bound back in a popular Lurrakian style. "You have to get it all out, so keep going until it's all done, alright?"

At Zain's nod, the guards began clearing the room so that people could tend their own newly ill friends and family. While Leuna tended Katti and the room emptied, the guard in charge explained everything he'd seen.

"And there's no doubt that it was Katti who poisoned Latz?" Zain clarified at the end.

"Well." The guard shrugged over at Leuna. "The doctor is confident. And the woman poisoned herself with her own glove."

"Take as many guards as you need and secure their chambers. Nobody goes in or out," Zain instructed. "Detain everyone attached to their party immediately." The guard nodded and hurried away.

"I feel like I swallowed sand," Katti croaked.

"That's because you're alive," Leuna stated pointedly. "We need a glass of milk, please." Pouring a glass of water from a nearby pitcher, she helped Katti rinse and spit, then wiped the woman's face with a napkin. Gingerly, she removed Katti's incriminating gloves. "I want her to have at least a few sips of milk every half hour until supper," she told Fiantza. "Please arrange it."

Finding Zain at her elbow, Leuna motioned for him to follow her to the window ledge where she'd been sitting with the queen when it all started.

Chapter 16

Succinctly, she informed Zain of everything that she could remember. Holding out the napkin-wrapped gloves, she finished, "Don't touch them. And when you're done with them? Incinerate them."

Still in shock, Zain accepted the parcel from her. "Thank you. I will." Running his fingers through his hair, he exhaled slowly. "I can't believe this happened. I mean, we knew about Latz, but," he shook his head. "Katti is a complete surprise."

"You knew," Leuna sternly disciplined her rising voice back to a conversational tone, "about *Latz*? How?!"

Zain regretted speaking, but it was too late to go back. "We knew from something Txoko learned while he was investigating in Ibilia."

"I knew I didn't like him." Thankfully, by now Latz' remains had been removed. "But if I'd known he was a poacher, well." She blew out a breath and rolled her eyes.

"Not just *a* poacher." The truth would come out shortly anyway, Zain told himself. "He was in charge of all of it. The poaching, the smuggling, storage, sales." He gestured broadly to include whatever he'd missed. "I guess that's why she did it, then." Meeting Leuna's startled eyes, he shrugged. "This was an attempted coup."

Sick to her stomach, Leuna sagged against the nearest table. "You're telling me that a woman tried to kill her brother so that she could be in charge of more killing?"

Concerned, Zain took her by the arm and led her over to the window ledge, where there was room for both of them to sit comfortably. "This could've been worse. Much worse. Latz was ruthless, so his death may actually have saved several lives in his organization. And Katti, she's still alive. So she can tell us who and where and so on. As for Txoko." He down at his hands. Cleared his throat. "If you hadn't been here, I…" Unable to finish, he set the napkin aside and pulled her into a hug. "Thank you for saving my brother's life."

Zain's last few words were spoken so softly she could've imagined them. Finally feeling safe enough to react, Leuna started to shake. Burying her head in Zain's shoulder, she stayed where she was.

"Easy, pixka," he murmured. "I've got you."

Comforted, she laughed a little. "Pixka?" Roughly translated, that meant 'little sister.' "I like it."

"The king and I are very close," he said for the benefit of the servants who had commenced the unenviable job of cleaning up the mess. "I love him like a brother."

"I love him, too."

"I know." Zain nodded and gently sat her up straight. "Your excellent work today should go a long way to overcoming any obstacles between you two and the altar.""

Leuna could feel herself blushing, but was too tired to care. "It means a lot to me to have your support."

Zain smiled broadly. "You won't mind, I suppose, that he's asked me to be his honor-bound?"

"His honor-bound?"

"It's an old and somewhat embarrassing tradition." Zain rubbed the back of his neck. "Our towns and villages are usually built very far apart. Also, some of our people spend their lives as traders, travelling with their families between the towns. If a couple from different towns meet and wish to marry," he shrugged, "what do they really know about each other?"

"Oh. Um, not very much, I guess?"

"Exactly. So it was the duty of the man's honor-bound to investigate the past of the woman he planned to marry, even if he had to travel to another town to do it."

"Does," she drew the word out a little, "that mean you're going to travel to Herrixka to ask people what kind of a person I am?"

"I already did." Zain had to look away. "While the embassy was being closed in Ibilia, I went to Herrixka to check on Jabea, the doctor of logura who helped Txoko, and, well. To ask about you."

Flabbergasted, Leuna slid back until she reached the windowsill frame. Leaning against it, she studied Zain. "I'm not sure how I feel about that."

"Everyone spoke highly of you," he hastened to assure her. "Your village elder, Zaharre, said his one happiness in losing you was that he knew you loved Txoko." Her frown deepened, so he tried again. "Ama sends her love and bade me remind you to 'carry a spray' on your wedding day."

That did it. She laughed. Sure, there were tears, too. She missed her old friends. Scrubbing at her eyes, she exhaled loudly. "Of course she did."

Hopeful that he'd eased her mind, Zain remarked, "I'm not familiar with that custom?"

"She meant a spray of herbs and spice," offered Merezi, who'd started over when she saw the distress on Leuna's face. Now she took her granddaughter's hand and smiled down at her. "Symbolic of the bride's readiness and ability to provide delicious meals for her family."

"Oh." Amused, he grinned at them. "Marroi women hang dried gozoa root over the door to their home to sweeten the words spoken there."

Leuna, willing to admit that there was at least some logic to the 'honor-bound' tradition, quirked an eyebrow at him. "Should I have someone checking into Txoko's past?"

"Leuna!" Merezi protested, startled.

"It's their idea," she laughed. "Zain got back from Herrixka just before we came here."

Zain coughed into his hand. "It's true," he admitted to Merezi. "However," he shot a look over at where Xelebre was talking quietly with Fiantza. "I think you already have your honor-bound. Yes," he nodded in answer to their surprised expressions. "Your grandfather has been quietly probing into Txoko's reputation since he returned to us."

Leuna turned the statement around in her mind. The more she thought about it, the more it sounded like something her grandfather would do. "Thank you for telling me."

Zain smiled and waved her thanks away. "If you will excuse me, I must consult with the queen."

Leuna caught his hand and squeezed it. "He'll be fine," she murmured. He left with a slight bow and she sat back, wrapping her arms about herself. She'd never truly be able to understand how the brothers felt about having to hide their true relation, but she was glad to be able to reassure him.

Xelebre joined them, slipping his arm about his wife's waist and looking at Leuna. "Fiantza has agreed to provide a light meal in our rooms," he advised them. "Since the festival starts tonight, she also recommends we rest if we can."

Leuna barked a soft laugh. "Rest?" Sliding off the marble window ledge, she hugged her grandparents. "I'm not really hungry or sleepy right now. I think I'll go check on Sparks and Presa. Make sure they've settled in."

"I will take you to them," Fiantza offered. Summoning an errand boy with a wave of her hand, she instructed him to take Xelebre and Merezi to their rooms in the visitors' wing. "Come with me, please."

Leuna fell into step beside her, appreciating the mirabe's silence as they wove through the hallways. What a disaster. While she could argue that she'd made a favorable impression on Ema, she really wished it could've been a normal luncheon. A little banter. Getting to know each other. Txoko not nearly dying. Yeah, that would've been nice.

"Here." Fiantza stopped at a meeting of the hallways. "See this?" She pointed at a carving and waited.

"It looks like a dragon?" Leuna guessed.

"Yes. Wherever you see a small, riderless dragon symbol at a junction like this, you can follow it to the stables."

Surprised, Leuna smiled. "But how do you know which way to go?"

"Follow the dragon," Fiantza repeated

cryptically.

Exhaling slowly, Leuna studied the carving. "He's flying straight ahead. So that's the direction we go?"

"Exactly." Fiantza let Leuna choose the way for the next several intersections, then began showing her other directional markings. "The knife and fork lead to dining rooms. Follow the knife."

"And the beds?" Leuna asked, thinking how nice it would be to not get lost in Koroa.

"Those lead to the visitor quarters," Fiantza clarified. "Follow the foot of the bed."

"The foot?" Leuna chuckled. "Because you have to walk to get there?"

Fiantza grinned back. She was developing a real fondness for this Lurrakian, and it pleased her to see how quickly she grasped what she was being taught.

"Is there a library here?" Leuna asked, pausing suddenly to study a hallway. At first, she'd dismissed the carvings that crowded the edges of the doorframes, but now that she knew what they were for, she wanted to know more about them.

"A very fine library," Fiantza promised.

"Aha!" Leuna touched the carving of a partially opened scroll. It would unroll to her right, so she guessed, "That way?"

"Very good." Fiantza took her arm and began

gently guiding her toward the stables again. "Sometimes the library is indicated by the carving of a book. For those, follow the spine of the book to find the titles in the library."

"This is amazing." Leuna stared at the walls with new wonder. "If I didn't know what I was looking at, I'd never see it."

"Just as the original architects intended," Fiantza observed. "With time, you will begin to recognize room and patterns. The colors of the walls, the sculptures' subjects. Soon you will not need the markings."

Touched by the vote of confidence, Leuna smiled shyly. "I'd like that." Curious, she asked, "Which markers lead to the royal quarters? I don't see a crown or anything. Am I just missing it?"

Fiantza shook her head. "For security reasons, there are no directional markings for that wing."

"Oh." Leuna nodded. "That makes sense." More so when she remembered that Koroa was begun in a time when the Marroi people were in constant danger from their stronger neighbors.

Seeing a group approaching, she squeezed in closer to Fiantza. As they got closer, she saw the dragon's claw emblem on their collars. Aditua. Elite dragon soldiers, such as Zain had once been. Despite their serious expressions, they looked so young! One of the silent group looked her in the eye and she dropped her gaze.

Abruptly, the group stopped. Bowed. Then proceeded on their way before she could even blink in surprise.

"They honor you." Fiantza kept her moving when she would've stopped to look after them. "Already word is spreading of how you saved the king."

Leuna bit her lip. The incline became steeper as they turned a corner and she pretended that was the reason she wasn't talking anymore. Truthfully, she was wrestling with the idea of how she should react to being praised for being herself. And wondering if they knew she'd also saved Katti. Given Fiantza's reaction, there were bound to be a few Marroi citizens who cursed her for that action.

"Do you think the poaching will continue," she asked, "now that Latz is dead?"

If they'd been outside, Fiantza would've spat. Poachers. She hated them. "If Katti's information is good, we may smash the rest of his organization." She shrugged slightly. "So long as there is money to be made at it, there will be poachers."

Reluctantly, Leuna admitted to herself that Fiantza was absolutely right. "Is that why those dragon soldiers looked so grim?"

"Grim?" Fiantza shook her head. "They are disappointed. This will be the first year in over a decade that the king will not be able to take part in the aerobatics."

"Oh!" Leuna tried to keep her elation to herself. She believed what the queen had said about their spotless safety record. Nevertheless, one of the knots in her stomach loosened at the news.

"Agurrak!" Fiantza called greetings ahead to three young men at the end of the hallway. "Where are the new gailens that arrived yesterday?" she asked in Marroi.

"Basking on the south face," they called back.

"I think I can find them from here," Leuna asserted.

Fiantza didn't even pause. "I will stay with you." She'd seen how the woman had vomited yesterday upon landing and wanted to be sure she would be alright. The average Marroi child was more or less raised on a dragon's back, and never learned to fear heights, just to respect them, but it was different for kanpotarraks.

"Alright." Leuna was glad for Fiantza's company when they reached the hole in the mountain that led outside. Somehow, she hadn't realized how far up they'd climbed. "South," she hesitated and studied the shadows. The sun was at a different angle here than she was used to, but… "This way?"

"Very good." Fiantza continued gently encouraging her as they made their way along a narrow track that led to the south meadow. This late in the day, it was no surprise that the heat-loving dragons would've gathered there to sun themselves. "Easy." She caught the girl's arm when she would've dashed through the flock to where the blue and yellow dragons were nestled together. "Startling a dragon can have very permanent consequences. We'll go slowly, yes?"

Swallowing hard, Leuna nodded her agreement. A swarm of gezi were bright winks of color, darting around the other dragons as they played some game that only they understood. A huge zaldiz dragon sprawled in the center of the meadow, with three or four relatively smaller dragons she didn't recognize stretched out across his back. A glistening, breathing shadow turned out to be a knot of gauean dragons, the kind favored for their swiftness. The gailens were scattered across the meadow in twos, usually one dark and one light, lying chest to chest with their heads on each other's backs.

"Wait." Fiantza stopped her when they were still a stone's throw away. "Call to them."

"Sparks?" Leuna instinctively spoke to the one she'd known the longest. "Hey, fella. Are you asleep?"

Seeing his ears twitch, Fiantza nodded for her to call again.

"If you've got room, I'd like to come sit a while," Leuna ventured. Sparks' head rose slightly from Presa's back and he looked in her direction. His wings fluffed, then he snuggled back down. Disappointed, Leuna sighed.

"Good." Fiantza urged her toward the dragons. "He knows you're coming now."

"Should I call Presa, too?" she asked.

"She heard you." Sure enough, the yellow dragon's eyes opened, inspected them, and closed again.

"Lazy little things, aren't you?" Leuna asked as they reached them. "Must be nice to sleep all day. Of course, you earned it, didn't you? Worked hard all the way here from Ibilia." She stroked their heads, then hugged Sparks. "Maybe I should've gone to our rooms with my grandparents." Turning, she seated herself beside Sparks' and leaned back against his shoulder. "I think I walked off the left-over adrenaline." Suddenly remembering something, she gasped. "My case! I left my case in the dining room!"

"All is well," soothed Fiantza from where she was busy scratching Sparks' neck. "I had an errand girl return it to your rooms. With all the vials."

Leuna groaned, her heart still racing. "Oh, what a mess. I'll have to sort everything out and put them back in their places."

Fiantza smiled absent-mindedly. Of all the dragons in Marroi, the species she most longed to see was still absent. By now, the festival distira should've been a common sighting. Shy creatures, it wouldn't have stayed long, especially once the noise from below picked up with festival activities. But try as she might, she couldn't think of a logical reason for *three* separate distira to come and go in such a short time period.

"What's bothering you?" Leuna met the older woman's sharp gaze directly. "Is it the king?"

Twisting gracefully about, Fiantza dropped into a seated position beside her. "He will recover."

"Yes, that's true." Leuna picked up a twig and twirled it between her fingers. Yes, she absolutely believed Txoko would make a full recovery. It was waiting to find out if she was right that was going to test her sanity. "What, then?"

"A second tradition." Fiantza leaned back against Presa's hip. "One that some would say is even more important than our aerobatics." Reaching out, she sketched a simple outline of a long-necked dragon. Added a neck ruffle.

"I've seen that before." Frowning, Leuna searched her memories. "My friend had a small tapestry on her wall at the Marroi embassy in

Ibilia. This dragon was on it."

Fiantza smiled. "The distira dragon is quite rare, and seeing one is thought to bring good fortune."

"Yes, that's it. She used to grumble terribly this time of year about how she was missing the festival and the zorte ceremony." Leuna chuckled softly. "I wonder if she'll be here this year."

"Perhaps," Fiantza nodded. "Our people come home from around the world for the dragon festival." A shadow crossed her face as she admitted, "But this year, there may not be a zorte ceremony." In answer to Leuna's puzzled expression, she gestured at the meadow. "Each year, their favorite food, a terrible, stinking fish, is brought to a high meadow and left strictly alone. By this means, we have for generations enticed a distira to join the domesticated herd for a time."

Leuna made a face, then sobered. "And this year?"

"Not one but *three* distira dragons have come and gone." Fiantza scowled in frustration. "The experts have tried everything they can think of."

"This is important to you."

"To you, too." Fiantza pulled a knee up and wrapped her arms around it. "You could save the king a dozen times and there would still be those who blame the distira's absence on his intentions toward you."

"A kanpotarrak." Leuna was glad Fiantza was being frank with her. So much simpler than having to dig the truth out of dull, polite phrases. "Yes, I see what you mean."

"You do not think they would be foolish to believe that?"

Conscious of Fiantza's watchful eyes on her, Leuna shrugged. "There's a lot I don't know about your culture. While I don't see how I could possibly have anything to do with the distira problem, I certainly do understand that traditions are usually grounded in logic. If having a distira at the festival is considered important, there must be a reason. And I hope there will be one." Stretching, she leaned back against Sparks, the quiet meadow and warm sun combining to soothe her frayed nerves. "Why won't the dragons stay?" she asked suddenly. "That doesn't make sense. I mean," she explained quickly, "if it's always worked before, it shouldn't just stop working for no good reason."

"This is the one thing all our experts agree on." Fiantza threw up her hands. "Yet none of them have hit upon a way to find a fourth distira in time for the ceremony tonight."

"That was supposed to be tonight?" Leuna groaned. "No wonder the queen is so tired." Fiantza looked sharply at her and she held up a hand. "I'm a doctor. Fatigue is the most underreported malady I've encountered, so I got pretty good at diagnosing it by sight." With that, she took the advice she usually gave to her patients: if at all possible, sleep when you're tired.

Chapter 17

"Leuna?" Txoko held out his hand to her. He'd never entered the royal balcony on a stretcher before, and wanted her near.

"Hey." Getting up from the lounge where she'd anxiously watched his servants assist him onto the stretcher, she laced her fingers through his and wrinkled her nose at him. "Having second thoughts about this?"

"For example?" He let his gaze linger on her lips, which were as distracting as always.

"Hmm." She stepped closer to his stretcher as the bearers moved into position. "You might be thinking that you should listen to your doctors and stay in bed." She'd arrived just as the Marroi royal physician was leaving, and knew full well that he'd given Txoko the same stern warnings she had.

"I basically *am* in bed." He patted the stretcher with his free hand. "And it's important for me to be there tonight when the festival starts." Inwardly he hoped she never found out about Zain's report earlier. They'd imprisoned over two dozen members of Latz and Katti's entourage, uncovered detailed maps, and sent soldiers to mop up the rest of the organization. Yes, that job was nearly finished—except for a whisper of something Zain and the others hadn't yet tracked to its origin. They would, though.

"Especially because the distira won't be there?" Leuna didn't expect to convince him to crawl back in bed, though she knew he should.

"Fiantza told you?" He was glad. That was the whole point of a mirabe.

She nodded and fell into step with the bearers. "Just promise me you won't do anything too crazy, alright? Don't try to stand on your own or lift anything. Will you promise me that?"

Txoko hesitated. "I'll have to stand, but I should be able to lean on something." Thankfully, the doors to his suite opened wide enough for them all to make the corner without bumping him.

Something about the way he said it prompted her to ask, "For how long?"

"Oh, not long," he said quickly. "At a time."

"Wait. How many times will you have to stand up?" she probed suspiciously.

"Ummm…"

"You were *poisoned* today, Txoko," she whispered fiercely. They were approaching the royal balcony and she could already hear some of the commotion inherent with large crowds of guests. "You should be in bed resting, not getting ready to…no, this doesn't count," she insisted when it seemed he was about to bring up the stretcher again. Gritting her teeth, she muttered, "If I had an ounce of sense I'd turn this stretcher around right now."

And then, it was too late. They came around a corner and into full view of the waiting royal guests. Peers and their families, dressed in their rich brocades, waited patiently to greet their king. Military insignias twinkled in the light from the firestones, and nearly a dozen of the older peers wore vanity sashes featuring an impressive array of military honors.

Leuna did her best to smile as he introduced her to the heads of some of Marroi's most influential families. The one good thing about the situation was that she'd allowed Fiantza to select her outfit, and she took comfort from the fact that she more or less blended in with the others. The sleeves of her knee-length yellow shirt whispered soothingly to her as she presented her hand to be bowed over, and the flowing, gauzy gerri of muted orange hid her trembling when she brought her hand back to her side. The cool linen pants covered the tops of her ankle-high slippers, which were really just short, nearly sheer stockings with heavy soles and did nothing to protect her toes. Vaguely, she wondered how the queen, who had entered on the other side of the room and was also working her way to the balcony, was protecting *her* toes.

Not much further into the room, a cluster of rounded hats sat atop the heads of the powerful visiting burus. They, like the peers, waited with their families, each wearing the subtly different styles of clothing distinctive to their corner of Marroi. Most of them expressed concern over the attack on Txoko, leaving Leuna hard-pressed not to agree with them that he should *very definitely* be in bed resting! Still. It was nice to see their genuine affection and respect for him.

She made eye contact with a powerfully-built, older buru standing near the balcony door, and missed a step. She registered when Txoko's grip on her hand tightened and instinctively knew she was looking at Nire's father, Buru Tipo Baden. Her stomach did a triple flip before settling uneasily back in place.

As he'd instructed, Txoko's stretcher paused along the way to allow him to exchange pleasantries with his guests. There was never enough time to speak with everyone, but tonight each handshake seemed to squeeze a little strength out of him so that he was sweating lightly by the time they reached Tipo. Belatedly, he realized he couldn't face his father-in-law that way. The older man would never accept it. Worse, he'd carry tales of the king's weakness home with him. Not maliciously. Just as a statement of perceived fact.

"Wait." Txoko raised a hand to his bearers. "Hold steady." His chest burned as he drew himself into a seated position, then swung his legs over the side of the stretcher. The room swam before his eyes but he hung on until he was able to force himself into a standing position.

"Welcome, good father." Txoko bent his head respectfully and nearly fell over. "Good mother." He cast a smile in the general direction of Nire's younger sister.

"Greetings, son." Tipo kept his arms folded. "We arrived early for the cenotaph." He didn't like leaving Deleku for any longer than he had to and believed himself to be perfectly justified in his irritation. The rumors he'd been hearing since their arrival three days ago, that Txoko was going to try replacing his Nire with a brat of a Lurrakian—was that her on his arm?—did nothing to improve his disposition.

Txoko looked at Nazka, her mother, and her sisters, then lowered his eyes. "And I was away. Forgive me, good father." Part of him wanted to point out that Nire should've been buried at Koroa, beside past queens. To remind Tipo that her body had been removed to Deleku at his own insistence. Leaving her bereaved husband to arrange a cold stone marker in memoriam. Instead, he bowed his head again. "Nire's cenotaph will be held at first light tomorrow on the eastern face."

"We will attend," Nazka promised. She ignored the white-faced Lurrakian lass on his arm.

"Excellent." Ema slipped her arm through

Txoko's left to give him someone else to lean on before he collapsed where he stood. Stupid, stubborn pride. Yes, her own, too. She probably could've persuaded him to rest if she hadn't been so worried about appearances. "We were so terribly saddened when you were unable to attend at our first invitation six lunars ago." Casually, she stroked her gerri as if its correct positioning was the most important thing to her at that precise moment. "Duty first, as you say." Now she patted Txoko's arm like the proud parent that she was. "It broke Txoko's heart to be called from his mourning, but thanks to his efforts, the poaching ring that has plagued us has been severely dealt with."

Txoko swayed slightly and Leuna raised her left arm so that their elbows were braced against each other. He needed to *sit* and now! Thankfully, she'd learned a long time ago to stay well clear of family disputes, or she'd have been only too glad to pitch into the bombastic clod blocking their exit. Verbally, that was. A wave of relief washed over her when she looked toward the balcony door and spotted Zain.

"Excuse me, my love," Zain whispered to Min. Taking a deep breath, he tried a tactic that had worked well for him in the past. "Doctor Oneko!"

Leuna suddenly found herself with her arms full of gurgling, drooling baby. Zain stepped neatly behind her and whispered something that even Txoko probably couldn't hear. From the corner of her eye, she saw Zain nod as if Txoko had responded, then take a firm hold of his king's arm and escort him away.

"Well." Leuna smiled at the adorable little girl. "Looks like it's just us." Settling the tyke comfortably on her hip, Leuna made her way over to where Min stood with two older children. At least, she assumed it was Min. "Good evening." Her simple greeting was met with an ear-to-ear grin that made her relax.

"I see you have experience with children," Min observed. That was her way of approving of the relative stranger continuing to hold her youngest.

"Oh yes." Leuna grinned back, especially glad for a safe topic after the tense encounter with Tipo. "My best friend has five children and she lets me…" Her voice faltered. "Let me," she corrected herself, "help with them sometimes."

Hearing sorrow in Leuna's voice, Min touched her arm gently. "Come. The festival is about to begin and we must be in our places."

Leuna followed obediently, grateful that Fiantza had spelled out the proprieties for them before lunch. The tumult from below reached deafening levels as Txoko and Ema stepped into view at the edge of the balcony. Since she and her grandparents weren't really family—yet—but also weren't typical guests, they were to stand with Min while Zain took over Txoko's duties in the evening's aerobatics.

"My people!" Txoko took two quick breaths and raised both of his arms to shoulder height. From the corner of his eye, he could see Zain, ready to pounce if he started to fall. Comforting, in a weirdly 'at least I won't die' way. Hearing his words echoed by the repeaters scattered along the lower ledges, he lowered his hands to the balcony railing and braced them there. "Welcome home!" A roar of approval swelled through the crowd, including those on the balcony, and he thought his head was going to burst from the noise. "We have come," he paused for the repeaters' sake, "to celebrate," another pause as they relayed his words, "our great nation!" His arms and legs were shaking now and there was nothing he could do about it. "Enjoy the festival!"

The sound of Zain's blaring signal whistle hit him like a club. Then Leuna was behind him, her arms around his waist, holding him up.

"Here!" Ema jerked her head toward the chairs the first king had carved into the balcony with his own hands.

"He's had enough." Leuna grunted with the effort of supporting Txoko, who had a good fifty pounds of muscle over her. "Call for the stretcher."

"We can't go," Txoko forced the words out. "Yet."

Anger coursed through Leuna, giving her the added strength she needed to swing him around. Ducking under his arm so that he could lean on her now that they weren't in fully view of the crowd below, she hauled him over to the chair. "Suit yourself." She all but dumped him into it.

"Leuna."

The single whisper stopped her in her tracks. She saw at a glance that he was sweating badly and his eyes were bloodshot. Summoning Fiantza, Leuna quietly spoke her command. The anger was gone. In its place was not-quite resignation.

"This is how it is, huh? Live or die, always the great king." She didn't bother trying to keep the bitterness out of her voice. Doing her best not to block his view of the all-important festival, which was presently featuring brightly colored explosions, she unbuttoned his shirt partway. "You're bleeding." No surprise there.

The balcony crowd thundered enthusiastically and she looked up in time to see Zain leap over the railing. Arms wide, legs bent as if he were trying to click his heels, he hung in the middle of nowhere for a horrifying second. Then landed as lightly as a feather on his dragon as it rushed forward to meet him.

She couldn't actually hear the retching, but her eyes were drawn to where Min bowed, half-hidden behind a pillar. Muttering about stupid, stubborn men under her breath, she ripped her gerri off and folded it.

"Like I said," she pressed the gerri firmly over where Txoko's blood was leaking out between stressed stitches, "you should've stayed in bed." She felt strangely numb as she watched him sink back into the chair. His symptoms registered and were ticked off in her head as if she was watching the deterioration of a stranger.

Fiantza, closing on them with the tray of items she'd been sent after, frowned. Her experience with medicine was limited to basic field training, but the detachment she saw in Leuna's eyes now worried her. The king must be in terrible condition for her to have shut off her emotions for self-preservation.

"He'll live," Leuna announced to Fiantza. "Hold this." She took the tray and balanced it on the arms of the king's and queen's chairs, which didn't quite touch. Selecting a vial from the three she'd brought along, she poured a few drops from it into an empty glass. Adding half a cup of tart citrus juice from one pitcher and half a cup of the mellow melon juice from another, she splashed the whole concoction into the second glass she'd asked for. It was a clumsy way to mix things, yet effective. Back and forth it went a few times before she was satisfied and handed it to the queen. "Make sure he drinks it all."

Filling the first glass with plain water, she turned on her heel and strode away. The darkening sky exploded behind her in rhythm with her steps, but she didn't look back. Weird shadows sprang up, including her own. *Step-boom!* Away from Txoko and his lunatic need to appear strong even if it killed him. *Step-boom!* Away from her grandparents, who were watching her with worried expressions. *Step-boom!* Toward Min. She might actually be able to help Min, assuming she didn't have a death wish.

"Easy." Leuna put her hand lightly on Min's back. A young, plainly dressed woman was holding the baby while the other two children screamed wildly for their father, too young and trusting to understand that the slightest miscalculation could end his life. "I don't think anyone important has seen you."

Min stiffened, then relaxed under the unexpected contact. "Good. I don't want to ruin this for the children."

Leuna closed her eyes and shook her head. "Drink this."

Min accepted the glass. Rinsing her mouth with some of its contents, she spat. "Water?" she asked doubtfully.

"Mostly." Leuna glanced around to make sure nobody was listening and made eye contact with

Nazka, Nire's mother. At this range and in the constantly changing lighting, the woman looked puzzled about something. Whatever. "There's nothing in there that will hurt your babies."

Min leaned against the pillar she'd been more or less hiding behind. "How did you know?"

"I'm a doctor." Leuna was getting tired of having to remind people of that. Or maybe she was just used to Herrixka, where she'd delivered half the population personally. "Speaking of which, have you been taking the nutrients your own doctor recommended?"

Confused, Min blinked at her. "Nutrients?" She tasted the water again. It reached her stomach and settled there soothingly. "What do you mean?"

Fiantza watched from her place by the king as the crowd cast speculative glances in Leuna's direction. Those who'd sung Leuna's praises just minutes ago before the festival started were now frowning at her. Unintentionally, she'd drawn attention to Zain's wife as well. They both should've been watching the aerobatics. Min should've been shouting herself hoarse at her husband's daring. Yet neither of them appeared the least bit interested in the show.

"It's a matter of standard practice in Lurrak to prescribe specific supplemental nutrients for expectant mothers," Leuna explained.

"I see." Min, who'd been exhausted before

throwing up, gestured to two chairs. "Sit with me. I am forgetting my duty to cheer for my husband." She tucked her arm through Leuna's, meaning to draw her along.

"I'm not sure I can watch."

Min paused, noticing the way Leuna's breathing had changed to short, sharp inhalations. "Relax." Finally noticing the sour looks being cast their way, she tugged harder. "Don't look at them. Look past them, at the stars."

"The stars." Leuna kept her eyes on the ground until they were seated. "I visited the stars once."

"With Txoko?" Min was impressed. "I didn't realize he could be that romantic."

Taken completely by surprise, Leuna laughed aloud. It was so…incongruous. There was nothing vaguely reminiscent of romance about tonight.

"Look at the stars," Min reiterated. "Think of what lies beyond them."

"Beyond the stars?" Leuna finally looked up. But not far enough. Three dragons were passing so near each other that their wingtips brushed. Abruptly, they folded their wings and dropped several feet in an instant. The riders jumped just as they began to fall, each aiming to land on a different beast.

"Breathe," Min commanded. "They've done

this thousands of times." They were also flying low enough, for the benefit of the crowd, that a falling rider would probably be caught, but she decided not to mention that.

"Why?" Leuna demanded. "Why do it at all?" Her exact words were drowned out by the crowd.

The wind shifted, carrying the dust and smoke from the explosions onto the balcony. Min raised her gerri to protect herself and noticed that Leuna wasn't wearing one. Odd. She had been earlier. "Here." Unwinding her own gerri, she offered one end to Leuna. "Breathe through this." Squeezing her hand, Min wondered uneasily if Txoko had chosen wisely. "Have you ever seen a battle?"

Leuna didn't have to think about that. The few fistfights she'd witness in her life were over inconsequential things like sporting events. "No." She shook her head.

"Neither have I." Min felt a fierce surge of pride as she looked out at the performance. "These men and women practice daily in case war comes to our land. They defend our citizens against poachers and other criminals." Gesturing broadly, she finished, "This? This is just a small sample of the techniques they learn."

Leuna's perspective shifted. Blurred like the time she'd had her vision tested during her third year at Ibilia. Min's words clicked into place and her vision cleared as though the right corrective lens had dropped into place before her eyes. "I'm so stupid." She stared at the performance again, but this time *she saw.*

Intricate, precision movements carried a dragon rider from a position of potential danger aboard her dragon's back to underneath it, where she hung for several seconds from the specially-constructed jarlekua. In a triumph of will over the laws of physics, she swung her legs to her right, her tired arms and torso forcing her body up around the dragon's side. The well-trained dragon dropped fractionally, allowing the rider to twist and drop back into position. Eight of the ten riders performed that exact same maneuver at the exact same time while the two remaining riders played the villains, firing practice arrows harmlessly over the empty dragons' backs. Such a tactic would save so many lives in an actual battle.

"Ema told me they hadn't had an accident in a hundred years." Embarrassed, Leuna shot a look toward where she'd left Ema and Txoko. They were gone. Swallowing a painful lump, she admitted that was good news. "I never even gave a thought to how all of this got started."

Chapter 18

The next morning, Leuna finished putting her medical case back together and went hunting for Min's room before breakfast. Apparently, festival mornings were for children and youth, and Zain had promised to take the children to some sort of dragon show, which meant there should be time for her to examine Min privately. According to Min, even Zain didn't know she was expecting!

She got lost twice despite the map Fiantza had grudgingly given her last night, but finally saw two gray marble doors with a dragon's claw knocker. Taking a deep breath, she raised the knocker and let it fall. As in the suite where she was staying with her grandparents, the knocker struck a small spring that passed through the width of the door and started a small bell ringing inside the suite.

Min opened the door almost immediately and motioned Leuna inside.

"You didn't sleep well," Leuna observed as she entered.

"The baby was fussy." Min shrugged and eased the door shut. Most of her 'neighbors' were here not just for the festival but also to complete important political tasks and had been up most of the night working. Being woken early would not be appreciated and, after years of visiting Koroa, Min knew just how loud 'small'

~ 235 ~

sounds could be. "Are you hungry?" She could think of no other reason for Leuna to be studying what was left of her breakfast tray.

"Starving." Leuna set her case beside the tray. "But you're not only having trouble sleeping, you're not eating."

"I told you." Min gripped her hands nervously. "The baby…"

"Was fussy." Leuna beckoned for her to come take a seat. "That's part of a nanny's job, isn't it?" She gently tipped Min's head up and examined her eyes. "Taking care of fussy babies?"

"Yes," Min agreed in a small voice. "I didn't want to admit it."

"That you're having trouble sleeping?" Leuna smiled. "If you don't tell doctors what's really wrong, they're not much good to you." Seating herself so that she wasn't looming over her patient, Leuna asked, "How long has it been since you got a good night's rest?" Over the course of the next half an hour, Leuna used gentle, probing questions in conjunction with a physical examination to learn what she needed to know.

"You can tell all of that from my hair?" Min was incredulous.

"It's amazing how much hair reveals," Leuna nodded, reaching into her case. "Now, your stomach is probably going to be a problem for the next several weeks. Until you're able to resume eating normally, I want you to do something for me."

"Yes?" Min cocked her head to one side as she watched Leuna produce a fist-sized bag, a wooden bowl, a smallish board, and a few vials.

"Once I've mixed these, I'd like you to take one of these nutrient pills daily." Leuna opened the bag and poured some finely-ground ezer powder into the bowl. "I checked with the royal physician and he told me you have no known allergies, correct?"

"Hmm? Oh." Min nodded. "That's right. But when did you see the physician?"

Leuna shook some of each of the highly concentrated vitaminic powders from the vials into her palm, then brushed them into the bowl. "I didn't sleep well last night, either," she confessed tersely. Using a clean fork from the breakfast tray, Leuna mixed the powders together until she had one, uniform color. A short drizzle of diluted gozoa syrup turned the whole thing into a damp mass, which she lifted out and set on the board.

"I've never seen anyone make pills before." Min watched, fascinated, as Leuna rolled the mass out from a ball into a long string, the way one might work bread dough. Then, she reversed her tool and ran it, cutting side down, along the board toward a depression at one end. Balls the size of the tip of her pinkie rolled out ahead of the tool and settled into the depression, making her laugh. "It's so terribly clever!"

"Yes." Leuna smiled at Min's interest. "They'll need a little time to dry properly, but this will help." Shaking a little more ezer powder into the depression, she rolled the balls around until they were thoroughly coated. Finally, she poured them out onto the clean plate Min hadn't used for fruit.

"Excellent!" Min clapped her hands and popped one of the pills into her mouth. Drowning it with a glass of water, she hopped to her feet. "I feel better already!"

That gave Leuna an idea how much stress Min must be under, for it was physically impossible for the pill to have even dissolved yet. "What's it like?" she asked as she wiped the pill roller down. "Being married to someone who jumps off of dragons?"

Min settled back into the chair slowly. "Not nearly as difficult as being married to a king." She wasn't sure she approved of Leuna's choice in confidant, but there weren't all that many options for this kind of a conversation. "Nire and I," she paused when Leuna almost dropped the pill roller. "We used to talk about it a little."

"You were friends with Nire?" Leuna instantly regretted her perplexed tone of voice.

"Yes," Min answered firmly. "Someone had

to be." Rising, she paced slowly over to the door, then turned to face Leuna. "Txoko never understood her. She didn't fit his expectations," she lifted a shoulder, "so their marriage was a strictly political decision."

Leuna winced at the disapproval now evident in Min's tone. If she knew more about the situation, perhaps she could've defended Txoko, but…hadn't she learned just last night how vast her ignorance of all things Marroi was?

"She left her home and almost everything she knew to come here, to Koroa." Min held her hands out and tipped her head back, placing exaggerated emphasis on the capitol city's name. "I suppose the honor of being queen should've been enough to compensate for the loneliness." Folding her arms across her chest, she took a single step toward Leuna. "You will be lonely if you marry him. A king's work is never done."

Leuna shifted uncomfortably. "I believe you. But my mother was lonely, too. And Ama. And Gaia." She looked Min in the eyes. "Not even a husband is there every time they're needed." Min's gaze dropped, confirming to Leuna that she was more upset with Zain than Txoko. It made sense, really. While with child, a woman's hormones sometimes betrayed her. Also, Min stated quite clearly that she hadn't told Zain yet because she didn't want to worry him. But she'd hunched her shoulders when she said it, as though her true concern was that he wouldn't be happy about the news.

"She was too young." Min hugged her stomach protectively. "She didn't have enough experience outside of Deleku to know how to handle the…culture at court." It was no wonder to Min that the poor child had gone running off to her family when she discovered that she was expecting a child. And her accidental death. Such a tragedy that she'd had to die because she didn't know how to communicate with her husband.

"I know what you mean." Leuna didn't flinch away from Min's disbelieving stare. "I was born in Herrixka, a small village where my mother and I spent hours locating and cataloging plants in the forest. I was perfectly comfortable in that relaxed culture, where everyone knew and trusted everyone else." Wiping her hands, she set the pill roller down. It wasn't hers, and she needed to find a way to return it to the royal physician. "Life at university was starkly different. Not every student who qualified to enter was able to adapt to the new rules and restrictions."

"And you?" Min softened as she reclaimed her chair. "Was it easy for you?"

"I grew into the new life." Leuna shrugged slightly. "And survived the requisite growing pains."

Min touched Leuna's arm. "Then perhaps you will do better than she." Seeing the pills, she remembered what had brought her to her feet the first time. "Come. Let's go find my family."

"Wait!" Leuna protested, hands still full of things she was putting away. "What about my grandparents?"

Min paused. "We'll send an errand boy for them. They'll love the dragon petting arena and the horticulture display and the plays." She continued rattling off a list of things they'd enjoy while Leuna finished putting her case in order.

"Alright, you've convinced me." Truthfully, Leuna was glad for Min's chatter as they hurried along the now-nearly empty hallways. She didn't know her—at all, as she'd discovered when the conversation turned to difficult topics—but she desired the woman's good opinion. Hearing her declare that 'perhaps' she would do better than Nire could've been a severe blow to her confidence. Somehow, instead it inspired hope. Hope that, although it would be hard, it could be done. Even by her.

"Boy." Min hailed an unoccupied errand boy stationed near an intersection. "Here. Take this to the Lurrakian suite in the visitor's wing," she handed him Leuna's medical case. "And bring the Lurrakians to the dragon show." The boy wasn't much older than Rena, so she had him repeat the instructions, then hurried Leuna through a bewildering array of tunnels. "At last," she announced, cheerily brushing past a pair of guards.

A burst of merry music drew Leuna into the sun, into the city-sized festival. Striped tents of every color and size stretched as far as she could see to her left and her right. Then they were in among them. They passed a juggler who was somehow keeping seven different items aloft. Ducked around an acrobat performing a dizzying number of backflips. She refused to be led past a stall offering fried meats and dough, though.

"Ah, I forgot." Min laughed. "You're starving. Here." She tossed a coin to the vendor, who dished up enough food to satisfy a teenage boy, then handed it out.

"I...may not be *that* starving," Leuna admitted even as she accepted the piping hot food. There were no utensils, so she tore off a piece of bread and used it to pinch some of the meat, cheese, and vegetables.

"How is it?" Min asked, carefully guiding her past clothing booths. It pleased her to see Leuna eating like the natives surrounding them.

"Hot!" Leuna breathed through her mouth as much as she dared in order to cool the food off, then gulped it down. "And soooo good!"

Anxious as she was to find her husband and children, Min allowed Leuna to linger here and there as her fancy struck. The puppet show. The magician. A jeweler? Min was intrigued. Leuna wasn't wearing a single piece of jewelry.

"It's incredible." Leuna stared at a sparkling orb just smaller than the pad of her thumb. "What makes it glow?"

"True love, m'lady," answered the elderly vendor, nodding wisely. "Someone hereabouts has fallen in love."

Min was opening her mouth to tell the simple truth, that it was a fleck of stardust captured in fish oil and would evaporate the second that air touched it, when Leuna surprised her.

"How much does it cost?"

Puzzled, Min waited while Leuna expertly haggled the vendor down to a reasonable price. If she wanted to prove she was still in love with Txoko after losing her temper with him last night, this seemed an odd way to go about it. "That is dragon glass," she told Leuna, who was handling the medallion as though it might shatter in her hand. "Very strong."

"That's a relief." As they left the booth, Leuna tucked the bauble into her gerri for safe-keeping. "I hope my grandmother likes it."

"Your grandmother?" Min cocked an eyebrow at her. "So you don't believe it's a spark of true love?"

"No, not really." Leuna obediently trailed along after her through the crowd to a roped-off section. "But I do love my grandmother."

Min smiled and slipped her arm around Leuna's shoulders. "Look."

Three youths stood in the center of the temporary arena, each of them beside a dragon. One dragon had wildly curving horns that reminded her of Gaia's naturally curly hair on a bad day. Another had distinct streaks of color down its sides that changed in shade as Zain came closer to inspect it. The third was enormous, easily as large as Jartz' fur shack, with two sets of glossy brown wings.

"Leuna!" Merezi and Xelebre pushed their way through the crowd to join them. "There you are." She hugged her granddaughter. "You might at least have left us a note," she half-heartedly scolded.

"Sorry," Leuna apologized, realizing that she had indeed forgotten to do so. She was about to surprise Merezi with the trinket when she noticed the unfriendly looks they were receiving.

"You found us," Min cut in quickly. "Just in time. Come, watch. Zain will test them to see how well they have trained their dragons." This was a critical part of the competition and the rest of the audience wouldn't appreciate it if they disrupted the event, however unintentionally.

Merezi gasped. "I've never seen dragons like that!"

"Nor I," Xelebre agreed, though he didn't seem as surprised. After all, how many dragons were there in Ibilia?

"These dragons are basically working pets," Min explained. "They haul a little wood, dig a few holes, that sort of thing. But the true objective is for them to teach our children about dragons."

"That's amazing." Leuna smiled her understanding. As a child in Herrixka, her parents had used the village dogs to teach her the first, basic lessons about interacting safely with animals. "I don't see any distira?" Based on what little she knew of the breed, it was extremely gentle.

"Oh no." Min shook her head vigorously. "They are much too rare. Much too shy. A man did capture a pair of them once, a few generations ago. They left no eggs when they died."

"How terrible," Leuna sympathized.

"That is why the festival distira," Min dropped her voice as far as she could and still be heard, "is so important. It shows us they have survived another year. That we can, too."

Leuna pondered that while Zain had the youths put their dragons through simple maneuvers and tasks. "Have they found a fourth?" she whispered, assuming that if Fiantza knew about it, Min would, too.

"Not yet." Min shook her head. "This could be very bad for Txoko."

"For me, too." Leuna blinked, surprised she'd said that aloud. "Something Fiantza told me," she explained. "There are those who'll blame me if one isn't found. And then…" Her words gave out, but Min nodded understandingly.

"Yes, some of our people can be very superstitious. Especially those from remote areas." Looking for a happier topic, Min mentioned, "Zain and I are thinking about getting a kizkur dragon." She pointed at the one with curly horns. "They're wonderful with children."

"So," Leuna coughed nervously, "what kind of a dragon should I get?"

Min hesitated. There were too many ears here for her to ask the necessary questions. "That's something you should ask him," she murmured at last.

Leuna sighed unhappily. She hadn't just gone to talk to the physician about Min in the middle of the night last night. She'd gone to Txoko's suite, hoping to at least get an update on how he was doing. The guard at the door went inside to inquire and came out with the physician. While she appreciated how gently he'd denied her access, it worried her. If she couldn't get near Txoko, how could she talk with him? How could she explain what happened last night?

That question niggled at the back of her mind for the rest of the morning, preventing her from really enjoying anything. Even when Zain suggested they go watch the puppet show, much to the children's delight, her gaze kept drifting back to the upper levels of Koroa, where the royal suites were located. Pity she couldn't fly.

Likewise, Txoko looked down from the suites. He could see it. Hear it. Smell it. Everything except be a part of it. His stupid, stubborn pride. He'd put in his obligatory appearance last night, then attended the cenotaph at dawn, and now he had to pay the price.

"Has the pain eased?" the physician asked. His own shoulder ached from an encounter with one of Katti's less savory companions the day before, but he kept that to himself.

"Considerably." It felt like a small fire was burning on his chest, but that was still an improvement.

"Take a deep breath for me." The physician kept a hand on Txoko's wrist while glancing over to check on the queen's relative position. "She came to see you last night," he informed the king, against his mother's recommendation. "You were…in conference, so I sent her away." His role as royal physician included making sure the king was up to discharging his duties, even if that meant mid-night conferences about poachers when he should've been sleeping. He just hadn't figured out how to explain that to Dr. Oneko.

"I see." Txoko shoved his fingers through his hair. "Has she been back?"

"No. But she asked me about Zain's wife, Min. I believe she intended to go see her."

"Odd." Txoko frowned. As far as he knew, Min was in perfect health. A little tired, no doubt. That seemed pretty normal, though, from what he'd seen of involved mothers.

"Nothing to worry about, I'm sure. Just a few questions about Min's allergies, a short conversation about vitamins and nutrients." From the corner of his eye, the physician saw the queen approaching. "If you're ready?"

Txoko eyed the syringe with distaste. However, it served the purpose of preventing his mother from approaching. "Do it." Among other things, the antidote made him drowsy. Granted, it was worth it given the alternative. In a low tone, he instructed, "When she comes again, let her in whether I'm sleeping or not. Let her wait for me if she will." Hopefully, there wouldn't be any interruptions. Though he was concerned that they hadn't yet sorted out whatever it was that was making their prisoners snicker when the guards passed.

"Understood." Withdrawing the needle, the

physician rose. "Be patient, Your Majesty. You're healing as well as can be expected."

"But not as well as I could be if I'd stayed in last night as you instructed me." Txoko didn't bother lowering his voice for that.

"You did what you had to do," Ema insisted, coming over now that the antidote had been administered.

"Now, Mother." Txoko took her hand. "Surely you'll concur that I could've used better judgement."

Ema sank onto the chair beside him. "Very well. Yes, we both could've used better judgement."

They sat silently for a moment, then he sighed. "You've changed your mind about her?"

Ema hesitated. She didn't have to ask to whom he was referring. "She also exhibited poor judgment last night." Rubbing at the ache in her forehead, she commented sadly, "I'm not sure she wants anything more to do with either of us."

Txoko wanted to laugh at that, but he couldn't. His court only knew what they'd seen. The woman he'd brought back with him, and given every indication that he planned to woo, had essentially deserted her place beside him during last night's opening ceremonies. He could forgive her—in fact, it would be easier to do that than to forgive himself. His court, on the other hand, would have to be convinced that she was up to filling the role of queen.

"I agree that she could've handled last night better. I also believe that she would have if she'd understood things better. I promised to help her, Mother," he said when it looked like she was going to interrupt. "I'd like to think I would've done a better job if I hadn't been… incapacitated. That I would've seen how much the idea of the aerobatics disturbed her." His mother squeezed his hand and he tried to smile. "Unfortunately, I didn't. And now the damage is done with the court."

Chapter 19

"Grandma." Leuna put her hand on Merezi's arm. "If it's alright, I think I'd like to wander around a bit. Look around."

"Alone?" Merezi couldn't say that she liked the idea. With so much noise and clamor going on about her, she'd found herself holding Xelebre's arm tighter than was strictly necessary. But to go off alone in all this?

"Of course it's alright." Xelebre patted Leuna's shoulder. "There's a lot to see. We'll have a long talk at supper, decide where we have to take each other tomorrow."

Grateful for his understanding, Leuna stepped back and lost herself in the crowd. It was a pleasant change. Refreshing to not be expected to smile. Or pay attention to and participate in conversation. She loved her grandparents, or she wouldn't have bothered. Oops! She patted her gerri to make sure the gift was still safe, relaxed when it bumped against her fingers. She'd forgotten it, and now she'd have to give it to her grandmother at supper. At least that was something to look forward to.

Meandering aimlessly along, Leuna tried to sort things out. Hindsight was a two-edged sword. It made things, complex things, seem so simple. Looking back, it was obvious that she should've used her time with Fiantza in the meadow to discuss the aerobatics. So much of embarrassment could've been avoided by an honest, earnest conversation.

"I guess a mirabe isn't any more useful than a doctor when people withhold information." Resting her head against a tent pole, she tried to laugh at herself. At any rate, she'd been wrong. So wholly and incontrovertibly wrong. On top of it, she'd behaved badly. She supposed she could excuse herself for at least some of that, though. Fear was a powerful emotion and she'd tasted fear last night, seeing Txoko so weak he could barely hold up his own head.

Suddenly the tents were pressing in on her. The music, the laughter. Covering her nose with the loose end of her gerri to block out the overpowering smell of the foods and perfumes, she headed for the thinnest point in the tents. She apologized after bumping into a couple of people, but finally reached her destination.

Which turned out to be the edge of the festival. Empty land rolled along before her as far as she could see. Back to back tents formed a nearly solid wall on her left and right. Where was she? Looking up to get her bearings, she turned around until Koroa was in front of her. Hmm. She could either try to wade through the revelers or try skirting the festival entirely. Frankly, a longer walk seemed more appealing than reentering the merrymaking.

She still got an eyeful, though. Dozens of performers practiced on the edges of the chaos. Sword-swallowers. Flame breathers. A particularly tall, pale magician pulled not one but *two* live gezi dragons from thin air as she walked past. Lacking coins to give him, she applauded enthusiastically. Singers, dancers, and even a baker darted back and forth from the chaos to their own fires in wonderful spectacle.

At last reaching the point where the shortest path to Koroa took her away from them, she looked along the line of tents, hesitating. A blast from a nearby horn sent pain lancing through her skull, deciding the matter. The festival would go on for several more days. If she didn't take care of herself now, she'd be in bad shape tomorrow.

Dust puffed around her slippers as she trudged along, making it seem hotter than it really was. Pausing to catch her breath in the shadow of a barrel cactus, she noticed an opening in the rock at the base of the mountain. A servants' entrance, perhaps? Eagerly, she hurried forward, stumbled, and fell flat on her face.

Spitting sand, she rolled over and sat up. Every bit of exposed skin was coated with dry, itchy dust. Sighing, she scrubbed at her face until it felt a little better. She didn't need a mirror, though, to know she looked frightful.

Yes, the entrance just ahead was definitely her best chance. With a little luck, she could keep her head down and slip past whatever guards were stationed there without being recognized. Rising, she slapped more dust off her slacks and sleeves while she made her way to the entrance. Finding no guards, she stepped inside.

"Hello?" The faint sound of water dripping invited her to move further in. Light poured in behind her, letting her see that she was quite alone. "Hello?" she called again. The dripping was closer now, tempting her. Licking her lips, she proceeded. This was clearly not a servants' entrance. Trailing her fingertips along the rough-hewn walls, she followed the sound to where the dripping water had worn a small depression in the floor.

Kneeling on the surprisingly smooth tunnel floor, she scooped the cold, clear liquid up in her hands and splashed it on her itching face until her skin felt better. By then she was wishing she'd found a way to take a drink first. Back on her feet, she stretched and peered curiously down the length of the tunnel.

Why build it if it went nowhere? And if it went somewhere, why not use it? But surely it had been used at some point. The walls bore chisel marks, yet the floor was smooth. Worn smooth by the passing of travelers? Her good sense pointed out that Fiantza probably knew the answer to those questions.

She was about to leave when the faintest of sounds caught her attention. There was someone at the entrance! Anxious, she moved still further into the cave. In the growing darkness, she kept one hand on the wall to keep from getting turned around. And then the wall cornered. Catching her breath, she stepped quickly around it, intent on hiding from the approaching footsteps. A faint breeze came down this new passageway, cooling her still further.

"Come on," one voice called irritably. "There's nob'dy in here."

"There was," countered another voice. "I know I saw a girl come in."

"A *girl?*" The irritation was replaced with resignation. "Was she pretty?"

"I only saw her back," protested the second voice.

"Sure. Well, look for her yerself." One set of footsteps began moving away. "I've got a business to tend and no time for playing hero."

"I ain't playing!" protested the second voice. "Ohhhhh…" A heaved sigh. "Fine. But if we hear later on that somebody's gone missing, just remember that it was *your* idea to leave."

"I can live with that."

Leuna grinned at the cynical tone. Clearly the two men were old friends. Anyway, they needn't worry. Once she was sure they were gone, she would… The breeze shifted just then, bring with it a strangely familiar smell. She sniffed to confirm it. What was a dragon doing down here? Shivering slightly, she took a slow step into the breeze.

Something pulled her along the passageway, her slowly numbing fingers tracing a path on the wall. It was almost her only connection to the world around her as the light faded to darkness. Except—she could hear an almost sound. Whatever it was, it made the tiny hairs on the back of her neck stand on end.

The wall cornered again, making her hesitate. Moving away from the wall until her arm was fully straight, she felt around with her other arm, searching for another wall. Nothing. Swallowing a lurch of fear, she stomped one foot, then the other on the floor of the tunnel. She hadn't vanished into blackness, never to return. She was there. Semi-lost in an unknown tunnel. There was still a wall under her fingers and she ought to turn back before something went wrong. Guards, equipped with bright firestones or even torches, could come back and investigate. Yes. That was the sensible thing to do.

Turning, she put her foot down, slipped, and went sprawling. *Cold.* Her fingers dug into the soft, damp stuff beneath her while she willed her mind to stop spinning. The floor beneath her was real. The…stuff on the floor beneath her was real. It was also soggy. Now that she was right down in the middle of it, it smelled revoltingly like rancid oil.

Righting herself with a groan, she wished that sogginess was as easy to get rid of as dust. Her brand new outfit was officially ruined. The only bright spot in the whole mess was a literal bright spot almost exactly over her head. Which she'd never have seen if she hadn't fallen over. Not that it helped. Not really. Her head was up and her feet were down. She knew that already. What she desperately needed to know was which way to go. Or even which way she'd been coming from.

Squeezing some of the sogginess out of her sleeves, she took a deep, calming breath. *Dragon.* It was stronger now. And coming from up ahead. Swallowing hard, she moved toward it.

"Ouch!" Hopping on one foot, she made a grab for the wall she'd stubbed her toe on. It was comforting, in a delusional sort of way, to be able to run her hand along it as she walked.

The scent grew stronger. The sound grew louder. Something was breathing. At least she hadn't come this far for nothing. A dragon could warm her up, light the way, and probably knew how to get out of there. Eager to find the dragon and return to the surface, she walked more quickly. Here and there small cracks in the roof sent thin fingers of light down, just enough to make her want more. And then something growled.

Leuna froze in place. That growl was close, much much *too* close for comfort. For the first time, it occurred to her that the dragon might not be as happy to see her as she was to see it. Wait…why didn't she see it? That had been a very threatening growl, so where was the fire? Not that she wanted to be roasted by a grumpy dragon, but this didn't make sense.

"I don't suppose you're a nice, tame dragon by any chance?" she asked the darkness. Another, fiercer growl was the response, then wheezing. "Wonderful. You're not only not tame, you're not well."

A short burst of flame lit up the surrounding space, so bright that she threw up her hands to protect her eyes. But it was worth the pain, because she saw it! Twenty paces ahead and to her right lay a weak, wheezing, *wild* dragon. Not far from its head lay a pile of what might've been broken boxes. Wouldn't it be ironic if she died of hunger in an old supply storage room? Shoving the thought aside, she focused on the dragon.

"I don't have any musker fruit." She inched closer. "Or even a dragon treat." A spurt of flame not much bigger than a flaring lamp showed that the dragon hadn't moved. "You're probably wondering what I'm even doing down here." She bit back a yelp when the dragon's teeth snapped shut. "Stupid girl, wandering around by herself without so much as a firestone. Am I right?" she joked shakily.

The dragon moaned softly. Tried, by the sounds of the scratching, to drag itself away from her.

"It's alright!" Forgetting to be afraid, Leuna dashed forward and plowed into it. "I really, really hope it's alright…" She felt the dragon's neck skim along her arm as it raised its head. A faint glow was visible at what must've been the back of its mouth, but that was it. With another moan, the dragon flopped back to the ground.

"Are you sure you're wild?" Leuna touched the dragon's head thoughtfully. The dragon shuddered, then held still. The scales felt cold, even to Leuna's already chilled hands. "I've worked with a few wild animals, and this is not how they react." Kneeling beside the dragon, Leuna pressed herself to it, trying to warm it. The orb poked her in the stomach, but she ignored it for the moment. "You're scaring me," she whispered to the dragon, who huffed a little smoke in response. "Dragons are supposed to be able to warm themselves from the inside. Why can't you do that? Are you really that sick? And," she stroked the dragon's soft neck, "exactly how sick is that, anyway?"

A soft noise, almost like purring, emanated from deep within the dragon.

"Yeah?" Leuna smiled for the first time in what felt like days. "You like that?" Her smile faded with the sound. "Alright." Blowing into her hands to warm them, she stood, her scraped knees protesting as she rose. "Neither of us is going to last much longer unless we find a way to warm up."

Pulling out the orb, she squinted and scrunched up her eyes, but its light was just too weak. Returning it to her gerri for safekeeping, she stepped over the dragon and floundered around until she ran into the boxes. One of which, at least, was still quite solid. Rubbing the bruises forming on top of her scrapes, she collected a few broken pieces of wood and began arranging them for a fire.

"I wish you weren't sick," she told the dragon. "We wouldn't be in any trouble at all then." Thinking back to the first growl, she hesitated. "Well, *you* wouldn't be in any trouble." She stuck herself on one particularly splintered piece of wood and grumbled to nobody in particular about it. "Here." She hated to do it, but her gerri was the driest piece of cloth she had, and they would probably only get one chance at this. Length-wise was the only way it would tear, so it was a mighty small piece she finally wound around the splintered end of the stick. Held it out tentatively to the dragon. "Do you think you can do it?" she pleaded. "Do you even know what I'm talking about? Fire?"

The dragon drew a great, shuddering breath. And exhaled a racking cough. Liquid splatted on Leuna's hand and arm, along with some weak sparks.

"It's alright, it's alright," she soothed the dragon, even as her heart sank. "We'll be alright." A few sparks lodged in the gerri and she drew it to her. Cupping her hands around the sparks, she blew a feather-soft breath on them. They glowed more brightly, then still brighter, making the fresh liquid stains stand out. "Wait. Is that…?" Gingerly, she nudged one of the darker spots nearer a spark and gasped when it burst into flame!

"You did it!" she laughed. Moving carefully, she placed the flame inside the stack of haphazardly arranged wood. The other pieces started smoking almost immediately, then caught in a blaze of glorious light! "That wasn't spit, it was…dragon fire…stuff." She laughed again. "Whatever it's called, it was positively brilliant of you to cough it all over the gerri." Tamping down on her disgust at having it also coughed all over her hand and arm, she picked up one of the smaller pieces of burning wood, held it up like a torch.

"What in the world…?" Leuna stared at what the light revealed. "You're the distira! Down here!   Down where?" Confused, Leuna shook her head, unable to take her eyes off the distinctively marked dragon. Her scales were nearly white in color, except around her neck, where bright reds and greens and blues hung in a triple thick ruffle, ready to be raised threateningly. "But *why* are you down here? And sick? What's going on?" She leaned back against a box, hardly feeling its corner digging into her back. "Txoko's been looking for you, you know."

The fire reached a knot in one of the boards and popped, snapping her out of her daze. Piling more wood on, taking care only to keep from smothering the flame, she stared in horror. This wasn't an old, abandoned storage room. This was very much in use!

Stacks and stacks of crates filled two thirds of the room. Every crate she could see bore a smuggler's mark that she recognized from her, um, adventure in a smugglers' shack outside of Ilun. They were probably filled with dragon claws and teeth. Two pristine dragon hides were tacked up on the far wall, drying. She pressed the back of her hand to her mouth as she faced the blunt truth of what had happened to the first two distira.

"We are in soooo much more trouble than I thought." The dragon's only response was a groan, but it served to redirect her focus. "Good point. There might be something down here we can use." Stretching her hands out over the fire, Leuna took stock of their situation. "Those boxes are different from the others. Well. More than one way to warm up, I guess."

It was only after she'd struggled for several minutes to open the top box that she managed to accidentally knock it off the stack. It landed on one corner and broke, spilling its incredibly smelly contents across the floor. The dragon roused itself enough to beg with moans and head motions, then collapsed back.

"Not how I pictured that happening," she muttered, "but worth the effort." Snatching up two handfuls of the stuff, she hurried over, nearly tripping over the thick chain that stretched from the dragon's hind foot to a metal pin someone had pounded into the stone wall. "Easy," she soothed, dumping the food into the dragon's mouth. "There's more." The dragon gulped it down and snuffled at her hands, its eyes wild.

"Coming, coming." Racing back over, she seized the box. Now that it was only half-full, it was fairly manageable. With grunts and heaves, she hauled it over to the dragon's head, dragging it over the chain one heave at a time. "You must've been pretty healthy when you got here," she observed, eyeing the metal restraint with distaste. "Not so fast," she admonished the dragon, holding some of the food back. "You'll make yourself… I mean," she closed her eyes and shook her head. "You're already sick." She cleared her throat. "But you'll make it worse if you fill your empty stomach this quickly. Too much air in it already. In fact. If you're starving, you're most likely also dehydrated."

Pulling the box back out of easy reach, she straightened. Looked around the room again. Studied the faltering fire. Spotted a wooden bucket. Good. Now, where was the water? Taking up the broken boards from the feed box, she added them to the fire. That was when she saw it. A long, roundish line amongst the stacks.

"Thank goodness." She allowed herself a quick drink first, then partially filled the bucket. "Open wide." The room was warming up, and she was nearly sweating with the exertion, but even as she poured water and watched the dragon swallow it, she knew it wasn't enough. In its chilled and weakened state, it was in dire need of…better. Better care, better food, better everything.

Chapter 20

The sound of wood striking stone caught her attention and she stared at the fire, where a burning board had just broken in two. The voracious flames leapt and danced wildly as if in a feeding frenzy. It was a crazy idea…wasn't it? Except it had worked once before. Sort of. On a healthy, adolescent gailen. She exhaled hard, blowing hair out of her face.

"Can you eat wood?" she asked doubtfully. "Or live coals, maybe?" Scrubbing her hands over her face, she began pacing. "I could go for help, I guess. Right. Hey, that's a good idea!" Grabbing the food box, she emptied it where the distira could reach it. "I'll stoke up the fire, take a torch, and…" The food remained on the floor where it had fallen. "No." Throwing the box in the general direction of the fire, she knelt to examine the dragon. "You can't die!" she ordered, her voice cracking in despair. It scarcely responded when she tried to lift its eyelid. "C'mon, we're so close. I promise! If you'll just stay alive, I'll get you out of this horrible place!"

Jumping to her feet, she scrambled over the dragon. "Let's get your foot free, shall we? Have to start somewhere." The scales were rubbed shiny underneath the shackle and she scowled at it. "I see you've already tried this," she muttered, touching the scratches on the surface. "Lucky for us both, I spent a lot of childhood afternoons at the blacksmith's." Actually, it wasn't that complicated for someone with fingers. Depressing the spring, she twisted the linchpin and out it came. "Ha! I did it!" she crowed as the useless hunk of metal slipped off the dragon to land on the floor.

"I bet you thought I…ugh!" Coughing and choking, she grabbed for her gerri. Belatedly, she remembered tearing it to make the fire. Tears streamed down her cheeks as she jerked her shirt up to cover her nose. "What is that smell?!" Blinking rapidly, she looked at the fire, which was mostly obscured by thick, black smoke. Thinking back to the food box, she muttered indignantly, "But I emptied it! Didn't I?"

Tears streamed down her face as she squinted at the fire until it suddenly clicked in her mind. "The treats! The box," she coughed, "soaked up the treat oil!" Patting the dragon, she leapt to her feet. "Yes. Yes! I know how to warm you up!"

Going back to the stack of boxes, she shoved the top one onto the floor. It only split partway open, but she was able to wrench two broken boards free. Gagging her way over to the fire, she used the boards to clumsily fish around in it for the pieces of dragon food she'd overlooked when she threw the first box over. Who knew they would burn?

"Open wide," she commanded the dragon, approaching it with a flaming treat balanced carefully on one end of a board. The smoke swirled around her and into the hallway. It also did what she hadn't been able to do—provoked a response from the distira. A dragon-sized sneeze followed by a growl was all the opportunity Leuna needed. Tossing the smoldering dragon food into its mouth, she ducked back to the fire for more.

"What do you think?" she yelled over her shoulder. "Can't taste any worse than it already did, right?" She must've been right, because it *swallowed*. "That's it!" she choked. "Want some more?" She tossed a couple more pieces over and it snapped them out of the air.

Rising with a weak roar, the dragon lumbered over to the fire where it helped itself to the remaining dragon-food-coals.

"Great!" Leuna dropped the boards she'd been using as tongs back into the fire. "Can we get out of here now? Please?" Her breath was coming in gasps now and she knew she didn't have long.

Ignoring her, the distira turned to the second broken food box. She raised her head and brought it down, striking the box with her jaw and splitting it wide open.

"Oh. Wow. I didn't know you could do that." Deciding to escape on her own while the dragon was busy with the food, Leuna pulled a flaming board from the fire. "Nice meeting you," she called as she backed out of the cavern.

She hadn't gotten far when she reached an intersection. Lifting the torch over her head, she took a moment to appreciate the relatively-smoke-free air even as she muttered, "Good thing I didn't go for help. Probably would've died of hunger before I found my way out." Glancing over her shoulder, she froze. "I, uh, don't suppose you know which way will take us out of here, do you?" she asked the distira, who was mere inches behind her.

The answering roar nearly stopped her heart. The torch landed in the soggy growth at her feet as her hands flew up to cover her ears. Something slender wrapped about her waist and she found herself deposited unceremoniously on the distira's back. Eschewing the tunnels, the distira leapt straight up. Yelping, Leuna flattened herself against the dragon while it clawed its way up a narrow tunnel she hadn't even realized was there.

"I hope," she gasped as small falling rocks struck her on the head and rattled down the dragon's scales, "that you know what you're doing!" More rocks tumbled down around her, forcing her to shut her mouth and eyes while she clung to the dragon for dear life.

All at once, the rock shower stopped and a

hot breeze swept over her. With a roar, the distira bounded out of the chimney. Leuna was still on its back when it spread its wings and took off. The dragon was too weak to get far, but they flew halfway up Koroa's south face before it sagged to the ground in a sloppy touchdown.

"You're safe." Leuna dove off its back and ran around to slip her sooty arms around its neck. "You're safe," she soothed again. "In about five minutes, people who actually know about dragons are going to be here. I promise." Wiping her eyes on her sleeve, she got a faint idea of just how dirty she'd gotten down in the cave. Shrugging it off, she continued trying to calm the dragon, her ears ringing with its ongoing roars. "Wait." *One dragon can't make all this noise…*

Frowning, she turned to look and gasped. "More distiras? Are you kidding? That's amazing! Hey." She looked sternly at the dragon beside her. "You're going to tell them I'm a friend, right?"

A squad of domesticated dragons appeared about then, making her distira snarl and curl into attack position.

Recognizing the defensive stance from her time with Sparks and Presa, Leuna did her best to wave the squad on. "Go away!" she shouted. "You're upsetting her!" They finally complied, leaving her to ask the dragon, "What now? You needed their help, you know." As if in answer, several ground-shaking thuds occurred simultaneously. "Or…not. Your friends are here, aren't they?"

She started to smooth her shirt, then laughed shakily. Oily soot formed erratic black streaks on her clothes and there were several small tears in her shirt from their perilous jaunt up the rock chimney. She could feel separate sections of her hair fluffing in the wind and, well. She was just generally a mess. Like the dragons would even care!

Breathing shallowly, Leuna turned by inches until she could see the other dragons. A massive white beast towered over the others, his ruffle raised. "You must be the aitak," she greeted him tentatively. "Is she part of your kabi?" Judging by the angry puff of smoke he shot at her, she decided she'd guessed correctly. "No problem. I mean, she's a little weak. Speaking as her doctor, I'd like to have her stay overnight for observation…" She cringed back against the dragon she'd rescued when the aitak rose on his hind legs and raised his voice in a cry that thundered across the plains surrounding Koroa.

That was when she noticed the festival tents out of the corner of her eye. Hundreds of small dots held perfectly still—the people? Inwardly she groaned and hoped they couldn't see her any better than she could see them.

"However, you make a compelling argument.

Just," she wearily stroked the smooth neck behind her, "be patient with her, please. Half an hour ago, I wasn't even sure she'd make it." Her stroking started the dragon almost-purring again, prompting a smile from Leuna.

The aitak settled back onto all fours and approached, stiff-legged. Extending his snout to sniff at Leuna, he eyed her up and down before blowing softly on her. There was no smoke this time, which she thought was progress. One of the other dragons growled and they all turned to face the up slope.

"Easy," Leuna implored. She didn't dare touch the aitak, but she patted her dragon. "Easy. Remember those people I told you would be coming to help? They're trying again." The aitak swung its head back and forth between her and the single advancing figure. "Tell you what. I'll meet them halfway. Will that be alright?" Patting her dragon again, she moved slowly away from her. "Everybody stay calm. Please."

Putting one foot in front of the other, Leuna stepped clear of the kabi and got her first good look at who was coming. "Ema!"

"Softly," Ema called back. Her shoulders had begun to ache from the buckets of fish she was carrying, but she came steadily on. "We don't want to startle them." Taking in the soot and dirt and…damp that was all over Leuna, she looked forward to hearing the tale. And telling and retelling it to anyone who would listen! An entire kabi of distira at the festival? It was unheard of! "I'm going to set these down. Then we can back away."

Leuna hesitated, looking over her shoulder at her dragon. Instead of leaving with the queen, she picked up the buckets. Whatever these fish were, they must be native to Marroi. She'd never seen anything like their short, squat bodies. She'd never smelled anything like them, either. Why was so much about dragons so smelly?

"I won't be long." Slowly, slowly she reentered the kabi. "This is for you, sweetheart," she told her dragon, bringing the buckets right up to her. "You're going to love it. I can tell by how badly they reek." Holding a fish on the flat of her palm, fingers well out of the way, she coaxed her into trying a bite. "See? I told you." The starving distira plunged her nose into the bucket, spilling its contents on the grass and scarfing it all down. A loud belch later, she launched into the second bucket. "You are going to give yourself the bellyache of all time!" Leuna warned, though she wisely stayed out of the way.

Taking a deep breath, she addressed the aitak. "I have to go now. But if you want to stay, all of you, for a while, that would be fine. Maybe let her rest and enjoy the sun for a couple of hours…you'll be safe here. The poachers are gone now."

Ema watched in awe as the slight woman bid the wild distira kabi a fond farewell, her mind reeling at the implications. No one would dare object to her marrying Txoko now. Not even Tipo.

"Is there someplace where I could wash up before we go inside?" Leuna asked as she returned. "I'm a mess."

"Yes, of course." Ema's first inclination was to pack her straight off to see Txoko, but she stifled it. 'Mess' was probably the understatement of a lifetime. Gingerly slipping her arm through Leuna's she asked, "How did this happen?"

Leuna shrugged, embarrassed. "I got lost. Well, I thought I knew where I was." Haltingly, and with a lengthy pause when they reached the nearest well, she related her story to the queen.

"A poachers' cave? Here, in Koroa?" Ema's body shook with anger. "I will have Zain clear out those old tunnels at once, then close their entrance permanently!"

"I'm glad." Leuna rinsed some grit out of her mouth and spat as politely as she could. She still needed a good scrubbing, but at least the top layer of soot was off. Her jagged, dirty fingernails might never recover, though. "I shudder to think what would happen if some children stumbled onto them." She nodded at Fiantza, who was just arriving.

"The children know to stay away from them." Fiantza did her best not to smirk. "I will have to keep a closer eye on you." While secretly embarrassed at all the trouble her charge had gotten into, she was simultaneously thunderstruck at everything the girl had brought about in so short a time.

"I'd appreciate it," Leuna agreed quickly. She hoped she'd learned her lesson. Twice ought to be enough, right? First with misunderstanding the aerobatics last night and then today with the cave that even children knew to stay away from? "I'm going to need all the help I can get, if I'm being honest."

"Well, now, let's get you cleaned up properly so you can see the king. He's waiting for you, you know." Fiantza hustled her off to the rain booth and into a fresh outfit.

"But the distira." Leuna returned to the subject of the dragons as Fiantza towel-dried her hair. "Did you get to see them?" Idly, she played with the orb she'd purchased for her grandmother. She should've given it to her at the festival.

"Yes, I saw them." Fiantza was touched at Leuna's concern. "The entire festival saw them. That's where I was when the aitak made his thunder." She couldn't help shivering slightly. "It's a story we'll all be telling our grand-children and great-grandchildren. *Six* distira at one festival!"

"I'm glad." Thoughts of the dragon hides from the cave intruding on her thoughts, Leuna couldn't quite manage a smile. There should've been at least eight distira there. Setting the bauble aside for later, she ran her fingers through her rapidly drying hair as Fiantza tossed the towel away.

"We must hurry," Fiantza said briskly. "Or the king will come find you."

"No, he mustn't do that!" Leuna settled back into her chair and let Fiantza work her hair into a loose chignon. "He's got to slow down until he recovers."

Frowning, Fiantza set the comb aside. "A king doesn't have that luxury."

"Convalescence isn't a luxury." Leuna bristled, her doctor's sensibilities ruffled. "If he doesn't take a little time now to get well, he will pay for it by being sicker much longer." Reaching for a pair of clean boots she asked, "How did Koroa manage when he was in Lurrak these past several weeks?"

Fiantza shrugged. "The queen was here. And the peers."

"The peers." Leuna sighed, a rush of hopelessness washing over her. "I have so much to learn."

"Haven't we all?" Fiantza asked gently. She'd made up her mind about something that morning

"It will be my pleasure to assist you."

Leuna smiled shyly at her. "Thank you."

"Going forward," Fiantza quirked an admonishing eyebrow at her, "you must ask me when things bother you. Then I can help you understand."

"I will," Leuna promised, warmed by her mirabe's concern.

Fiantza tapped the comb lightly against her palm, then nodded. "You'd best go see the king now."

Leuna hesitated. It seemed ridiculous not to follow through with what she'd just promised, though, so she took a deep breath. "There's something I need to know first. What's the Marroi law regarding the queen?"

Fiantza nodded slowly, considering the question that lay behind the question. "I know of no law requiring that she be Marroi herself."

"And are there any laws requiring the king's wife to be queen?" Leuna almost couldn't bring herself to ask that one. Except that she *needed* to know

Fiantza's head tilted to one side in thoughtful surprise. "The peers will know better than I," she said at last, "but I believe it is only tradition which requires it. For the king's sake."

For the king's sake. Leuna's stomach bottomed out. She didn't want to be a fair weather wife, partaking only of the good her husband could offer while refusing the trials.

"Thank you," she murmured to Fiantza. She walked in a daze until she encountered the first group of ecstatic citizens. They recognized her, probably because she was almost the only Lurrakian woman in Koroa at the time, and shouted good wishes at her until she waved and darted into a side tunnel.

After that, she was able to steer clear of the crowds she heard coming, taking a side tunnel or a byway around them. She hugged herself when she heard how happy they all were about the distira. The feeling that she was a part of the celebration lightened her heart considerably. And this time, the guard at Txoko's door opened it wide, bowing to her as she passed through.

"There she is." Merezi hastened over from where she'd been watching the distira from Txoko's balcony. "My darling, are you alright?" She'd almost fainted when Xelebre had cautiously identified the person standing with the wild dragons as their Leuna!

"More or less." Leuna happily returned her hug. "Nothing that a little fresh air won't cure." She'd already dosed herself with a tonic for the smoke damage, thankfully.

"You may have all the fresh air you want," Xelebre promised, pulling her into a rib-cracker of a hug. "But you'll forgive me if I don't let you out of my sight for the next few years, I trust?"

Laughing, Leuna hugged him back. Then, someone else spoke.

"Koroa will always have room here for you, Jaurle and Jaurla Izan. Stay as long as you like." Txoko watched Leuna's eyes widen as he entered the room in a wheeled chair. "It is my hope, Doctor Oneko, that you will remain permanently."

Leuna folded her arms across her chest. "Not unless you ask me properly." She wanted to talk to him, to discuss what had happened the night before. Preferably, *without* an audience. Her grandparents seemed to get the hint, because they both winked and slipped out.

Txoko moved to rise and she darted forward. Her hands were on his shoulders, holding him against the chair back. Relenting, he took her hands as she lowered herself to her knees beside him.

"Don't even think about getting up," she hissed. Blushing, she rushed on. "I don't care if you're kneeling or standing on your head, I just…I can't even consider staying unless… We have to be clear about what it is that we're talking…"

"I love you, Leuna Oneko," he interrupted her babbling. There. She seemed to like that better. He'd find time to explain the honor he'd been offering when he'd addressed her by her title and family name. Later. "I know I haven't been there for you like I promised. In fact," he lowered his gaze, "I can see now that we will have to enlist the aid of others to help teach you the Marroi ways, and I'm sorry. I'm *so* sorry about what happened last night. About everything that happened last night."

"We can count on Fiantza's help," she offered shyly when he paused. Turning her hands, she laced her fingers through his. "I've been thinking, too," she added. "I have to trust more. Trust you, your people, your customs. I promise that, going forward, I'll do a better job of using the resources surrounding me. I'll even try not to disgrace you again."

Txoko slipped one hand free and gently stroked her cheek. "If we're both doing our best, everything will be alright." Slipping two fingers under her chin, he tilted her head up so that she was looking at him again. "Marry me?"

She regarded him thoughtfully, taking a moment to consider the dozens of things she didn't yet know about how this decision would affect her future. Knowing that she wasn't alone, that she'd have Fiantza's support, and Ema's, gave her courage.

"Yes." Rising slightly, Leuna met him halfway. Her fingers slid into his gloriously silky hair as she lost herself in their betrothal kiss.

Thank you so much for reading the Coddiwomple series!

I hope you enjoyed them!

Other titles by Lea Carter:

<u>Silver Sagas Series</u>
Silver Princess
Silver Majesty
Silver Verity
Troubled Skies
Dress Blues
The Seeker's Storm
Heartwood
Wedgewood
Fission (Coming 2020)
Fusion (Coming 2020)

Visit leacarterwrites.wixsite.com/flinch-free-fiction for the latest news!

www.ingramcontent.com/pod-product-compliance
Lightning Source LLC
Chambersburg PA
CBHW070603170726
48291CB00003B/680